A MINOR DECEPTION

A Joseph Haydn Mystery

Nupur Tustin

Foiled Plots Press

A Minor Deception
A Joseph Haydn Mystery
Foiled Plots Press

First Trade Paperback Edition, 2016
Copyright © Nupur Tustin, 2016
Cover Design by Karen Phillips

This is a work of fiction. Names, characters, places, and incidents are either a product of the author's imagination or are used fictitiously. Any resemblance to actual persons, living or dead, business establishments, events, or locales is entirely coincidental.

ISBN-13: 978-0-9982430-1-6

Printed in the United States

For Matt Tustin, my husband and best friend. Your loving support makes everything possible.

ACKNOWLEDGEMENTS

My first thanks must go to my husband, Matt, for watching and analyzing innumerable television mystery shows with me; for reading two or three versions of every scene, and as many versions of every other sentence; for always believing in me; and for ensuring I had the resources I needed to write this book.

Musicologist David Wyn Jones kindly answered questions on eighteenth-century musical practice. Thank you!

Susu, Christine, Michael, and all your wonderful friends, thank you for taking such loving care of Rena, Gunner, and Hunter while *Mumsie* worked on her novel.

I would also like to thank Sisters in Crime, in particular the Guppies chapter. Special mention must be made of Kathleen Chalmers, Susanna Calkins, Ellen Bryon, Lourdes Venard, Terrie Farley Moran, B.K. Stevens, and Leslie Karst. Your wisdom and your graciousness in sharing it have brought me where I am.

Cindy Sample, Amber Foxx, Jane Gorman, and Sasscer Hill offered invaluable advice on publishing. Thank you!

A number of people read a part or all of the novel. Your advice, feedback, and comments were invaluable in shaping my work. Thank you Julie Biando Edwards, Bhuvaneshwari Jayaram, Kathi Tustin, Sally Carpenter, Lori Robbins, and Marta Tanrikulu.

CAST OF CHARACTERS

Optional Reading for the Curious
In the Year of Our Lord, 1766

HISTORICAL PERSONAGES MENTIONED

Political Figures, In Order of Rank

Her Imperial Majesty, Empress Maria Theresa (Ruled 1740-1780): Archduchess of Austria, Queen of Hungary & Bohemia, daughter of the Holy Roman Emperor Charles V and widow of Holy Roman Emperor Francis I. The lure of Joseph Haydn's music has tempted her to come out of mourning for a state visit to Eisenstadt, a Royal Free Town on the Hungarian side of the river Leitha.

Although technically Dowager Empress of the Holy Roman Empire—only men may be elected rulers of this loose confederation of Habsburg domains and German states—the reins of power for both the Habsburg lands she inherited from her father and the Empire remain firmly in her hands.

Archduke Joseph, Emperor Joseph II (Ruled 1780-1790): Maria Theresa's eldest son, a miserly man of little tact and unfortunately autocratic tendencies. Elected King of the Romans, he automatically became Holy Roman Emperor upon the death of his father in 1765. His mother has appointed him co-regent over the Habsburg Domains as well, but mother and son have a contentious relationship.

And as long as she is alive, the Empress will never fully relinquish control to him or abdicate in his favor. He is referred to by his title of Archduke of Austria in this novel.

Ferenc II Rákóczi (1676-1735): A long-dead Prince of Transylvania, who led an uprising against the Habsburgs between the years 1703 and 1711, attempting to free Hungary from Habsburg control and re-unite Transylvania with Royal Hungary. The revolt was led by nobleman like Ferenc II, but the Hungarian peasantry joined in as well.

The Empress's grandfather, Leopold I, was Emperor at the start of the uprising. By the time it was successfully crushed, her uncle, Joseph I, had ascended the throne for his very brief reign.

His Serene Highness, Nikolaus Esterházy, Prince of the Holy Roman Empire: A member of one of the wealthiest and most powerful Hungarian noble families, the Prince is known for his love of splendor. He is also the employer of the composer Joseph Haydn.

Steadfastly loyal to the Habsburgs, the Esterházy family received the hereditary title of Prince of the Holy Roman Empire from the Emperor Leopold I. Their position as court favorites, however, may be jeopardized by Archduke Joseph's recent rise to power. The Prince hopes the lavish entertainment he has planned for the Empress will induce her to use her influence on his behalf with the Archduke.

Count Harrach: A noble family with estates in Haydn's hometown, Rohrau. They, too, are quite influential in the imperial court. Haydn's mother worked as their cook.

Count Pergen: A man who is helping to develop a vast network of spies and a sophisticated police state for the Archduke Joseph.

Peter Ludwig von Rahier, Estates Director: Haydn's immediate superior in the Esterházy court, Rahier is responsible for the smooth working of the court. He is rather jealous of Haydn's position in court, though, and takes every opportunity to tread upon the Kapellmeister's authority.

MUSICIANS AND THEIR FAMILIES

Joseph Haydn, Court Kapellmeister to the Esterházy family: Hired by the reigning Prince's older brother, Paul, Haydn has quickly become a composer of international renown. His instrumental works, symphonies, quartets, and concertos, all in the new style, have helped to catapult him to the position of Director of Music to one of the most powerful magnate families in the Austrian court. The court newspaper hails him as the "Darling of the Nation."

Maria Anna: Haydn's wife. Known for her shrewish temper and her extravagance with his money, she has little interest in music, in general, or in her husband's work. Haydn has been known to remark that he could have been an innkeeper at one of the many heurige (wine-taverns) that dot the countryside for all she cares.

Johann: The Kapellmeister's youngest brother, a singer in the Esterházy chapel. Although a capable singer, Johann is no virtuoso, leaving him free to act as his older brother's assistant in many capacities. He is also staunchly loyal to Haydn, and serves to preserve the peace between his older brother and sister-in-law.

Michael: Haydn's, pompous, slightly belligerent middle brother. A composer, like Haydn, Michael is employed at the court of the Archbishop of Salzburg. He is better known for his sacred compositions.

Mathias: Haydn's father, now dead, God rest his soul. He was a wheelwright in the small market-town of Rohrau, and was later appointed a local magistrate of the area.

Leopold Mozart: Michael's colleague in Salzburg, and father of the little genius, Wolfgang.

Wolfgang Mozart, Wolferl: The little genius from Salzburg whose performance on the keyboard and violin and whose compositions are taking Europe by storm.

Oboist Zacharias Pohl and cellist Xavier Marteau: In real life, two of Haydn's best musicians. An ill-fated bar-fight between the two resulted in the oboist losing his right eye, causing an eternal enmity between the two men. Minor characters in the novel.

Luigi Tomasini: A virtuoso violinist, Haydn's trusted friend and Konzertmeister. Unfortunately for Haydn, he is on loan to the court of the

Archduke Joseph in Vienna, a move engineered by the Estates Director to curry favor with the new Emperor.

Gregor Werner: Haydn's predecessor until his death in May 1766.

FICTITIOUS CHARACTERS

Albert: The Estates Director's nephew, Albert is a violinist of little talent, whom Haydn is compelled to employ.

Bartó Daboczi: A violinist formerly employed at the court of the Archbishop of Salzburg, Bartó arrived in Eisenstadt a few months back to take on the position of principal violinist and temporary Konzertmeister. His immense talents barely make up for a surly temperament.

Count Nádasdy: Haydn's friend, also a powerful Hungarian magnate and distantly related to the Esterházys. He was the impetus behind the string quartets the Kapellmeister is so famous for.

Herr Hipfl: Eisenstadt's barber-surgeon, a man who, in addition to cutting hair, performs surgical operations. Since the unpleasant tasks of examining corpses and performing autopsies are consigned to barber-surgeons, he also serves as the small town's medical examiner.

Herr Groer: Bürgermeister, or mayor, of the Royal Free town of Eisenstadt, his authority is circumscribed by that of His Serene Highness who acts as High Sheriff of the county. And thanks to Archduke Joseph and Count Pergen, it is also constrained by the Police Commissioner.

Herr Lichtenegger: Police Commissioner (PC) of Eisenstadt, he reports directly to Count Pergen. Ordinarily small towns are not assigned their own PCs, but the Prince, in a zealous effort to go along with the Archduke Joseph's reforms, insisted the little Hungarian town have one assigned to it.

Lorenzo: Principal of the second violinists, he had hoped to be promoted to acting Konzertmeister in the absence of Luigi Tomasini.

Niklas: Principal cellist and new father. The Kapellmeister and his wife are godparents to the cellist's son. The infant's christening ceremony is to take place shortly before the imperial visit.

Greta: A buxom, blond all-purpose maid assigned to the musicians and artists at court.

Rosalie Szabó: A pretty maid from the Kapellmeister's hometown of Rohrau, and Greta's friend. She obtained her position as all-purpose maid to the musicians and artists by virtue of Haydn's recommendation. Her mother, too, worked as a cook in Count Harrach's kitchen.

Sándor Szabó: Rosalie's brother, an extraordinarily gifted violinist, but discouraged from pursuing his musical interests by his parents, who wish a more secure living for him.

OVERTURE

On a chilly December morning in the year 1766, the inhabitants of the little town of Eisenstadt bustle about in a state of feverish anticipation. Eisenstadt might be no different from any other obscure free town in Royal Hungary; too insignificant to merit a spot on the postal route. Nevertheless, it has drawn the attention of the entire Empire upon itself.

The widowed Empress Maria Theresa is to grace the little town in her Hungarian domains with a visit in three weeks; bringing to an end a year-long period of mourning for her beloved husband.

But the man whom the town credits for this remarkable event is at this very moment beginning to fear something might go amiss in the weeks to come.

CHAPTER ONE

The sound of two violins, a cello, and a bass playing a section from a string quartet wafted out from the open window of the Music Room of the Esterházy Castle. Franz Joseph Haydn—resplendent in his livery of blue and gold—waved his baton.

He was still waving it when the music came to an abrupt close.

"No, Bartó! No!" Haydn shook his head, baton suspended in mid-air. "The phrase continues there. Your solo begins on that note." He tapped the sheet music on his ornate silver stand with his baton.

The expression on the faces of Haydn's second violinist, the bearded cellist, and the youthful blond bass player mirrored his own exasperation. They had played the same phrase twenty times at least, and his principal violinist, Bartó Daboczi, recently appointed to the post, had made the same mistake every time.

Bartó put his violin down, his thin lips compressed into a stubborn line. "Herr Kapellmeister, I do not understand."

Quite forgetting he was wearing a wig, Haydn dragged his hand through its locks, pushing it so it sat askew on his head. God grant him patience! At this rate, they would never be ready for the imperial visit.

"What is it you fail to understand, Bartó?" Haydn strove to keep his voice down. The Estates Director, hearing their voices raised in argument earlier, had already availed himself of one opportunity to read them a lecture on decorum. Haydn was determined not to give him any more.

"Why must this new phrase begin here, Herr Kapellmeister?" Bartó jabbed a finger at the score. "It is the middle of the measure."

"Yes, Bartó, that is the middle of the measure," Haydn conceded the point. He dabbed at his forehead with a handkerchief, wishing he could dispense with propriety and, like his musicians, relieve himself of his jacket and waistcoat. Arguing with his principal violinist could make even a cold day such as this seem unbearably warm.

"But that is the beauty of the piece, you see. Your solo begins on the very note on which the four instruments playing in unison ends."

Bartó folded his arms and sat back in his chair, staring impassively at Haydn. "And what purpose does it serve, Herr Kapellmeister, to begin my solo on the same note?"

The cellist and the bass player muttered impatiently. But Lorenzo, the second violinist, had clearly reached the end of his tether.

"Ach, you dolt!" he growled, grabbing the music off the stand. He thrust the score before his colleague, and prodded at the offending note. "Don't you see your solo develops the theme from the section before in which we all play together?"

Bartó was on his feet in an instant. "Whom do you think you're calling a dolt, you idiot!" He thrust his face close to the second violinist, his clenched fist inches away from the other man's jaw. "What can you know of composition, you talent-less donkey?"

"That is enough, Bartó!" Haydn braced himself against the principal violinist. How had the two men come so easily to blows?

Bartó struggled to move toward Lorenzo, who was rising to his feet, a murderous expression on his face. But Haydn kept his hand firmly on his principal violinist's chest, pushing his second violinist back into his chair at the same time.

"You are musicians and officers of the court, gentlemen. Endeavor to behave as such."

He took a deep breath, aware that his second violinist was staring at him, expecting him to hold his ground. But the Kapellmeister had no desire to continue the argument.

"Very well, Bartó. If it will allow you to play the piece better, we can move the note to the next measure." He took a silver pen out of his pocket to make the changes.

Bartó, seeming mollified at this capitulation to his demand, sat down. He adjusted the ruby ring on his forefinger, and put his violin under his chin.

"Let us play through the entire piece now, Herr Kapellmeister. I think you will agree it sounds much better."

The Kapellmeister did nothing of the sort, but, in the interests of preserving the peace, said not a word in reply. The session over, the musicians began to file out of the room, but Lorenzo lingered by the door.

"There was no need to yield to him, Herr Kapellmeister," he said. "What is it about him that makes you so tolerant of his behavior? He is just asking to be dismissed, and you know it!" He stared Haydn squarely in the eye, then left.

"How long you will continue to tolerate his behavior is the better question."

Haydn, about to close the door, spun around in the direction of the voice. Peter von Rahier, elegantly clad as always, leaned against a marble figurine, his arms crossed. How long had the Estates Director been standing in the hallway?

Rahier, his arms still folded, came forward. "We all know why you tolerate it."

He walked past Haydn into the Music Room, stopped to inspect the fortepiano for dust, and turned around.

"You begin to recognize the importance of his talents to the success of our upcoming program, then?" Haydn stood near the doorway, an eyebrow raised in mock surprise.

""Do not quibble with me, Herr Kapellmeister. You know exactly what I mean. It is because the man came armed with references from your brother in Salzburg that you hired him in the first place. And now, despite his intolerable attitude, you are willing to keep him on."

"The question of hiring a violinist would never have arisen, if Tomasini were here."

It was at the Estates Director's advice that the Prince had loaned Haydn's Konzertmeister to the Archduke Joseph, the Empress's son and co-regent. It was a temporary absence, but it had come at a most inopportune moment, the Empress having already consented to the Prince's invitation to undertake the journey of thirty miles or more from the capital, Vienna.

The Estates Director sniffed. "The Archduke specifically asked for your Konzertmeister. To ignore his request at any time would be unthinkable. More so now that he is Holy Roman Emperor... But the subtleties of cultivating political favor are completely lost on you, are they not, Herr Kapellmeister?

"As for Tomasini—he is not the only virtuoso in the Empire. All you had to do was hire another man. How difficult could that be?"

"And, so I did." Haydn's grip tightened on the door handle. "Bartó was the only applicant whose abilities came even close to Tomasini's."

"Pah!" The Estates Director dismissed this with a contemptuous motion of his hand. "You know full well that my nephew could have filled the position admirably. Why you wouldn't hire him is beyond me!"

Rahier's nephew? In the position of principal violinist? Haydn almost choked at the thought. A deferential cough behind him saved him the necessity of a response.

"Dietzl?" Haydn hoped the harassed expression on his horn player's features had nothing to do with his principal violinist.

"It is Bartó, Herr Kapellmeister"—The principal violinist's name brought forth a loud snort from the Estates Director—"He insists upon keeping every score in the Rehearsal Room, and—"

"If these are scores for the upcoming program, that is quite all right, Dietzl." Haydn steered the horn player into the hallway, conscious of Rahier's gaze boring into the back of his head.

"Your violinist's behavior grows increasingly insupportable, Herr Kapellmeister." The Estates Director had noiselessly advanced across the room to the door. "And your tolerance of it even more so."

Haydn forced himself to stay calm. "It is only—" he began to say, but was interrupted.

"I have made no mention of his conduct to the Prince." Rahier brushed a speckle of dust from the ruffles of his fine linen shirt. "But"—he turned his attention from his ruffles to Haydn, his pale blue eyes meeting the composer's in a steady gaze—"I cannot promise to stay silent for very long."

Haydn had no trouble pushing the Estates Director's words out of his mind, but Lorenzo's remarks had left him discomfited. He sat down at his desk, drawing toward him the last of the set of baryton trios he was composing for the Prince.

The faint breeze from the open window carried the sound of the Bürgermeister's rich baritone singing the arpeggios he had assigned him: "Do

Mi So Mi Do." In the distance, he could hear the soft, melodious strains of the barber-surgeon's violin. Even the most unmusical of the townspeople was able to take simple directions without argument, but Bartó...

A loud outburst reverberated through the hallway beyond the Music Room. Haydn was on his feet in an instant.

God in Heaven! Whatever was the matter now? Could Bartó get along with no one?

He rushed into the Rehearsal Room, aghast to see chairs lying overturned before him and violin cases strewn all over the blue and gold patterned marble floor.

Bartó struggled to wrench a beautiful amber-colored instrument out of Lorenzo's hands."How often must I tell you to keep your paws off my belongings?"

"Enough!" Haydn stepped between the two men just as Lorenzo wrested the violin out of the principal violinist's hands. "That Stadlmann is no longer yours."

The corners of Lorenzo's mouth twitched at the Kapellmeister's words. Like every other member of the orchestra, Bartó had been obliged to sell his violin, crafted by the finest luthiers in the Empire, to the Esterházy family. The requirement was common enough among noble families of sufficient means to command an orchestra. But the principal violinist had treated it like an imposition he had never encountered elsewhere.

Bartó glared at the second violinist. "My contract—"

"Your contract"—Haydn's voice was firm—"only allows you to buy it back if you choose to leave at the end of your period of service or are dismissed."

Bartó had insisted the clause be added to his contract, and Haydn regretted giving in on that point. It had only encouraged Bartó to regard the violin as his own; and, along with his usually churlish behavior toward his colleagues, spurred them on into baiting him. One or the other musician would bring out the gray case with its embroidered emblem, taking care to call Bartó's attention to his actions as the second violinist must have just done.

"And you will be dismissed if your unmannerly conduct continues," Haydn added, but it was an idle threat. His principal violinist knew it, for his cantankerous behavior continued without respite.

———❧———

Evening had turned to dusk by the time Haydn was ready to leave. The musicians had all departed. Haydn began to put his scores into his leather case, preparing to set out when a knock on the door startled him. He turned slowly around.

God forbid it should be Bartó! The man's broad, dark features and the ruby ring he constantly fiddled with were getting to be quite tiresome.

But it was his second violinist who strode into the room, his face beaming with pride.

"Herr Kapellmeister! I've mastered the rhythm and articulation for the solo in the quartet we played this morning. May I show you?"

Haydn set his scores down, and smiled. "Yes, of course, Lorenzo."

His second violinist, although lacking the technical prowess that enabled Bartó to dazzle his listeners, was always eager to improve upon his limited capabilities.

"Let me accompany you." Haydn seated himself at his Schantz fortepiano, and opened the lid.

Before Lorenzo could begin the solo, however, the door opened again. Bartó, standing at the entrance, his violin tucked under his arm, peered out into the hallway, and then softly closed the door behind him. He took a few paces into the room, apparently oblivious to the presence of both the Kapellmeister and the second violinist.

"Bartó! Is there something you need?"

The Kapellmeister's voice brought the principal violinist to a precipitous halt. After a moment's hesitation, he spun around.

"There you are, Herr Kapellmeister." Bartó attempted a smile. "I have a quest—" He stopped short at the sight of Lorenzo. A frown replaced his smile.

"What is he doing here?" The principal violinist turned to face Haydn, his lips pressed into an obdurate line.

"Surely, that is none of your affair—" Haydn began, but Bartó's harsh voice broke in before he could say another word.

"How can it not concern me when that dolt"—Bartó thrust his bow at the second violinist—"conspires at every turn to usurp my position?"

Lorenzo rolled his eyes, but fortunately kept silent.

"Your accusation is ridiculous!" What had gotten into his principal violinist, Haydn wondered. "Lorenzo was only demonstrating his ability to play one of the violin solos."

"And my willingness," Lorenzo added, his lips broadening into a mischievous grin, "to play it just as the Kapellmeister has written the piece."

Haydn caught his second violinist's eye, and imperceptibly shook his head. He sympathized with his musicians' desire to bait Bartó—Lorenzo was not the only one—but he could ill-afford any strife among his men so close to the imperial visit. He certainly could not afford to lose Bartó.

Bartó's features darkened. "Your willingness to thwart me at every turn, more like it." He spat out the words. "You think I fear your willingness?" He came closer to the second violinist, his bow stabbing at Lorenzo's chest.

"You think your willingness will earn you any favors with the Kapellmeister? Your willingness has been pitted against my prowess from the day I came here. God knows, the Kapellmeister sees fit to let you get away with your insolence. But it will yield you nothing, mark my words!"

Lorenzo drew back. "My insolence! I have served longer than both you and the Kapellmeister. But I have always known my place in the orchestra. And I have always abided by the Kapellmeister's decisions."

Although he was addressing the principal violinist, Lorenzo's gaze was directed at Haydn.

Haydn was conscious of a growing sense of discomfort at Lorenzo's words and at the pain evident in his eyes. His second violinist had expected to take Tomasini's position during his temporary absence. At the time, Bartó's mastery of the violin had made him the obvious choice. Lorenzo, despite the length of his service and his unswerving loyalty, had never even been in contention.

His mind struggled to find some words to mitigate his violinist's wounded feelings, but Lorenzo was already at the door. Watching him leave, Haydn could not but wonder if he had made the right decision.

CHAPTER TWO

Haydn was still mulling over the day's events when he left the castle grounds that evening. A few minutes' walk in an easterly direction brought him to the green doors of 82 Klostergasse, the house he had bought that May upon his appointment as Court Kapellmeister. He let himself into the cobblestoned courtyard, too preoccupied to stand outside, as he usually did, and revel in the possession of his first house.

Through the kitchen window, Haydn saw the frail form of his youngest brother, Johann Evangelist. Maria Anna, Haydn's wife, was ladling out a steaming bowl of stew for her brother-in-law. Haydn made a wry face. He was late yet again for the evening meal.

Maria Anna whipped around the moment Haydn stepped inside the warm kitchen. "Can you never be troubled to come home on time? I have almost run through my entire supply of wood for the winter keeping your meals warm for you."

"It was work, my dear, and not a perverse desire to exhaust your supply of wood that kept me from home," Haydn replied, his eyes drawn toward the enormous pile of wood neatly stacked near the stove. It would quite easily last them the entire winter, but he did not think it wise to point that out in her current ill-tempered state. He hung up his coat, took off his wig and set it aside, before joining his brother at the kitchen table.

Maria Anna thumped down a bowl of stew before Haydn. "Your brother manages to come home on time," she grumbled.

Haydn forbore to speak. As always, his wife sought to clang against him like a discordant note. As always, he refused to be drawn in.

Johann looked up from his bowl, and stepped in as always to dissolve any hint of dissonance. "That is not a fair comparison, sister-in-law. With all the preparations for the Empress's visit, my duties have been rather light these past few weeks. Why, we have sung the same mass at every service, the Prince shows so little interest in sacred music!"

This was not entirely true, and Maria Anna's muffled snort and the skeptical glance she gave her brother-in-law out of the corner of her eyes suggested she was well aware he did more than sing at church services. He was indispensable to the opera director, and Haydn himself relied on Johann's assistance in training singers, arranging works, and making necessary changes to compositions. His younger brother had even on occasion conducted the orchestra during rehearsals.

Maria Anna opened her mouth to speak, but Johann had already turned toward Haydn. "I hear Bartó's behavior grows more outrageous every day," he said, his eyes warm with sympathy.

Haydn closed his eyes. The mere thought of his principal violinist grated on his every nerve like an out-of-tune violin. But his brother's invitation to unburden himself was such a balm to his sore feelings, he could contain himself no longer.

"The man must be losing his mind! Do you know he accused my second violinist of scheming to take his position?"

He would have said more, but Maria Anna looked up from the loaf of bread she was slicing. Her knife made a sharp clack against the wooden board. "Well, then dismiss him! I am tired of having to hear of that Bartó's doings all day."

"Why, what have you heard?" The words burst out of Haydn's lips. It was so unlike his wife to take note of anything pertaining to his music or his musicians. She had long since ceased to feign an interest in either.

Maria Anna flung her arm toward the window."The way the townspeople keep bringing their complaints to me, they must think I share your duties with you!"

"But what has Bartó done?" Haydn asked again. When Maria Anna remained silent, he turned toward Johann.

"Apparently, he has threatened the Bürgermeister with dire consequences if the 'old fool,' as Bartó calls him, continues to spy on him," Johann replied.

"Why would he think Herr Groer wants to spy on him? That is absurd!" As he pictured the jovial, apple-cheeked Bürgermeister, the absurdity of the situation struck Haydn with even greater force.

"Oh, who can know what your violinist's motives are!" Maria Anna's knife sliced the air with an impatient whoosh as she flicked her wrist up.

"Herr Groer saw him hurrying by, and asked him whether he was going for his usual walk in the woods. Whereupon Bartó turned upon him, fists raised. Herr Groer said he quailed at the malevolent glint in his eyes."

Haydn grunted. "More evidence the man is losing his mind. Why, no one goes into those woods."

"In all likelihood," Johann said, "he was headed in the direction of that wine tavern in Kleinhöflein he enjoys frequenting. Gerhard, the owner, refuses to let him in now."

It was not news Haydn had been aware of, but the reason could not be clearer. "I can well believe it. What fool would ply a disputatious man with wine? It would only exacerbate his quarrelsome nature."

Maria Anna put a few slices of bread and a hunk of cheese on a plate, and pushed it toward Haydn. "I doubt Gerhard's reasons have anything to do with the effect of his wine on your violinist."

Haydn, about to bring a spoonful of stew to his mouth, put it down again at her words. He and Johann exchanged a glance, but Maria Anna, apparently quite oblivious of the effect of her words, went to the cupboard opposite the stove to get out another plate.

"What could you have meant by that?" Haydn addressed his wife's back

Maria Anna turned around with a plate in her hand. "Oh, you have your nose forever buried in your music, husband, and can see no farther than the notes on the page." She sniffed disparagingly. "You never should have hired that man. The fact that he is a Hungarian should have told you all you needed to know."

"I hire men on the basis of their musical ability, not their nationality." His wife understood nothing of music, still less the intricacies of his position. But when had that ever stopped her from expressing an opinion, however wrongheaded? "Besides, what have you against the Hungarians?"

"They are disputatious like your violinist. They loathe the people of Austria. And, though your violinist may be excused on this count, they tend to follow Luther." Maria Anna held out a thumb, her forefinger and third finger as she enumerated the diverse vices of the Hungarian race.

"Not every Hungarian is hostile toward Austrians," Johann protested. "No one could be more loyal to the Empress than the Prince. Or a more staunch supporter of the Empire."

Haydn fought the urge to smile. Maria Anna disliked being contradicted. But it was not a fact that could be refuted. One would be hard put to find a single Hungarian magnate who resented the protection of the Habsburgs. Their employer, Nikolaus Esterházy, Prince of the Holy Roman Empire, was no exception.

"His Serene Highness is no follower of Luther, either. He is a devout Catholic," he added.

Maria Anna glowered at him. "Be that as it may. Your violinist despises Austrians, of that I am quite sure. I heard him myself hurling insults at the barber-surgeon. A toady, that is what your violinist called the barber-surgeon. A servile Austrian toady without a backbone."

The brief good humor Haydn had enjoyed dissipated at her words. "It is bad enough that Bartó cannot get along with his colleagues. Why must he antagonize the townspeople as well? What can he possibly have against our Herr Hipfl?"

If only he had no need of a virtuoso like Bartó. The situation called for a reprimand. But it would have to be issued with the utmost restraint. Or, his violinist might simply leave. Not that Haydn believed he would. Still, it was best not to test Bartó's resolve given his veiled threats of late.

His fingers tightened around his spoon. "I cannot imagine what Michael was thinking when he referred him to us! I would dismiss the man this very instant if it were not for Her Majesty's visit."

Maria Anna looked at her husband out of the corner of her eyes. "Are you certain it is only the Empress's visit that keeps you from getting rid of your troublesome violinist?"

Haydn searched her countenance. Was there a veiled insinuation in her words? "What other reason is there to keep him on?"

Maria Anna merely shrugged. Haydn turned to face Johann. His brother, at least, could be trusted to be honest with him.

But Johann's eyes slid away. He shifted uneasily in his seat. "The Estates Director has put it about town that you refuse to dismiss Bartó because he was sent to us by Michael," he said eventually.

"Is that all?" The move was typical of Herr Rahier, Haydn thought. An attempt to force his hand, no doubt. "I ought to have known he wouldn't be content with making the accusation to my face. I trust the townspeople know me better than to think a brother's recommendation is all it would take to hire someone!"

Rosalie Szabó, the newest addition to the palace staff, inched down the hallway, eyes glued to the black and gold patterned floor. Her arms ached from the strain of carrying a heavy silver tray piled high with breakfast dishes. Unable to see over the mound of dishes, she peered around the side, and placed one foot before the other with extreme care.

She heard the West Wing doors slam open. But by the time she discerned the figure storming toward her, it was too late. All she saw was a brown blur as the form collided into her. The tray slipped out of her arms, and crashed to the floor.

"Master Bartó!" Rosalie cried, surveying the broken china in dismay. Brown streaks of coffee along with remnants from the musicians' breakfast stained the floor.

But Bartó had already brushed past the palace maid. "Out of my way, you stupid girl!" He rubbed at the coffee stains on his white stockings, and hurtled on to the staircase as though the devil were at his heels.

Rosalie's violet eyes darkened. Really, Master Bartó's rudeness knew no bounds! She might be just a maid, but was it too much to expect a modicum of courtesy from the principal violinist? She sniffed. But for the gift of music, Master Bartó would be a mere servant no different from herself.

She had overheard him boasting to one of the other musicians of the patents of nobility he had bought for his family with the gulden he earned from his music.

"A tall tale, if ever I heard one," she muttered, as she bent down to pick up the shards of painted ceramic. "He must believe it, he gives himself such airs! Oh, just look at this mess!"

She was about to go in search of a dustpan and mop when the Estates Director emerged from his office. The noise from her collision with the principal violinist must have reached his ears. She might've known it would, the man had such sharp ears!

Rahier threw her a look of icy contempt, then surveyed the mess around her with growing disgust.

"That will be a gulden out of your salary every month until you have repaid the price of those dishes you were so careless with. The Kapellmeister's favor may have obtained this position for you. Do not think to retain it by his favor alone. Any more such clumsy incidents, and you will be dismissed without a reference."

It would be pointless to protest, Rosalie knew, that this was the first such incident. And not her fault either. She made a face behind the Estates Director's back as he strode away. Herr Rahier needed but the slightest excuse to dismiss her, and she was determined not to give it to him. She swept the mess onto a dustpan, mopped the floor clean, and set the few pieces of china that had survived the fall back on her tray.

She was making her way to the kitchen when she saw the tall, broad figure of a stranger before her. He peered first to the right, then to the left as he walked slowly backward.

Rosalie tried to step aside to avoid him, but as the stranger swung around, he almost knocked the tray out of her arms. She gasped as a pair of muscular arms reached out to clasp her and the tray.

"Ach, what a clumsy dummkopf I am, Fräulein!" The man grinned ruefully down at Rosalie, his handsome features wearing an expression of regret. "I can't apologize enough for my blundering behavior."

Rosalie found herself gazing into a pair of blue eyes with a merry glint in them. "It's quite all right—" She bit her tongue. She had been about to address him as "Mein Herr," a salutation reserved only for the gentry.

This man, judging by his rough garb, was a peasant like herself. Even so, he was more deserving of a "Mein Herr" than that coxcomb Master Bartó!

"No, no, Fräulein. My carelessness could have cost you your job if you hadn't masterfully saved that beautiful china from dropping to the floor." He shook his thick mane of chestnut brown hair. "What a big, bungling lummox I am, to be sure! You're not hurt, I hope?" He regarded the maid with concern. "Here, let me help you with these dishes."

He took the tray from Rosalie, and followed her to the kitchen. "I am quite lost in this huge palace," he confessed. "My friend has mentioned the Esterházy family's enormous fortune. Their magnificent palace. But nothing could have prepared me for this." His head turned in a slow sweep around the exquisitely patterned wallpaper, the ornate vases of jade and brass, the intricately carved tables. "Such grandeur! No words can adequately describe it."

"Does your friend work here—" Rosalie stopped herself just in time. She had been about to address him as "Mein Herr," yet again. What was the matter with her?

27

In the Music Room upstairs, Haydn sat deep in thought at his Schantz fortepiano. Should he dispense with Bartó's services or not? The question preoccupied his mind as his fingers moved idly over the keys. The melody was one he recalled singing with his childhood companions in the market-town of Rohrau: "La Ti Do Ti La, La Ti Do Mi Ti Do La."

He had apologized to the townspeople. But was an apology sufficient to quell the rumors of favoritism the Estates Director had spread about town? Haydn's third finger struck and held down "Mi" with unusual force, disrupting the rhythm of the tune. His rebuke to Bartó—too mild to be called that, he supposed—had done no good at all.

Any other Kapellmeister, Haydn was quick to realize, would have instantly dismissed a musician for the kind of belligerent behavior Bartó persisted in exhibiting. But the Esterházy orchestra, while it numbered a great many capable musicians, had none who quite matched Bartó's expertise. Haydn would have to hire another virtuoso, and where was one to be found at such short notice in the small town of Eisenstadt?

The sound of Bartó's raucous voice drifted in to the room. Jolted out of his thoughts, Haydn swung around to face the open window.

Bartó was supposed to be in the Rehearsal Room with the rest of the orchestra practicing the violin concerto that would greet the Empress upon her arrival. What in God's name was the first violinist doing outside the castle grounds?

Haydn pushed his piano bench back, the force causing the brass fittings on its legs to scrape against the marble floor. He strode toward the window and thrust the burgundy curtains aside.

The window of the Music Room gave on to the undulating landscape dotted with vineyards at the foot of the Leitha Mountains. Haydn could see a part of the town to his right. Beyond the town, far in the distance, the waters of Lake Neusiedl glimmered on the horizon.

He propped himself against the window sill with his hands, and leaned out as far as he could. But the wide stone ledge skirting the window obstructed his view. He could see neither Bartó nor his companion.

The first violinist was speaking in lowered tones, even so his words were audible to the Kapellmeister.

"It is no fault of my own, I am sure. What can I do if the Kapellmeister chooses to dismiss me?"

Haydn was taken aback as much at the querulous note he detected in Bartó's voice as at his words.

28

"Then you had best make sure you remain in his favor," his companion responded in a manner that sounded vaguely forbidding. Haydn thought he had heard the voice before, but try as he might he could not place it.

"There is too much at stake..." were the next words Haydn heard, although they were so faintly uttered, he could not be sure of either the words or who had spoken them. The men must have walked on for despite straining his ears to the utmost, Haydn failed to discern the rest of the conversation.

He stood still for a time, contemplating the landscape outside. The snippet he had overheard set a welter of thoughts jostling in his head. What mischief was Bartó up to now? Nothing in his conduct had suggested to the Kapellmeister that his principal violinist feared for his position. Quite the contrary, in fact.

He heard the slow, heavy rumble of wheels coming to a halt on the cobblestoned inner courtyard. His brain absently identified the sound as that of the mail coach from the Esterházy station in Großhöflein, where the postal coach dropped off letters bound for Eisenstadt.

CHAPTER THREE

Some time before the mail coach arrived, Rosalie stood over the kitchen sink, her thoughts on the man she had encountered in the hallway. They had chatted for a while after he carried her tray into the kitchen for her, and put the dishes in the sink.

Such a friendly man. So very polite. Why, he would've addressed her as Fräulein Szabó if she hadn't stopped him! How someone as churlish as Master Bartó could have won the friendship of a man like that, she didn't know. There were not two people in the world more unlike each other than those two.

He seemed to know exactly who she was. Only because Master Bartó spoke so often of her, he'd explained. But Rosalie found that hard to believe. The principal violinist's manner toward her, on the rare occasions that he acknowledged her presence, was nothing other than brusque. She was sure Master Bartó's friend was...

Lying?

Rosalie brought her head up so sharply, the muscles in her neck almost cracked. She gazed out the kitchen window, her large violet eyes shrouded in uncertainty. Was it possible? But why lie about such a trivial matter?

Besides, how else could he have known so much about her? He knew she was from Rohrau. Just like the Kapellmeister. Who else but Master Bartó could have told him that? She didn't think he knew anyone else from the palace.

She considered the nameless man. Now, that was strange, too. He had asked for her name, but not given her one in return. Why not?

And now that she thought about it, there was something odd about his person, too. Rosalie couldn't quite put her finger on what it was. Her mind brought up an image of the peasant with his immense height, his boyish good looks, and charming smile.

A peasant? That was it! His clothes were such as any peasant might wear. Coarse gray-green coat and trousers of serviceable loden. Plain linen shirt. A rough wool cloak. She'd thought he was from Master Bartó's hometown. A simple peasant. But now, she wasn't so sure.

She'd thought nothing of it when he asked to meet the principal violinist beyond the castle grounds. Convinced it was a matter of some urgency, she had hurried straight up to deliver the message to Master Bartó. Now she wished she had gone to the Kapellmeister instead.

Despite his clothes, the man didn't seem like a peasant. No more than His Serene Highness would, were he ever to don such garments. Rosalie tried to picture the Prince in the rough, durable garb of a farm-hand. Now, what would mark him as a nobleman even in such rude gear?

She struggled over the question. His speech, perhaps. Or his gait. But she could recall nothing remarkable in either. No distinct feature that set the stranger apart.

If he was really a peasant, why had he...? Well, not lied. But he had been cagey, merely smiling when she asked if he brought news from Master Bartó's family. Deflecting all her questions. Drawing her out, but revealing nothing. All she'd gleaned was that he needed to speak with Master Bartó. Privately. She supposed there was no harm in that.

Unless he wasn't a peasant. But a member of the nobility, instead! What business could a nobleman have with the principal violinist of the Esterházy orchestra? And why had he come disguised?

Oblivious to the warm, soapy dishwater growing cold, Rosalie stared out the window, an uneasy stirring in the pit of her stomach. She clutched a silver dish in one palm, held a sponge in the other, but her hands, growing wrinkled and numb in the water, remained motionless.

Finally, she wiped both hands on her apron. The dishes could wait. She would follow Master Bartó and the stranger, and see if she could overhear any of their conversation. There was mischief brewing, she was sure of it.

Just then, she heard the mail coach rolling into the inner courtyard. She hesitated for just a moment. Could she put off fetching Herr Haydn's mail while she followed her hunch?

But the Kapellmeister, she knew, would be impatiently awaiting his mail. Most likely he leant over the banisters at this very moment, like an impetuous young schoolboy, eager to know if the mailbag brought any letters from Vienna.

———

The coachman had brought the mail bag into the hallway. A footman sifted through the enormous pile of envelopes left on the polished table, dividing them into five smaller stacks. One for the family. One for the guests. The third for the staff under the Estates Director. The fourth for the musicians. And the largest pile for the diverse artists and artisans in temporary employment at the castle.

Rosalie took up a position behind the Prince's valet and the Princess's maid, and waited for the footman to finish his task. She swirled from side to side, and tapped her foot lightly on the floor. She would have to bide her time until they picked up the mail for Their Serene Highnesses.

Her thoughts returned to Master Bartó's curious friend. Should she inform the Kapellmeister of the stranger's visit? All she had was the vaguest suspicion that the man wasn't a peasant. If Herr Haydn pressed her on the issue, what would she say?

She was still undecided when she entered the Music Room, bearing his letters on a silver tray. But the Kapellmeister was so lost in thought, he didn't so much as turn around.

"Ah, thank you, Rosalie. You may put my letters on the fortepiano."

Rosalie was so surprised, she couldn't prevent herself gaping at him. "But you have letters from Vienna." She pushed back the curly tendril of hair that had fallen over her forehead. "Are you sure you don't want to open them right away?"

The Kapellmeister held up his hand. "Whatever it is, it can wait," he said with an abstracted air.

"But there's one from Herr Tomasini." Rosalie held out the letter from the absent Konzertmeister. Herr Haydn showed no signs of having heard her. He stroked his chin, and studied the dark rose rug on which he stood.

Rosalie peered closely at the Kapellmeister. Something must be eating at him. She had never seen him respond with so little animation to his correspondence. What had Master Bartó done now?

Once again she wondered if she should broach the subject of Master Bartó's odd friend. Then she saw the lines of weariness that marked the

Kapellmeister's features, and decided not to bother him with what was most likely a trifle.

Master Johann was coming up the carpeted staircase when Rosalie came out of the Music Room. The maid considered approaching him with her suspicions, but they hung upon so slender a thread, she thought better of it.

The Kapellmeister's younger brother paused at the top of the stairs. He rested his hand on one of the marble figures that decorated the banisters, and took a few deep breaths. He was still standing there when Rosalie neared the staircase.

"Herr Haydn seems very troubled, Master Johann," she said.

"I have overheard the most intriguing conversation," Haydn greeted Johann the moment he set foot within the Music Room.

"It must have been more than that. Your correspondence lies untouched!" Johann walked toward the fortepiano, and flipped through the unopened envelopes. "What troubles you so, that not even a letter from our Luigi elicits your interest?"

Johann's gentle tone did much to ease Haydn. He stood before the Kapellmeister, head tilted in concern, grey eyes crinkled. Haydn thought his youngest brother had never looked more like their father. He felt his misgivings recede. *Let the problem be what it may, Sepperl. There is always a solution,* Mathias Haydn, God rest his soul, had often said.

But his qualms returned as he began to recount what he had overheard.

"There is some devilry afoot, and Bartó is at the bottom of it," he declared when he had finished. "He knows well enough I cannot dismiss him. It would be foolish to do so."

Johann, leaning against the fortepiano, head still tilted, straightened up at these words. "Perhaps he has realized you are at the end of your tether." He swept his arm in the direction of the town. "Who would not be with a man of his quarrelsome nature? Besides, did you not issue a warning to him the other day?"

It was a plausible enough explanation, and Haydn wished he could accept it. "Yes, but there has been no change in Bartó's conduct. He was lying, I am sure of it. I only wish I knew why."

33

"Now, why would Bartó want anyone to think you intend to dismiss him, brother?"

"It makes little sense, I know." Haydn gnawed at his lower lip. His brother would never say it outright, but Johann must suppose he mistook a mere ripple murmuring across a puddle for the raging of the Danube. He searched his memory for any detail that could convince him.

He recalled Bartó's tone. "He was pleading. I would take my oath on it. Bartó sounded genuinely desperate to impress upon his companion that I would dismiss him. And through no fault of his own."

He snorted. "No fault of his own, indeed! The man's behavior is preposterous."

"Yes, but his own fear for his position may well account for his ill-temper. You did say he seemed unreasonably jealous of Lorenzo?"

Haydn considered this as he paced about the room. It seemed unlikely. What cause did his principal violinist have to be jealous of anyone? His mind moved to a different question. "I wonder who his companion was. I could see neither man. The other voice sounded familiar, but I still cannot place it. Judging by the little I heard, a person in a position of some authority over Bartó."

"Herr Rahier?" Johann ventured a guess.

"The Estates Director is the last person to want to intimidate Bartó into remaining in my favor. He would be quite delighted to get rid of Bartó in order to foist his bumbling nephew on my hands."

"Ah yes, that nephew! I remember him well." A look of utter distaste flared across Johann's features. "He has a positive talent for making his violin screech. Still, this man holding a stick over Bartó does you a favor. You can use Bartó's fears to issue a stronger warning to him. Keep him on until the imperial visit is over, and then, unless his manner improves, dismiss him without a reference."

Haydn felt the weight of his burdens fall away from him. He might have known Johann would find a way out of this vexing situation.

"I will do it this very evening."

Even so, he wondered what was at stake for Bartó to live in such fear of losing his position.

When would Bartó return? Haydn heard a heavy footfall, and peered over the banisters for the fifth time. Bartó climbed slowly up the stairs. Haydn had never seen him so subdued. He waited until the violinist stepped heavily onto the landing, then confronted him.

"Your absence during rehearsal sets a poor example to the other musicians. What if they were to follow your lead, and came and went just as they pleased?"

Bartó's eyes narrowed as Haydn spoke. He scanned the stretch of hallway over Haydn's shoulder, then directed a piercing glare at him.

"You have your spies, I see, Herr Kapellmeister." He swallowed several times, and clutched the banister. It seemed to take him an effort to rein in his temper.

When he spoke again, he had wiped the scowl off his face. "It was not by choice that I left in the middle of practice. Still, I will endeavor to keep your objection in mind. Have you anything further to say or will that be all?"

"That is all for now. But I would like a word with you at the end of the day." Haydn replied, not sure what to make of his principal violinist's manner.

Bartó had curbed his contrariness, most likely at the insistence of his mysterious companion. But his habitual distrustfulness seemed to have turned to paranoia. Accusing the Bürgermeister of prying into his affairs was preposterous enough. Thinking his Kapellmeister employed informants to spy on his every move savored of madness!

Haydn watched him go, unable to shake off the uneasy sense that Bartó had some evil planned. Why else would his principal violinist be so suspicious of everyone?

Bartó's bizarre behavior continued through the day. He refused to rise to the bait no matter how much the other musicians provoked him. He played through every piece without raising the slightest objection to Haydn's manner of indicating phrases or changes in dynamics and articulation.

His manner toward his colleagues, though distant, was polite. But Haydn noticed Bartó kept his beloved Stadlmann so close, no other musician had the opportunity to touch it. More than once, Haydn caught him guardedly watching the other men. A man alone in a den of suspected villains could not be more vigilant!

Every so often, Bartó's keen gaze raked over Lorenzo's features. The suspicion on his face was unmistakable. Haydn thought he detected a flicker of terror as well. What could Lorenzo have done to inspire it?

At the end of the day, Haydn was still trying to persuade himself all was well. Bartó had, at least, displayed no show of temper. The warning Haydn meant to issue might not be necessary after all. He pushed aside the baryton trios he had been working on, and leaned back in his chair. His fingers felt cramped from the effort of writing.

Haydn glanced up at the gilded porcelain clock on the wall. In a quarter of an hour, his musicians would be ready to leave. He was still pondering Bartó's behavior when the door to the Music Room was thrust open, and the principal violinist burst in, dragging his violin case behind him.

Haydn's head pivoted instantly toward the door. He was not overly offended by the musician's boorish entry, but it would not do to let it pass unacknowledged. "I prefer you announce your presence with a knock, Bartó. Instead of charging in the way you just did. Other than that, there is nothing I wish to say. You are free to leave." No need to issue his ultimatum, he decided.

Bartó, if he heard Haydn at all, showed no sign of it. He approached Haydn's desk, and held up a broad, flat palm to silence him.

"Herr Kapellmeister, whatever it is you wish to say to me, let it wait. Hear me out first, I beg of you. The matter is urgent."

Haydn frowned, but nonetheless invited his principal violinist to take a seat in one of the gilded chairs near the window.

Bartó ignored the offer. He held himself rigid, hands hanging stiffly down. "I am in urgent need of money, Herr Kapellmeister. I must have one hundred gulden in the next day or two."

Haydn's frown deepened. The amount was far in excess of the small advances he sometimes made to his musicians to tide them over until they were paid. "Why Bartó, what urgent need can you possibly have?"

Bartó stared at Haydn in silence. His swarthy complexion darkened to a deep purple. "Is that really any of your concern, Herr Kapellmeister?" he said at last as he pulled his violin case closer. His knuckles showed white against the burnished handle.

Haydn felt his hackles rise. Was Bartó being insolent?

"Your financial needs would ordinarily not concern me at all. But when you ask me to authorize an advance of a substantial amount, it does become my concern. You are paid well enough to make any request for money very unusual. Not to mention a sum of this size."

Bartó harrumphed. "Ach, Herr Kapellmeister. Who says it has to be a loan? Let it be the difference between the paltry amount I make and the amount I should be making were I being paid as befits my virtuoso status. If you make the necessary changes to my contract, the sum you give me will simply be the money owed to me rather than an advance."

Haydn leaned forward. His grip tightened on the tortoiseshell writing case he had been fiddling with. "You are not owed any money, Bartó. Nor are you owed a raise."

"How long must I wait for a raise in salary, then?" Bartó came closer to the Kapellmeister, his fists clenched.

For a brief moment, Haydn said not a word, too stunned to reply. Bartó glowered at him, and the Kapellmeister glared back at his principal violinist.

"Your musical proficiency and the stellar reference my brother Michael provided you do not exempt you from the rules that apply to all my musicians." Haydn brought his fist down on his cherry wood desk with unaccustomed force. "You are here on probation, and you have only served three of the six months of that period. Need I say more?"

Bartó's thin lips seemed to become even thinner. "I need money, Herr Kapellmeister. How am I to support a family on the two hundred gulden I am paid? How, I ask you!" The principal violinist was almost quivering in rage.

"The amount you scoff at suffices well enough for the other musicians and their families. Besides, you receive room and board, and rations of grain and meat as well. And even without those extras, you are paid a generous amount."

Bartó lowered the fist he had begun to raise and took several deep breaths. "Look around you, Herr Kapellmeister." He swept his arm around the room at the gilded furniture and the ornate jewel-encrusted picture frames that surrounded them. "We work for a man who lacks nothing, and who can afford to pay his musicians what they deserve. Only think of the money the Prince lavishes on renovating that hunting lodge of his. Yet, you and I, simple peasants, are to be content with the crumbs he throws us?"

The words propelled Haydn to his feet. "I do not know about you, Bartó. But I myself would still be a poor musician in Vienna with barely two kreutzers to rub together despite working myself to the bone were it not for the magnanimity of His Serene Highness.

"I have tolerated your squabbles with your fellow musicians. I have been silent despite hearing of your run-ins with the townspeople. But, be warned, Bartó, you go too far in your criticism of the Prince. Mend your behavior, or you will be dismissed after the Empress's visit. Your services are not indispensable; and your talent, though exceptional, not unusual."

Bartó brought his right fist against his left palm with a forceful thwack. "I will not be dismissed, Herr Kapellmeister. I will be long gone before you can dismiss me. You wait and see."

CHAPTER FOUR

A vein throbbed in Haydn's temple as the day's events roiled out of him into his brother's sympathetic ears later that evening. They sat in his wife's warm kitchen, but he barely tasted his food.

"The temerity of that man never ceases to astound me." Haydn's voice crescendoed to a finish. He thrust his knife into his breaded veal, and regretted it instantly. A small section of his schnitzel flew of his plate, and landed on the table. Reason enough for Maria Anna to voice her displeasure, and she seized it.

"You will chip the rose pattern on my china if you continue on in that manner, husband." She watched Haydn retrieve the piece with a quick stab of his fork. "The meat is not so tough that you need wrestle with it so."

"I suspect it is Bartó's antics, and not the veal, that cause brother Joseph's agitation," Johann rose to Haydn's defense.

"This is the most succulent, flavorful piece of meat I have ever tasted," Johann added with a smile. He speared a piece of meat, brought it to his mouth, and chewed and swallowed with a relish that appeared to mollify his sister-in-law.

His smile dimmed when he turned toward Haydn. "Your principal violinist's behavior is inexplicable! A man in fear for his position would exercise greater caution. But Bartó persistently acts in a manner sure to precipitate that very outcome."

Haydn set his knife down. "I never thought he feared for his position," he said quietly. "But I can make no sense of it, either. Why should Bartó choose this very moment to carp at the terms of his contract?"

Maria Anna rose to bring out her cherry kuchen. Haydn waited until she neared the oven, then leaned closer to his brother. "If it were not for the snippet I overheard this afternoon," he said, his voice low, "I would think his companion had put ideas in his head or brought an offer from some noble family that thinks to rival the Esterházy orchestra. He believes he should be paid three hundred gulden a year!"

Johann appeared to digest this bit of information. His mouth closed over a piece of schnitzel. He stared at his plate as he chewed. It must be bad indeed, Haydn thought, if his brother had no words at hand to allay his concern.

Maria Anna returned to the table, just then with her kuchen. She set it down, and looked curiously from her husband to Johann.

"Why does your violinist want three hundred gulden?"

Haydn hesitated. She had already heard the worst of it. Bartó had threatened to leave. What matter if she heard the rest? "He seems to have acquired a family. And with it, a concern that two hundred gulden along with perquisites cannot suffice to support one." He braced himself. What portents of doom would his wife discover in this incident?

"Well, I dare say the additional hundred gulden a year will suffice for that purpose," was all Maria Anna said. She brought a dish of cold, sweetened cream to the table. "It is a generous enough sum for any woman with a child. I have known quite a few make do with less."

It was such a ridiculous comment, Haydn had trouble keeping his eyes still. His wife *made do* with six hundred gulden. In her opinion, he supposed, that was barely enough to keep one's head above water. Only a spendthrift like Maria Anna would consider two hundred gulden wholly inadequate to support a wife and child. And three hundred gulden barely sufficient to do the job. Besides, what child did Bartó have? Or wife, for that matter?

"By the by," Maria Anna went on, ignoring Haydn's reaction, "I shall need fifteen gulden for my dressmaker."

Haydn stared at his wife. "You have spent fifteen gulden? On a dress?" What kind of dress required so outrageous a sum? It was almost as much as some of his musicians earned in a month.

Maria Anna crossed her arms. "What would you have me do, husband? Go to our godchild's christening in my old rags?" She shook her head impatiently. "Oh, do not tell me you have forgotten all about it! It is your cellist Niklas's firstborn son."

"It has not completely escaped my mind, Maria Anna," he retorted. Although it had, thanks to Bartó. Not that he would admit it to his wife. At

40

least, his musical preparations for the event were complete. "I may have omitted to lavish fifteen gulden on a new set of clothes. But there is a mass composed in honor of the occasion."

Maria Anna merely sniffed, and continued to fan the hot kuchen with a cloth.

"Do you suppose Bartó is in debt or under some financial obligation?" Johann, deep in thought until now, roused himself to ask. "An obligation he is eager to get out of? Maybe his visitor sought to spur him into discharging his duty. It would explain what you overheard and his subsequent behavior."

Haydn nodded. His violinist, stubborn beyond belief, was just the kind of man to need prodding. And to lie about his own imminent dismissal only to plead off his duties, apparently!

But Maria Anna chimed in before he could say a word: "So eager, he must have hoped his demand for money would get him dismissed."

Haydn could only stare at her in stunned silence. He hoped she was merely babbling, but his wife had tossed out the remark as though she knew something. Could Bartó deliberately be trying to get himself dismissed? It would explain his outrageous behavior. But then, he could hardly be so averse to paying off his debts as to go to the trouble of getting dismissed from a lucrative position.

"If Bartó owes money, it may be to Gerhard in Kleinhöflein." Haydn addressed Johann, but gave his wife a quick glance out of the corner of his eyes. He hoped his remark would spur her into revealing any knowledge she had. A direct question, he knew, would yield him nothing. Maria Anna delighted in being evasive.

Her elusive reference to the tavern-keeper the other night returned to Haydn's mind. Could she really know why Gerhard and his principal violinist were at odds with each other?

Far more likely that she knew nothing at all, he told himself, when Maria Anna ignored his remark. She took out a knife, instead, and began slicing her kuchen with swift, deft strokes. As though she hadn't heard him! She busied herself in this manner until Haydn loudly cleared his throat.

Then, she sniffed again, disparagingly, but refused to look up. "If you kept your eyes and ears open, husband," she said, "instead of burying yourself in your music, you would not find your violinist's behavior so inexplicable."

She paused to heap a spoonful of cream onto a slice of kuchen for Johann, and pushed the plate toward him. "Still, it would be well to hire another violinist to take his place."

"Why?" The question erupted out of Johann's mouth. "He will not be needed after the Empress's visit. And brother Joseph intends to keep him no longer than that. He has already issued an ultimatum to that effect, have you not, brother?"

Haydn nodded, but was prevented from saying anything more by Maria Anna's next words.

"Well, let us hope he stays as long as that."

Rosalie rubbed her forehead as she stared at the letter the mail coach had brought for her. She had decided to read it while waiting in the kitchen for some of the other maids. But its contents had begun to make her head throb.

"I grow tired of this tedious business of printing," her brother Sándor had written. "What could our parents have been thinking to make me work here with Antal Péchi? The endless pamphlets and treatises on the Hungarian situation we have had to print. The eternal disputes on the best way for Hungary to get the House of Habsburg off its back. My dear sister, you cannot imagine how tiresome it all is!"

Rosalie closed her eyes and kneaded her forehead with her fist. "It is just an honest day's work, Sanyi, and good money, besides."

She shook her head. It took very little for her younger brother to lose all interest in a position merely because of the repetitive nature of the work. She had lost count of the number of positions with excellent prospects he had left because the work failed to stimulate him any longer.

Rosalie glanced up at the plain wooden clock that stood against the wall near the window, and wondered how long the other maids would be. The cold, fresh air on the long walk to their quarters behind the extensive palace gardens would do much to ease the pain of her headache.

She squeezed her eyes shut, and gently massaged the eyelids with her fingertips. A moment passed. Then, she smoothed out the pages covered in her brother's fine hand, and resumed her reading.

"My musical talents are wasted here in Pressburg. Why must it be either the Church or bookbinding and printing for me? You have only to look at Herr Haydn's success to realize our parents were entirely mistaken about the lack of prospects in secular music."

Oh, foolish Sanyi! Rosalie clutched her forehead. Her fingers threaded into the glossy strands of her hair as she raked her hand through her scalp. Everyone in Rohrau knew of the years of poverty the Kapellmeister had endured. How close he had been to starvation in Vienna. How he had eked out a meager living as a musician. And if, God forbid, the Prince should lose his wealth and have to disband his orchestra like Herr Haydn's first employer, there would go all his success!

"God did not intend for me to be a mere journeyman helping to run a small Catholic printing press in Pressburg, Rosalie. If He did, you, my dear sister, would not find yourself in such close proximity to the greatest composer of our time."

Rosalie pushed Sándor's letter away from her. How could her brother expect her to prevail upon Herr Haydn to employ him? As though it was the Kapellmeister's responsibility to find positions for everyone in the Szabó family. Hadn't he done enough by securing a position for her?

Not that her parents had sought any favors from the Kapellmeister. Old Mathias Haydn, their neighbor, had urged his son to provide what aid he could on his deathbed. And Herr Haydn had made good on his promise as soon as he was appointed Court Kapellmeister. Asking him to do any more was out of the question.

"Besides, a musician's work is every bit as tedious as any other work, Sanyi," she muttered to herself. The daily drudgery of rehearsals would soon wear Sándor out. "Why, even Master Bartó has to practice a piece twenty times over, or more, to perfect it!"

The thought of Master Bartó reminded Rosalie of the strange peasant who had visited him that morning. But a commotion in the hallway interrupted her thoughts.

She thought she recognized the icy voice of the Estates Director. She went out into the hallway just in time to hear him say: "And it is more than you should have heard."

Herr Rahier pointed a long finger at the group of maids huddled near the staircase. "Have you nothing better to do than stand around in the hallway gossiping?"

"And you!" He turned his attention to the plump, blond maid in the middle. "What business do you have listening in at doors. You should be ashamed of yourself!"

The plump maid glared after the Estates Director's retreating back. She held her head high, and marched primly toward the kitchen door.

"I was not listening in at the door," she said as she brushed past Rosalie. "I was emptying the vases in the hallway outside the Music Room." She pointed a pudgy hand in the direction of the Estates Director's office. "He was up there, too, you know. What business did he have there, I should like to know!"

Rosalie followed the maid into the kitchen. "But what did you hear Greta?"

Greta turned toward Rosalie, a broad smile on her face. "You will never guess?" She caught sight of the letter on the kitchen table, and smirked. "Let us just say Herr Haydn might soon be in need of the services of a violinist such as your brother."

Rosalie's hand flew to her mouth. "It is Master Bartó, is it not? What has he done now?"

Greta sat down, brushing a fine strand of golden hair from her pale face. "He has threatened to leave! But not before Herr Haydn gave him his marching orders." She leaned over. "I can tell you I will be glad to see the last of that awful man."

Rosalie sank down into the chair next to Greta. It hardly seemed possible. Could Master Bartó have grown so audacious? What could have caused it? His strange visitor? The lure of a better offer, perhaps?

Whatever it was, it might be just the opportunity for Sándor. Who knew, given the chance to use his musical talents, he might just buckle down to work.

Some days later, Haydn and Johann sat at the window of the Music Room, and went over the music for his godson's Christening. The service would be held shortly before the imperial visit. The mass Haydn had composed for his godson lay in an untidy stack on a black lacquer table painted with roses that stood between their armchairs.

As he worked, Maria Anna's premonition rang persistently in Haydn's mind. Bartó had, fortunately, not left. But his wife's conviction that he would had impressed itself upon the Kapellmeister's mind. He found it hard to shake off her warning. Or her constant reproof that he was deaf and blind to everything around him other than his music.

Haydn expelled a heavy breath, and glanced up. Johann pored intently over his sheet music, pen in hand to mark changes. His brother, eleven years younger than Haydn, had a wisdom beyond his years. The Kapellmeister was in sore need of it this morning.

"What knowledge can Maria Anna possibly have of Bartó that I do not?" he said out loud.

Johann looked up, reluctantly, Haydn thought. "You cannot take her words to heart, brother. She spoke in anger, no doubt, and only sought to alarm you." He put his music down on the stack covering the lacquer table between them. "How could you do your duty as Kapellmeister and manage your men if you were as unaware of what goes around you as she accuses you of being?"

"But what is this dispute with Gerhard that she hinted at? There is some dispute. What obligation is Bartó so desperate to rid himself of?" Haydn gripped the silk-covered armrests on either side of him, and pulled himself forward.

Johann smiled and tilted his head in a way that reminded the Kapellmeister of their father. In just this way had his father regarded him when he had despaired of his future, convinced it was ruined unless he became a castrato.

"She knows nothing more than either you or I do, brother. I am sure of it. In all likelihood, she was merely taking our own conjectures a little further."

Haydn chewed his lower lip. Was it as simple as that? Ever since their relations had worsened, Maria Anna took great relish in pointing out doom where none existed. But when it came to his failings, she had always been more clear-sighted than he could have wished. Even in the early days of their marriage when she had liked him—or pretended to.

He was about to question Johann further on the matter when a loud rapping on the door interrupted his thoughts. Before he could respond, the door opened, and the Estates Director stepped into the room.

"Ah, Herr Kapellmeister. Master Johann." Rahier nodded at each man in turn. "I see you are both hard at work." He approached their armchairs.

Haydn stiffened. What did the Estates Director want now?

"A word with you, if you please, Herr Kapellmeister." Rahier gazed pointedly at Johann, evidently expecting him to leave the room. Johann was about to rise, but sat back readily enough when Haydn, with a slight movement of his head, motioned for him to stay. It was not for Rahier to give orders to his singers and his musicians.

The Estates Director heaved a loud sigh of resignation. "Well, stay if you must." He turned toward Haydn. "I want to draw your attention once more to my nephew's musical skills, Herr Kapellmeister."

"It has come to my ears," he explained when Haydn stared at him, bewildered, "that your principal violinist demanded a substantial sum of money. Which you denied him."

Haydn's eyes met Johann's. How, in the name of God, had the Estates Director known that? Did he make a habit of listening in on his conversations with Bartó? Most likely, the man had his ear pressed avidly to the door at the time.

"You did well not to give in to his demand, Herr Kapellmeister."

"I am glad you approve, Herr Rahier." Haydn shifted in his chair to face the door. "But what does Bartó's demand for money have to do with your nephew?"

He wished Rahier would go. His younger brother, he noticed, was no more ruffled by the visit than he would have been by a fly or the annoying demands of an unreasonable toddler. But not he. He stared pointedly at the stack of music on the table.

But the Estates Director was not one to take a hint. He drew up a chair, brushed a few imaginary speckles of dust off the crimson seat, and sat down. His icy blue eyes settled unblinkingly on the Kapellmeister.

"It is not in my nature to gloat. So I will not point out how greatly you erred in your judgment, Herr Kapellmeister, when you passed over my nephew in favor of your principal violinist.

"But I must point out, in the friendliest spirit, of course, that in tolerating the man for two more weeks, you make a grave error."

Haydn sat back in his chair and folded his arms. "On the contrary, Herr Rahier. Dismissing a key musician before the Empress's visit—which, I need hardly remind you, is an event of the greatest importance to His Serene Highness—would be the worse error."

Rahier held up a hand, bowing his head at the same time as though in acknowledgement of the Kapellmeister's objection. "I have taken note of the circumstances, Herr Kapellmeister. Were it not for His Serene Highness's desire to put on a lavish display for Her Majesty, I would demand an instant dismissal of your principal violinist."

Haydn's lips tightened at Rahier's easy assumption of one of his own duties. They both knew it was the Kapellmeister and not the Estates Director who determined which musician would be hired and which one shown the door.

Oblivious to Haydn's reaction, Rahier went on: "As it stands, I only ask you to consider the wisdom of keeping on so troublesome a man as your principal violinist. Despite the circumstances, your hands are not tied." .

Were they not? Haydn deliberately allowed his left eyebrow to arch up, and met the Estates Director's gaze.

Rahier must have read his expression. He pursed his lips, and leaned back in his chair, his elegantly shod feet planted firmly on the floor. "Ach, Herr Kapellmeister, you know as well as I do that my nephew is more than capable of stepping into your principal violinist's shoes."

Haydn exchanged another glance with his brother. Johann lifted his shoulders in an amused shrug. His hands were tied worse than he had supposed if the fallout of dismissing Bartó meant having to deal with Rahier's dreaded nephew. He turned back to the Estates Director.

"To put it plainly, then, Herr Rahier, you wish me to dismiss my musician and hire your nephew in his stead. And I suppose I can reasonably expect your nephew to master in as little as two weeks material that it has taken Bartó nearly three months to prepare." Haydn allowed his voice to rise to a question as he uttered the last word.

Rahier stood up, a steely glint in his blue eyes. "I will leave you to ponder my words, Herr Kapellmeister." His lips were still compressed as he turned on his heels to leave the room. "But mark my words. No good can come of your hesitation to dispense with your violinist's services." He banged the door shut.

CHAPTER FIVE

The storm clouds that hung low over Eisenstadt and the first dusting of snow they brought with them that evening drove all thoughts of Rahier and his nephew from the Kapellmeister's mind. It had been two days since Bartó made his threat to leave. His principal violinist would not, Haydn decided, be rash enough to abandon his position.

"If nothing else, the thought of losing his beloved violin will prevent him from any foolhardy actions," Haydn said to himself as he put on his overcoat, eager to leave before the precipitation grew any heavier. The wind, blustering outside, was already strong enough to push drifts of snow before it.

A glimmer of light was visible under the Estates Director's office door downstairs. As he walked past, Haydn idly wondered what Rahier was doing within the castle at so late an hour. He shrugged. It was none of his affair. He strode out onto the inner courtyard, bracing himself against the wind as he struggled toward the drawbridge.

God forbid this storm should continue to rage beyond the night. Their Hungarian roads, never in good repair, would be quite impassable if it did. The Empress would then be compelled to turn back to Vienna. Head bent against the wind, Haydn shuddered at this dreadful prospect.

Maria Anna was alone in the kitchen when Haydn arrived home. He vigorously stomped the snow off his shoes before setting foot on the polished wood floor.

"Where is Johann?" he asked, as he hung his coat on a peg behind the kitchen door.

"Your brother has retired for the night." Maria Anna brought a steaming bowl of soup to the table for Haydn. "I was at the Parish Church in Kleinhöflein this morning making arrangements for the Christening service," she began.

Making arrangements to spend my hard-earned money, no doubt, Haydn thought as he blew on a spoonful of soup to cool it. He ate in silence, grunting a response now and again as Maria Anna rattled on about her day and the gossip she had picked up about town.

His ears pricked up at the mention of his principal violinist. Bartó had been seen storming out of the Parish Church a few days back, shouting and shaking his fist at the pastor as he stalked away.

"Your principal violinist seems to think a confession of his sins can buy him divine protection." Maria Anna snorted.

What devil could Bartó fear, Haydn wondered, that he felt the need for divine protection? He chewed thoughtfully on a piece of bread, his attention drifting away again from Maria Anna's conversation. Had Bartó's reluctance to fulfill his obligations earned him a threat? Or was it something else altogether? Something that prompted his strangely leery attitude toward his colleagues?

Still, bizarre as it was, Bartó's behavior was causing the Kapellmeister less trouble than his former belligerence. *And in a few more weeks, he will be gone*, Haydn said to himself. His eyes flickered in quiet gratitude toward the crucifix on the wall opposite him.

Hearing Bartó's name again, he returned his attention to Maria Anna. The gist of her story had escaped him. He had only caught the name Marlene along with that of Herr Hipfl, the barber-surgeon.

"...refused to give over a single kreutzer," Maria Anna said as she tipped over a generous slice of kuchen onto a plate for Haydn.

"Ach so." Haydn reached for his dessert, his curiosity piqued. Who was Marlene? And what did either she or the barber-surgeon have to do with Bartó? He would soon find out. His muttered encouragement should keep his wife talking.

But Maria Anna looked up sharply at his words. "You have not heard a single word I've said, have you husband?"

Haydn, about to bring a forkful of kuchen to his mouth, put his fork down with a sigh. How had she caught him out this time?

"That is not true! I have listened to every word."

Maria Anna glared at him, her chin thrust out. "What have you heard, then?"

Haydn glanced at the crucifix again, and fingered his fork. The sullen refusal to part with even a kreutzer sounded just like Bartó. Had someone asked Bartó for money, and been denied? It was unlikely to be the barber-surgeon. It must be the woman, Marlene, whoever she was.

He turned back to Maria Anna, confident. "Marlene wanted money from Bartó, but he refused to give her a single kreutzer. It was churlish of him, I agree. But entirely in character. Besides, given his own financial obligations, one can hardly expect Bartó to be generous with his money."

Maria Anna rose to her feet. "It is just as I suspected. I have been trying to convey news of some importance to you, but I could have been speaking to my pots and pans for all you care."

She swept his dessert plate away.

"I have barely touched my kuchen, Maria Anna," Haydn protested. His eyes lingered on the sweetened cherry preserves and cream heaped on his untouched dessert. His wife's singing might be as pleasant as the crowing of a jackdaw. Her tongue as sweetly mellow as souring wine. But there was not much to fault in the food she cooked.

"You are so lost in your thoughts, I doubt you have tasted a morsel of my cooking." Maria Anna began clearing the table in a huff.

Seeing Haydn still at the table, she put her hands on her hips. "Well, be off with you, husband! I cannot wait upon you all day."

She was still vexed at him the following morning.

Rosalie stood near the entryway of the West Wing, huddled inside her coat. She crossed her arms over her chest, and tucked her hands under her armpits. It was bitterly cold, but at least the storm clouds had passed leaving the sky a pristine blue.

Hearing heavy footsteps behind her, she looked over her shoulder. Buxom Greta hurried down the hallway, carrying a silver pail with brooms, mops, and dustpans over her left arm.

"Here, take the dustpans and the brooms." Greta crammed the last bite of a sweet, buttered roll into her mouth, and held the pail out to Rosalie.

"Let us be off, then." Rosalie took the proffered implements. "The sooner we can get the Musicians' Quarters cleaned, the better. I still have to mop the Music Room floor and make Herr Haydn's coffee."

She set off at a brisk pace across the inner courtyard. She had almost reached the forecourt, when she saw a tall, cloaked figure treading carefully on the wet cobblestoned path that skirted the snow-laden mounds of grass.

"Sándor!" Rosalie stopped short. There was no mistaking the vivid chestnut-colored, wavy locks that tumbled out from under the hood covering the man's head.

"Is that your brother?" Greta gasped, the abrupt change in momentum making her totter dangerously on the slippery path. She flailed her arms in an effort to regain her balance.

"I thought you had told him not to leave his job just yet." Greta peered over Rosalie's shoulder at the man approaching them.

"Sister!" Sándor drew Rosalie into a warm hug. "I thought it best to get here and acquaint myself with Herr Haydn before he has a chance to hire someone else for the job." He drew back, and flashed a radiant smile at Greta.

Rosalie handed her brooms and dustpans to Greta. "Go on up the hill, and get started, Greta." She prodded the other maid forward. "My brother and I must talk."

"Do not tell me you have left your position at Antal Péchi's printing shop, Sanyi," she declared once Greta had left them.

"What would you have me do, sister? Antal was forever complaining the business was doing so poorly, he didn't know how much longer he could afford to run it."

"Antal complains about money incessantly. No matter how well his business is doing. What will you do now? There are no prospects here for you."

"Why? Has Herr Haydn found himself a new violinist already?"

Rosalie sighed. "Sanyi, Herr Haydn has no need of a new violinist just yet. Didn't I tell you not to give up your position until I had more news?"

Sándor shrugged. "Well, I am here now, sister. It is just possible, Herr Haydn will find some use for my services."

Haydn was relieved to see the storm had spent its force, leaving only a blanket of snow all over Eisenstadt. The air that greeted him as he stepped out of his courtyard was cold and crisp.

Maria Anna thrust her head out of the window. "Come in and get your breakfast, husband. You may have nothing better to do than loll about in the snow, but I have work to do."

Haydn took his silver timepiece out of his pocket, and gave its dial a quick glance. "As do I, Maria Anna. I had best set out for the palace. I will eat there."

Maria Anna shut the window with a bang that made Haydn wince. "Making me slave all morning over a breakfast he won't eat," he heard her grumble so loudly he was certain all of Eisenstadt had heard as well.

He was about to return to the house for his music case, when Maria Anna opened the window and hurled it at him. It flew open, its contents drifting onto the snow before Haydn could catch either the case or the manuscripts it contained.

"Be off with you, then. Although I greatly doubt Her Majesty will be coming to Eisenstadt, after all."

Haydn ignored this sentiment of doom. There was no reason for the Empress to cancel her visit. The storm had abated. If this fair weather continued to hold, she would encounter little trouble on her journey south from Vienna. He gathered his manuscripts, brushing the powdery grains of snow from each sheet before returning it to his leather case, and set off.

He had just neared the town hall when Herr Groer, the Bürgermeister, hailed out to him urgently as he hurried up the path from the castle.

"Herr Haydn!" he huffed, coming to a halt before the Kapellmeister. The unaccustomed exertion had flushed his cheeks a deeper red than usual. "The imperial visit—" Herr Groer put one hand on his hip and clutched at his heart with the other, still panting. "Do you have any news?"

A blast of cold air wrapped itself around Haydn's neck. He ignored it. "News? What news, Herr Groer? What have you heard?" How badly, he wondered, had the previous night's unexpected snowstorm affected the roads?

The Bürgermeister had regained his breath. He shook his head. "That is just it, Herr Haydn. I have heard nothing. The Hungarians are always rumbling on about something or the other. To my mind, they are more bark than bite, but Count Pergen must think otherwise."

Haydn squinted at the Bürgermeister, struggling to take in his words. "Count Pergen?"

"He is the head of state police," the Bürgermeister explained. "A man of a deeply suspicious nature from all I have heard."

"Yes, yes, I do know who Count Pergen is, Herr Groer. But why should his suspicions concern us?"

The Bürgermeister gazed heavenward in silent prayer as he ran his hand through his thatch of thick, white hair. "Ach, Herr Kapellmeister, did I not tell you? The Police Commissioner, Count Pergen's man in Eisenstadt, went to the castle early this morning, and has just left. Shortly thereafter, the Estates Director was rushing around in a frenzy, looking for you. Even you must see that can only mean one thing, Herr Haydn."

The color faded from Haydn's cheeks. "My principal violinist," he began.

The Bürgermeister brushed aside the Kapellmeister's principal violinist with an irritable wave of his hand. "Never mind your principal violinist! There are more important matters at hand. God forbid, the Hungarians' infernal griping should cost us the imperial visit."

But His Serene Highness, when Haydn found himself in his presence a few minutes later, made no mention of the Police Commissioner or the imperial visit other than to enquire about the entertainment his Kapellmeister was preparing.

"I will be out of town attending to some business for a few days, Haydn. And since I will be leaving shortly, I decided to see you earlier than the appointed hour."

Haydn expelled the breath he had been holding, and inched himself back from the edge of his seat. "You will not be disappointed, I assure you, Your Serene Highness."

The Prince set his coffee cup on the marble-topped table that stood between them, and rested his hands on the white ruffles covering his ample stomach. "I am glad to hear it, my dear Haydn. We must put on a splendid show for the Empress. No effort must be spared. Your own career—and mine—depends upon it."

The Prince paused before continuing. "On my return, I would like to hear some of the chamber music you have composed for Her Majesty, Haydn. You may treat it as a dress rehearsal of sorts."

Haydn inclined his head in assent, only to bring it up sharply at the Prince's next words.

"I trust your principal violinist performs his duties diligently. Is he a worthy successor to our absent Konzertmeister, Luigi Tomasini?"

What had the Prince heard regarding Bartó, Haydn wondered, once more sliding forward toward the edge of his chair.

"He is not, Your Serene Highness." There was nothing for it, but to tell the truth, he decided. "My brother Michael did not exaggerate Bartó's dexterity on the violin. He appears, however, to have been entirely mistaken about his suitability as an employee of the Esterházy court. I am afraid I cannot retain his services beyond the imperial visit."

The Prince brought his coffee cup up to his lips, and took a sip. "I am sorry to hear it." He directed an unblinking stare at his Kapellmeister over the rim of his cup. "I trust you will have him sufficiently under control for the duration of the imperial visit. I cannot afford to have anything disrupt Her Majesty's stay here."

───※───

The Estates Director must have had his ear pressed close to the door of the Prince's chamber for Haydn walked right into him as he left the Prince's chamber.

"Herr Rahier!" Haydn rubbed his nose where the button on the Estates Director's coat had scratched it.

The Estates Director ignored Haydn's protest, and put a firm hand on the Kapellmeister's neck to propel him forward. "What did His Serene Highness have to say?"

Haydn shook Rahier's hand off. "It does not concern you. Still, if you must know, the Prince was enquiring about the program of entertainment for Her Majesty."

"And he made *no* mention of the Police Commissioner's visit? None at all?"

Haydn bit back the retort that had sprung to his lips. "The Police Commissioner's visit is none of my affair, Herr Rahier."

The Estates Director gazed at Haydn through eyes narrowed in suspicion. "Is it not, Herr Kapellmeister? And yet no sooner had the Police Commissioner left than His Serene Highness sent for you."

Haydn felt his mouth puckering as he eyed the Estates Director. Why must everyone persist in believing the Police Commissioner's visit had anything to do with him? Or the imperial visit? Aware that he was holding his breath, he let it out.

"There is no great mystery in that. His Serene Highness is leaving on business shortly. His impending departure necessitated that we meet before mid-day. If it will set your mind at rest, we discussed the chamber music and my principal violinist, and nothing more."

The Estates Director had been stroking his chin as he scrutinized the floor. At Haydn's words, he looked up. "What crime can the Police Commissioner suspect that he should come running to His Serene Highness?" he muttered to himself.

Johann was waiting for Haydn at the top of the staircase in the semicircular carpeted landing between the Music Room and the Rehearsal Room. He came forward with a look of immense relief when he saw the Kapellmeister.

"There you are, brother! What took you so long?"

"His Serene Highness wished to see me. Why, what is it?"

As he spoke, an excited buzzing drew Haydn's attention toward the Rehearsal Room. The door was slightly ajar, but no strains of music emerged from the room. His brows drew together. Where was his principal violinist?

"What can Bartó be thinking of?" His eyes returned to his brother's anxious face. "The Prince wishes to hear all of the chamber music for the imperial visit. In three days' time, no less. But far from conducting rehearsal, Bartó allows the men to idle away the morning!"

"The imperial visit will still take place, then." Johann's voice sounded tentative.

Haydn wondered why, but there was no time to press the issue. More urgent matters awaited his attention. Head bowed, he stepped briskly toward the Rehearsal Room only to find Johann in front of him, barring his progress.

The Kapellmeister raised his head. The mists of preoccupation parted. He noted his brother's pale face and tightly pressed lips.

What was so amiss for Johann to look like that?

His younger brother coughed, eyes flickering away. "I wish I knew how to break the news to you, brother." He coughed again. A moment passed.

Then he turned resolutely toward Haydn.

"Bartó is gone, brother."

CHAPTER SIX

"Gone!" Haydn repeated, struggling to understand. "What do you mean Bartó is gone? Where can he have gone to?"

A maelstrom of thoughts whirled through his brain. He recalled the Estates Director's mutterings about some crime the Police Commissioner suspected. Could that have anything to do with his principal violinist? Surely not. His Serene Highness would have said something were that the case. Nevertheless, he was perturbed.

Johann opened his mouth to speak, but Haydn took no notice.

"Bartó must be somewhere in town." He uttered the words with as much firmness as he could muster as he strode toward the Rehearsal Room. "I will send one of the musicians out to look for him."

"I have already done so, brother." Johann placed a restraining hand on Haydn's arm. "I sent your principal cellist out as soon as I heard Bartó was not in the castle. Niklas has just returned." Johann's voice was gentle, tinged with regret. "Bartó is nowhere to be found."

Haydn stopped mid-stride, and turned to face his brother. "Not even in Kleinhöflein?"

Johann shook his head.

"At Gerhard's wine tavern? The Parish Church?"

At each question, Johann shook his head, an apologetic expression on his face. "We have looked everywhere, brother. I am afraid there is only one conclusion to be drawn."

Haydn was silent, scouring his mind for some other explanation. His principal violinist could not have left. The sun blazed uncomfortably into his eyes. He turned his head to avoid it, and caught sight of Rosalie coming up the stairs with his breakfast tray.

57

Struck by a thought, he approached her. "Which of the maids went up the hill to clean the Musicians' Quarters this morning?"

Rosalie rested the tray on the marble cherub that capped the newel post on the landing. "It was Greta and I, Herr Haydn." Her voice registered uncertainty. "Why, is anything the matter?"

Haydn ignored the question. "Was Master Bartó in his room?" The Kapellmeister turned toward his brother. "It is unlike him, but he may have overslept."

Rosalie looked curiously from the Kapellmeister to his brother. "He was not in the Musicians' Quarters when Greta and I went up there." She hesitated before continuing. "In fact, he may not even have been in his room all night. His bed had not been slept in."

Haydn's brows drew together. "Not been slept in!" he repeated, his voice stern. "Why did you not report this matter immediately to either me or Master Johann here or even to one of the other musicians?" he had unconsciously raised his voice.

Rosalie drew back. She shifted the weight of the tray on her arm. "B-but we thought nothing of it. It is not the first time it has happened."

"Then his things were still in his room?" Johann probed gently.

Rosalie pondered the question. "Master Bartó doesn't like to keep very many personal belongings in his room," she began slowly. "Doesn't want the likes of us 'snooping around,' he says. Why, he got very upset one day when he saw Greta tidying up some of his papers and putting them back in his writing case."

She fidgeted with her tray, eyes crinkling in concentration. Had there been anything odd about the room? She had only entered briefly. Greta had almost finished cleaning the room by the time Rosalie joined her. Besides, she had been so upset by Sándor's unexpected arrival, she didn't know that she would have noticed anything.

"Everything seemed as usual. Two suits of livery in the closet along with a few other clothes..."

"I suppose I was somewhat hasty in my conclusion," Master Johann began doubtfully. He turned toward the Kapellmeister. "But where can he have gone to? He did not breakfast in the Officer's Mess with the other musicians. And no one has seen him this morning."

Rosalie eyes moved inquisitively from Master Johann to the Kapellmeister. If Master Bartó had really left, Herr Haydn might have need of another violinist after all. But there had been no signs of a departure. His clothes...

Had been dwindling!

"And his travel trunk has been growing lighter!" She almost tipped the contents of her tray over in her excitement. "Why, it must be a week or more since I last needed help moving it!"

Herr Haydn extended his arm, and grabbed the edge of the tray before Rosalie could spill its contents. "I am glad to hear it, Rosalie. Is there anything else you can tell us that is more pertinent to the matter at hand?"

Rosalie shook her head vigorously. "No, no, Herr Haydn, you don't understand. Master Bartó's trunk used to be so heavy, it would take two of us maids to lift it and move it out of the way while we were cleaning. But it seems to have been getting lighter and lighter."

Haydn exchanged a glance with Johann. Bartó had made good on his threat, then? Somehow, he could not bring himself to believe it. And yet—he turned back to the maid.

"As though he were preparing to leave?" he asked. "And did not want anyone to know it."

Rosalie nodded. She hesitated, glancing down at her thumb rubbing back and forth over the raised edge of her tray. "I cannot say I am surprised." She looked up, the words tumbling out of her mouth now. "Master Bartó had a visitor last week, you see. I should have told you, but—"

Haydn held up a hand. "There is no need to say any more, Rosalie. I am aware that Master Bartó left the castle grounds without permission to see someone. It was his responsibility, not yours, to inform me of the fact.

Haydn stepped aside to let Rosalie walk past him into the Music Room.

"But that makes no sense. Bartó had already threatened to leave," Johann began the moment the maid had gone. "It seemed an empty threat at the time, but he was quite clear on the subject. Why go to any trouble to conceal the fact?"

Before the Kapellmeister could reply, Lorenzo, the second violinist, emerged from the Rehearsal Room.

"Herr Kapellmeister, how long must we continue to wait for Bartó?" The second violinist gazed steadily into Haydn's eyes. "If he is gone—as indeed, seems most likely—would it not be best to come to a decision on who should be in charge?"

Haydn gnawed at his lower lip. His second violinist was right. A decision on the best way forward would have to be made. But it seemed so unlikely that Bartó should have left.

"Yes." He forced himself to nod. "Yes, I suppose it would be best if you took charge, Lorenzo. Temporarily. His Serene Highness has asked for a rehearsal in three days time. One can only hope Bartó will be found by then."

Lorenzo balled his hands into fists. "Bartó is gone, Herr Kapellmeister. It would be best to accept that fact." He took a deep breath. "I am a capable musician, and I have been patient. You cannot pass me over now. Make me your Konzertmeister. You will not be disappointed."

Haydn could only nod. Seeming satisfied, Lorenzo returned to the Rehearsal Room. But an uneasy thought snaked its way up into his consciousness as he watched his second violinist go.

His anxiety must have been apparent, for Johann leaned over to say in a quiet voice: "Never fear, brother. There are a few alternatives that will not necessitate re-writing all the parts for solo violin to suit Lorenzo's capabilities."

Haydn drummed his fingers on the wings of the cherub supporting the staircase balustrade at the landing. Should he voice the thought at all? His brother, he realized, was still waiting for him to speak.

"It is not the re-writing, considerable though it will be, that concerns me, Johann," he said at last.

He led the way into the Music Room, and shut the door behind them.

"I am willing to accept that Bartó is gone. It is the suddenness of his departure that troubles me."

"Then you expected him to leave? It did not seem like an empty threat, to you?"

"No—that is to say—" Haydn stopped himself. His brother was right. Despite his apprehension, he had never for a moment expected Bartó to carry out his threat. But that he was preparing to leave... Now, why was he not surprised by that?

He began to pace the floor, needing the rhythm of movement to clear his head. He was aware of his brother's eyes following him as he walked to and fro, head bent, hands clasped behind his back. He stopped at last.

"There are some minor details that make Rosalie's supposition entirely plausible. Bartó's constant fear that he was being spied upon. His suspicion of his colleagues. Of Lorenzo, in particular. And the little I picked up from Maria Anna last night about his extreme dread. Of what exactly, I know not. I can only suppose he was making some clandestine plan. To desert his post, perhaps. It is entirely in breach of his contract, so it would have to be clandestine."

"As to Lorenzo." Haydn paused, making an effort to collect his thoughts. "This cannot be the first time that Bartó, instead of being in the Rehearsal Room leading the orchestra, is elsewhere. Yet, Lorenzo seems absolutely certain Bartó has left. Never to return."

Haydn dragged his hand through his wig, unwilling to follow his train of conjecture any further. "Bartó seems to possess a peculiar talent for rubbing people the wrong way. But I am afraid, the animosity he and Lorenzo have for each other could..." He hoped his brother would understand. He could not bring himself to name his fears.

Johann regarded him for an uncomfortable moment. "It was but yesterday that the Estates Director promised dire consequences unless you dismissed Bartó," he quietly reminded the Kapellmeister. "It would be as plausible to suspect *he* had some hand in Bartó's disappearance."

Haydn felt his teeth pressing into his lower lip. "The Police Commissioner's visit seems to have ruffled Rahier's usual calm." He faced Johann squarely. "He thought the Police Commissioner was at the castle in connection with a crime—"

"A crime that might result in the imperial visit being cancelled, which is quite likely the reason for Rahier's alarm. At any event, agonizing over the question does not help us, brother. Surely, there is no way of knowing whether or not Bartó left of his own accord?"

Haydn absentmindedly ground his heel into the carpet as he pondered his brother's question. A moment later, he straightened up.

"The Stadlmann, Johann! Bartó would never leave without it."

Rosalie rapped her knuckles on the door a little louder than she had the first time, grimacing slightly at the pain the effort caused her. She pressed her ear against the door. She could hear no music from within the Rehearsal Room. What were the musicians so preoccupied with that not one of them had responded to her knocking?

Well, there was nothing for it, but to barge in. She had work to do.

She set the heavy tray laden with a coffee pot and ceramic cups on top of a wooden cabinet painted with hunting scenes, and opened the door. A loud bark assailed her ears, causing her to lose her grip on the door handle and stumble back.

"That no-good, thieving swine!" Lorenzo's back was rigid with disbelief. His forefinger was still held against the painted gem that caused a picture of the demigod Amphion to slide open, revealing the closet in which the musicians stored their instruments.

Rosalie brought the tray in, her eyes fixed on the scene before her as she carefully made her way toward a table at the back of the room.

Niklas, the orchestra's principal cellist, pushed past the men crowding around the closet. "Why, what has he done?"

"The Stadlmann!" Lorenzo turned to face his colleague, his features rigid. "Bartó has made off with it!"

Rosalie remained bent over the table, oblivious to the cold edge of the tray pressing hard into her palms. *Then, Master Bartó really had left.* She had wondered about that, despite what she had told the Kapellmeister about his travel trunk. But the missing violin settled the question.

Haydn surveyed the now-empty closet and the instruments that lay strewn on the floor before him. Together with his second violinist and principal cellist, he had taken every instrument out of the Rehearsal Room closet. But neither the Stadlmann nor its charcoal-gray case were anywhere in sight.

Johann stood beside him, peering down at the instruments. "I would not have taken Bartó for a thief," he said.

Johann's voice reflected Haydn's own disbelief. The Kapellmeister was not sure what he had expected to find. There could be no doubt now that Bartó had gone. Undoubtedly, the implications of the violin being left behind would have been far worse. But even so... He roused himself to attend to his brother.

"Why, by his contract, the violin would have been his again on the day you had set for his dismissal," Johann was saying.

Haydn remained silent, teeth set against each other. Only a few minutes before, he had feared for his principal violinist's well-being. He had gone so far as to suspect his second violinist, a man he had known for close to six years, of doing Bartó an injury.

He might have known Bartó had just deserted his position with no thought as to the consequences.

Haydn turned toward Lorenzo. "Take charge of the orchestra. We have not a moment to waste." His gaze passed to the other musicians as he spoke. "His Serene Highness has called for a rehearsal in three days, gentlemen. I trust you will not let this little mishap disrupt your practice."

His eyes returned to the closet. "I expect the Estates Director will have to be informed about this matter. He may even wish to bring the Police Commissioner in."

Lorenzo, ushering the musicians back to their seats, started visibly at these words.

"The Police Commissioner, Herr Kapellmeister!" He twisted around to face Haydn. "What crime has been committed that the Police Commissioner must be brought into this matter? Bartó is gone. Let him go, I say!"

Haydn was taken aback at the vehemence of his second violinist's response. His mention of the Police Commissioner had been quite casual since Rahier would in all likelihood apprise him of Bartó's disappearance.

Haydn was still struggling to formulate a reply when his principal cellist, Niklas, burst out: "*What* crime has been committed? Why Bartó has stolen a valuable violin! Who else but the Police Commissioner could help to find him and the instrument?"

He rested his chin against his cello, his expression grave. "I doubt he has come to any harm. Still, I suppose it must be considered."

"If he has, it is no more than he deserves," Lorenzo muttered, scowling deeply.

CHAPTER SEVEN

Haydn was lost in thought when he and his brother left the Rehearsal Room. His second violinist's outburst had re-kindled his earlier fears.

"I hope Lorenzo has not done anything foolish," he said quietly once they were back in the Music Room.

He went to the window, and threw it open. The rush of fresh air felt pleasantly cool against his fevered face. He heard Johann's footsteps come to an abrupt halt behind him.

"You cannot still suspect Lorenzo, brother? He is fearful of losing his position as Konzertmeister, and must feel any effort to bring back Bartó undermines his position."

Haydn sighed. His brother was right, no doubt. And yet...

"There is something about this whole affair that troubles me." He turned around.

Johann regarded him, his gaze troubled. "The violin is gone. It is the proof you required to believe that Bartó had willingly left. Why do you question the fact, then?"

Haydn had no immediate response. He cupped his chin in his hand and studied the carpet, following the colorful tapestry of its interwoven strands.

"That is just it," he said slowly. "We all knew Bartó would never leave without the Stadlmann. What better way to convince us of his departure than to take the violin as well?"

His fingers closed over edge of the window sill behind him, hands pushing deep against the cold stone. "Why was Lorenzo even looking for it? The only reason he ever played the instrument was to get on Bartó's nerves."

"It would require a more devious mind than your second violinist has to plan such a nefarious act, don't you think?" Johann approached the window as he voiced the objection..

A sharp rapping on the door startled them both. The horn player in charge of the Music Library entered the room.

"Herr Kapellmeister, do you have the master copy of the works composed for the imperial visit?"

"There should be a copy in my closet. Why, Dietzl?" Haydn walked toward the painting of Terpsichore that served as his closet door. He brushed his fingers against the lyre strings, and looked around at his musician as the painting slid aside.

The horn player's face reddened. "We seem to be missing almost every solo piece written for Bartó. I cannot imagine where he might have put them. They are not in the library or in the Rehearsal Room."

At Haydn's frown, the horn player continued in a defensive tone: "For the past few weeks, Bartó has been insisting we keep all the music in the Rehearsal Room closet instead of returning them to the library after practice. There was no reasoning with him…" He spread his hands out.

Haydn could say nothing. He recalled the disputes. Dietzl had sought his intervention, but they had never seemed grave enough to warrant it.

He turned toward the closet, and began leafing through the scores neatly stacked on the shelves. The scores for the operas, the masques, and the dances were all intact. But where was the chamber music? The symphonies and concertos for the upcoming performance were missing as well.

He swept the entire stack of music into his arms and brought it to the fortepiano. Although it was most unlikely that he would place the scores for an upcoming performance beneath old scores.

"Rosalie must have re-arranged my music," he said more for his own benefit as he began to meticulously scan each score before setting it aside in a separate stack. His agitation grew. He went through the pile of music once more. It was not possible, and yet…

"It is gone, Johann! All the music composed for the Empress is gone!" Haydn turned a face as white as the snow outside toward his brother. "But who…?" His eye fell on the horn player.

Dietzl's consternation at the news was apparent. "Bartó..." he stammered, his Adam's apple bobbing convulsively. He looked wildly from the Kapellmeister to his brother.

Johann laid a hand on the horn player's shoulder. "Calm yourself, Dietzl. What does Bartó have to do with this mishap?"

"For some time now Bartó has been staying behind after all the musicians have left. To work on his cadenzas, he said. Last evening he said he was quite sure there was a mistake in one of his parts. That he needed to consult the master copy. But you had already left, Herr Kapellmeister. I did not think..." Dietzl's voice trailed off unhappily.

"It is not your fault, Dietzl." Haydn tried to give the musician a reassuring smile. "I have, fortunately, quite extensive notes on every composition..." He attempted to shrug his shoulders, but a far more unpleasant thought than having to re-write every piece of music weighed him down.

"There is an extra set in your study at home, brother." Johann quickly ushered the horn player to the door. "I will have it brought here," he assured the dazed musician as he gave him a gentle push into the hallway.

Johann shut the door and turned toward Haydn. "The violin may not have been sufficient proof for you, but with the theft of the music, there can be no doubt."

Haydn nodded, swallowing hard. "He must be found, Johann. Bartó must be found. God forbid, the music should find its way to a printer or some publisher in Italy or France or England. His Serene Highness..." Haydn gripped the fortepiano.

The thought of what the Prince would have to say regarding an unauthorized publication, in particular of works he himself had yet to hear, made him blanch.

Rosalie stood over the kitchen sink, scrubbing vigorously on a porcelain creamer. Pausing in her task, she looked over her shoulder at her brother. "I cannot tell whether Herr Haydn means to hire another musician. He has said nothing about it so far."

Sándor's shoulders appeared to lift ever so slightly, but his eyes remained on the plate of sweet rolls Rosalie had placed before him. "From what you've told me about the Kapellmeister and his orchestra, the prospect of hiring a virtuoso rivaling the one he has just lost will not be without some appeal."

Rosalie could have sworn she saw his mouth stretch into a small smirk But when Sándor looked up a moment later, there was only a beseeching expression in his dark blue eyes.

"You will do what you can for me, will you not, sister?" He held up his palms. "I have lost my livelihood, and have no means of supporting myself now."

Rosalie turned back to the sink, nostrils flaring. Would Sanyi never learn? Her younger brother acted rashly on every impulse that entered his head. Then looked to *her* to protect him from the consequences! It had been so from the day he was born, eight weeks before his time. No one had expected the pathetic, mewling infant to survive. But survive he had. Would anyone with a less remarkable birth have been indulged quite so much?

She looked down at her hands. Should she scrub the china quite so vigorously? The delicately painted flowers and the gold edging on the rim were looking a little less bright since her exertions.

The kitchen door swung open just then, and Greta barged in, eyes bright with barely-suppressed excitement. The maid peered around her as though afraid of being overheard.

"Herr Haydn thinks Master Bartó may be..." Greta seemed to be struggling to keep her voice from ringing out. "Well, that Master Bartó may be in danger," she finished flatly, evidently responding to the disapproving frown on Rosalie's face.

Rosalie's forehead was still furrowed. "How do you know that?"

She had not liked Master Bartó any more than anyone else. But to wish him ill? Why, Greta was positively glowing at the idea of the principal violinist in danger.

"Because I heard him say so with my own ears," Greta said. "I was outside the Music Room, polishing the mirror and picture frames in the hallway. Herr Haydn thinks Master Lorenzo may have...well, that he may have made Master Bartó disappear."

"But..." Rosalie didn't understand. "But then, the violin would still be in the palace."

"Oh! No one told me Master Bartó's violin was gone, too! Is that why you came charging out of the Rehearsal Room? Well, in that case..." Greta brought a plump hand up to support her rounded cheek.

Her head jerked up a moment later. "Then, why does Herr Haydn want the Police Commissioner to be brought in? I...er"—she reddened under Rosalie's stern gaze—"I was under the staircase when Herr Haydn came sprinting down with Master Johann—"

"The Police Commissioner!" Sándor's hand, clasped around a roll, hovered motionless in front of his mouth. "For the theft of a violin?" He set the uneaten roll back on its plate. "It must be a priceless violin, indeed."

Rosalie glanced down at her brother. "It was a Stadlmann," she murmured. Her mind drifted back to the principal violinist's room. Greta had already swept and mopped the floor when she looked in, but— "Master Bartó's travel trunk was still in his room, wasn't it?"

Greta nodded.

"I thought he was preparing to sneak away," Rosalie went on. "But why do that when he'd made no secret of his decision to go? And why leave the trunk behind?"

"Ah, his travel trunk!" Sándor lightly fingered a roll. "He must have forgotten it in his hurry to get away" He brought the roll to his mouth, and took a large bite. "Still, if it is important, who is to say he won't return for it?"

"Ah, so your principal violinist has gone, has he, Herr Kapellmeister?" The Estates Director rose from his straight-backed chair, and walked to the window his hands clasped behind his back.

His self-satisfied tone made Haydn grimace. Tired of waiting to be offered a seat, he drew forth a couple of chairs for himself and Johann on the other side of Rahier's wide cherry wood desk.

Rahier turned around, an eyebrow going up in mild outrage at the Kapellmeister and his brother seating themselves without permission.

"And, so you come running to me, do you, Herr Kapellmeister? Did I not warn you of some such untoward incident, if you did not dismiss him when you had the chance?" Rahier walked back toward the writing desk.

Haydn clenched his teeth. He might have known the Estates Director would gloat. "I have come to report the matter to you not to complain of my predicament." He struggled to keep his tone even. "The issue involves

Bartó's contract and the theft of a valuable piece of Esterházy property. If I am not mistaken, these are matters that come under your purview."

Best not to mention the stolen music, he thought as he watched Rahier flick his handkerchief over a pearl-encrusted velvet writing case. The news would give Rahier even more pleasure than the unexpected departure of his violinist.

"You may even wish to report the theft to the Police Commissioner," Haydn added since the Estates Director appeared not to be listening.

Rahier's head came up with a sudden, sharp movement. "The Police Commissioner?" His eyes narrowed. "And why would the Police Commissioner be interested in a trifle such as this? Do you suppose Herr Lichtenegger has nothing better to do than concern himself with your missing principal violinist and a violin he has purloined?"

Haydn stared. Had the Estates Director taken leave of his senses? "How, then, do you propose to bring Bartó back and recover the violin?" he demanded. "Surely, this is a matter for the Police Commissioner and his men."

Rahier stood over him, his icy blue eyes gazing into Haydn's from what seemed like an immense height. "Herr Lichtenegger is concerned with security, Herr Kapellmeister." The Estates Director's arm swept the air in a semi-circular motion. "The security of the Empire. What threat to the Empire does your pernicious principal violinist and his violin pose? I would look like a fool were I to bring this business to his notice."

Haydn was silent, struck by the strength of the Estates Director's opposition to calling in the Police Commissioner. He shifted uneasily in his chair. God forbid that it should be so, but was there a more malevolent reason for Rahier's opposition?

"I am sure my brother did not mean to call into question your abilities." Johann glanced at the Kapellmeister as he spoke, but Haydn had no objection to his brother smoothening matters as best he could. "No doubt, you can handle the matter yourself."

"Handle the matter, Master Johann?"

Surely, some action should be taken," Johann persisted.

"And I am expected to take it?" Rahier turned toward Haydn, a hint of a smile on his features.

Haydn shuffled his feet. The Estates Director was clearly enjoying his discomfiture. He had frequently complained of the other's open meddling in matters entrusted solely to him. But in this case...

He rose slowly to his feet. There was nothing more to be said. But he found himself unable to shake off the sense that something was amiss. Rahier was wont to insist on the musicians' contracts being enforced to the very letter. Yet Bartó's sudden departure and the loss of the Stadlmann had elicited no comment from him. It was quite unlike the man to be so unconcerned about such a flagrant violation of contract.

"Very well, then. I shall leave you to do as you see fit."

His shoulders were bowed as he turned toward the door. He could hear the scuffling of Johann's chair being pushed back on the plain white carpet as his brother prepared to follow him out.

"Herr Kapellmeister! A moment please!"

Haydn turned to find the Estates Director at his side. He regarded Rahier in silence.

"What will the loss of your violinist mean for the program you have prepared for the Empress? Will you be able to continue as before? His Serene Highness sets great store by Her Majesty's visit, as you well know."

Haydn scrutinized Rahier's features, trying to read the expression on his face. Since when had the Estates Director allowed himself to be troubled by what befell the orchestra?

"We shall likely need another violinist," Haydn began, but seeing Johann shake his head imperceptibly, added, "although we may well be able to continue with our present contingent."

Rahier rocked on his heels. "I am not unaware of the bind you find yourself in, Herr Kapellmeister, having lost an accomplished violinist. My nephew"—Rahier stopped rocking—"Albert is a capable musician. Hire him, and the difficulty of your situation may be somewhat eased."

"Meaning," Haydn fumed to his brother as they strode down the hallway toward the staircase, "that he will overlook the fact that I hired a musician who has not only reneged on his contract, but has also pilfered a violin."

Johann hurried to keep pace with the Kapellmeister. "It did occur to me that he might try to use the opportunity to foist his nephew on us. He would have raised the issue sooner had you not reminded him of his own concern in Bartó's disappearance."

The thought of Rahier's strange reticence regarding his principal violinist's violation of his contract brought Haydn to a halt. He had been about to climb the stairs, but now stood still, one foot resting on the crimson carpeted step. His younger brother had not been impressed by his suspicions, but surely even Johann would agree there had been something peculiar about the Estates Director's response to the news.

Aware that Johann was waiting for an explanation, Haydn lowered his foot and turned to face him.

"What did you make of the way Rahier took our revelation?"

"Why, he had nothing to say..." The bewildered expression on Johann's features dissipated. "Ach so! Now that I think about it, it was quite odd." Johann pondered the cherub decorating the baluster at the bottom of the staircase.

"It seemed to have come as no surprise to him," he spoke slowly. "As though he were already aware of the fact. And, yet how could he have known unless..."

He looked sharply at Haydn. "But that is inconceivable! Although... But how?"

Haydn shook his head. "I wish I knew." He paused, trying to collect his thoughts. A few stray words from the previous night's conversation with his wife returned to his mind.

"I wonder if she meant that Bartó was asking around for money?" he murmured. Noticing Johann's confusion, he waved his hand dismissively. "It was something Maria Anna was saying last night. Nothing important, in all likelihood."

He perused the carpet as though it might be capable of offering up some explanation for the Estates Director's bizarre behavior. His principal violinist had been in need of money.

And Rahier knew that!

"Do you suppose," Haydn asked, raising his head slowly, "that a sufficiently large sum of money might have persuaded Bartó to leave his position? We know he was in need of money."

Johann considered this suggestion. "And this large sum of money, I take it, might have been offered by the Estates Director?" At Haydn's nod he continued, "I suppose it is possible."

Haydn gripped the balustrade. "Clearing the way for his wretched Albert, while at the same time making me appear to be an incompetent buffoon of a Kapellmeister!"

The thought made Haydn tighten his hold on the balustrade. "It is just as well I have already informed His Serene Highness of my decision to dismiss Bartó. I may have misjudged his character when I hired him, but at least I was not deceived for too long.

"And it would not surprise me at all to learn that it was Rahier who put the idea of stealing the music into Bartó's head.

Johann spread his hands wide. "But even if all this were true, what can we do about it? We are still a musician short. And if you mean to give Bartó's parts to your second violinist, there are considerable changes that will need to be made to every score that contains a part for solo violin."

Haydn turned to ascend the staircase. "I do not know yet." He looked over his shoulder. "But once we have settled the musical problems posed by Bartó's departure, I intend to approach the Bürgermeister. If Rahier will not report Bartó's disappearance to the Police Commissioner, maybe Herr Groer will."

CHAPTER EIGHT

The door to the Rehearsal Room was slightly ajar. An energetic burst of music emanated from the room, swelling to a crescendo as the Kapellmeister and his brother set foot on the landing.

Haydn swayed his head in time to it, his mouth widening into a smile of pure bliss. "Excellent!" he said, forgetting his worries about Bartó's untimely departure and the theft of his music. "Lorenzo will make a capable Konzertmeister, yet."

The music grew imperceptibly faster. Haydn held his breath, waiting for the climax. But instead of building up to a fortissimo fury of notes, the music ended in a loud, discordant clang that brought forth a clamor of protest from the musicians.

"If you must make changes to the score, Lorenzo, get them approved by the Kapellmeister first," growled a voice Haydn recognized as that of his one-eyed oboe player.

"Or acquaint yourself with the theory of counterpoint and harmony before making any rash attempts at composition," grumbled one of the cellists.

An amused smile spread slowly over Haydn's features at this unexpected agreement between his oboe player and the musician he held responsible for his disfigurement.

"If nothing else," Haydn said, turning to his brother, "Lorenzo appears to have achieved a reconciliation of sorts between those two. They have not agreed on any subject since the drunken brawl in which poor Zacharias lost his eye."

Johann followed his brother toward the Music Room. "I am glad you are amused, brother. But unless we come to some decision about Bartó's parts—and quickly at that—I am afraid your program for the Empress will be an unmitigated disaster."

Haydn's smile faded. Johann was right. Lorenzo, however capable, lacked the musicianship to play the solos incorporated into almost every piece to showcase the brilliance of his principal violinist. Worse still, his second violinist had no talent for improvisation, and would be unable to tackle a cadenza unless Haydn wrote it into the score for him.

"And that defeats the purpose of a cadenza entirely," Haydn said aloud, coming to a sudden halt. "Not to mention that if I included them in the score, they would come off as rehearsed rather than spontaneous. Who, but a talentless hack, memorizes a cadenza?"

"Be that as it may, it might be our best way forward in this situation, brother." Johann nodded in the direction of the Rehearsal Room, wincing at the sound of Lorenzo practicing the passage they had just heard. "As it stands, his rendition of some parts of the written music are quite painful to hear."

The suggestion was not without merit, Haydn thought, gazing at a woven tapestry on the wall of the Greek god Pan playing his flute. "But it will be quite evident that the Esterházys either lack the means to employ a virtuoso or have a Kapellmeister of no discerning at all."

Haydn shook his head. "And neither impression is conducive to my retaining my position here, Johann. This morning, the Prince reminded me yet again that his political ambitions, and therefore my career, ride upon the success of our program. Some other solution will have to be found, although I cannot for the life of me, think what."

"Would His Serene Highness object to my conducting the orchestra, brother?"

Haydn did not see how that would make any difference, but waited for his brother to continue.

"It is surely the crowning glory of your career that the Empress allows herself to come out of mourning for the sole purpose of giving into the enchantment of your music. Your eagerness to take on the role of principal violinist would be a fitting acknowledgement, I think, of the singular honor she bestows upon you."

"Ah!" Haydn beamed at his brother. "An ingenious solution, Johann. It really is quite perfect!" He strode toward the Music Room and pushed open the door.

❧

A considerable weight behind the door seemed to give way under the force of Haydn's arm.

"Rosalie!" Haydn wondered what the maid was doing in the Music Room. She stood before him in apparent agony, twisting the corners of her apron.

"I did not mean to overhear your conversation, Herr Haydn." Rosalie's violet eyes were bright with dismay. She rolled and unrolled the edge of her apron, looking nervously from the Kapellmeister to his brother.

Rosalie cleared her throat. "If you should have need of another violinist, my brother..." She turned toward Johann, as though expecting him to come to her aid. "You will remember him, Master Johann. Sanyi..."

Johann's lips widened into a smile. "Ah, little Sanyi. Has he kept up with his music, then?" Johann turned toward Haydn. "If only you could have heard him, brother, but you had long left Rohrau by that time. He could make that old, battered fiddle his family possessed sing as though it were a Stadlmann."

"Sanyi. Sándor." Haydn pronounced the name carefully. The name seemed familiar but he could not recall when he had heard it before.

"I have mentioned him to you. He was just such a prodigy as Michael claims Leopold Mozart's boy to be. He had but to hear a melody once and he could reproduce it perfectly," Johann explained as the Kapellmeister continued to stare at him, a glassy, vacant look in his eyes. "Had Sanyi the advantages of Kapellmeister Mozart's child, he would have taken the world by storm just as little Wolfgang appears to be doing now."

Haydn peered down at Rosalie, intrigued despite himself. "And does he still retain those prodigious skills? Can he sight-read besides, and is he well versed in music theory?"

"Oh yes, Herr Haydn." Rosalie nodded after each question. "Sándor received very good instruction at the parish school in Bruck an der Leitha. My parents hoped he might use his musical talents in the Church, but that was not to be."

She hesitated, twisting her hands together. "I did not mean to overhear your conversation, Herr Haydn, but if any music needs to be re-written, Sándor has a beautiful hand as well. He has worked as a copyist in addition to his other jobs..." Rosalie's voice faded away.

Haydn chose not to comment on this veiled reference to her brother's inability to retain a position. He had only a temporary position in mind for the boy, and should he desert it as Bartó had done, Johann's plan would serve the purpose admirably.

"It can do no harm, I suppose," he said, turning to Johann. "I shall have to subject myself to Albert's screeching before long. Sándor will provide a welcome respite to my ears."

"Very well, Rosalie."

But Rosalie continued to stand before him. Haydn wondered why. He glanced down at her apron. Her exertions had left it quite wrinkled.

"I do not think..." Rosalie smoothed out her apron. "That is to say..." The maid swallowed hard. Finally, she looked up, her mind evidently made up.

"I don't think Master Bartó has left," she blurted out. "His travel trunk was still in the closet this morning."

Haydn stared at her for a moment. "I have had doubts about his departure myself," he muttered, conducting the maid to the door. He needed to ponder this tidbit she had provided him with.

Rosalie opened her mouth, and then closed it again. She threw Johann a look of utter confusion as she went past him.

"Left his travel trunk behind, has he?" Haydn murmured once Rosalie had left. He began pacing about the room, hands clasped behind his back, head inclined toward the floor. His perambulation took him to the window. The snow-whitened landscape beyond extended to the frozen Lake Neusiedl.

The snow storm! Small wonder, Bartó had left his travel trunk behind. He must not have expected to leave last night.

Haydn turned to face Johann, a determined glint in his eye. "Bartó cannot have gone far. He must be hiding in the vicinity somewhere. Did I not tell you the suddenness of his departure troubled me?"

"And yet he has left..." Johann faltered, his tone doubtful. He appeared to be having trouble following the Kapellmeister's train of thought.

"Rahier must have made his offer last night," Haydn said under his breath. He turned away from Johann and walked toward the window again. "He was still at the castle when I left yesterday. Why, it was but yesterday that he foretold disaster unless I dismissed Bartó immediately. And today, Bartó is gone. That can be no coincidence."

He pivoted on his heels, and strode toward the door. "We must go to the Bürgermeister at once, Johann."

The town hall was but a short walk east from the Esterházy castle. Its snow-capped oriel windows were visible from the castle gates. As Haydn and Johann approached the pink and white building, they could hear the Bürgermeister's stentorian baritone and the barber-surgeon's milder tenor engaged in argument.

"Cause, indeed! What cause do they have, then, Herr Hipfl?" the Bürgermeister was saying.

Haydn sent Johann an amused glance. The Bürgermeister, they both knew, had no patience with the Hungarians nor any sympathy for their complaints. That the barber-surgeon's sentiments on the issue were quite contrary to his colleague's was evident from what they overheard next.

"The peasants complain about the ever-burgeoning tax burden, and with good reason, my dear Herr Groer. The Empress says she loves all her subjects as a mother loves her children, but what mother favors one child over another? Taxing Hungarian goods as imports in the Austrian market is hardly fair!"

"Pah! Not fair, indeed!" The Bürgermeister let out a derisive snort. "But you have no complaint with the advantage it gives you in the beef market, do you, Herr Hipfl?"

A brief silence ensued. The barber-surgeon like many other inhabitants of the small town raised cattle; the money helping to supplement the small income from his official position as medical examiner for Eisenstadt and the villages surrounding it.

"I was only commenting," he began in a defensive tone, "that we might not have any trouble with the Hungarians were the circumstances slightly different. What harm could there be, for instance, in uniting Transylvania with Royal Hungary? If the Empress would but give in on that demand, I am convinced it would do a lot toward calming the dissent in the region."

Haydn and Johann were close enough now to see the Bürgermeister roll his eyes at this last statement. "God forbid the Empress should ever give in on that count! All the troublemakers come from Transylvania."

"I had no idea the Hungarians had such a litany of troubles." Haydn smiled a greeting at the two men. Their argument had momentarily diverted him from his worries.

"Pah! The Hungarians need someone to blame for their own lack of industry, and the Empress serves as a convenient target." The Bürgermeister came out from under the arched portal of the town hall, his hands outstretched in eager greeting. "But what news do you bring, gentlemen?"

Haydn let out a deep breath. "I have nothing good to report, Herr Bürgermeister. A situation of the utmost gravity has befallen us, and we require your good offices in remedying the matter."

"This has something to do with the Police Commissioner's visit to the castle no doubt," the Bürgermeister replied, his voice filled with misgiving.

Haydn shook his head. "No, Herr Groer. It has to do with my principal violinist."

<hr />

"Ach so!" murmured the Bürgermeister. His eyes had been closed during Haydn's narrative. His elbows rested on the large oak-wood table in the meeting room within the Town Hall, his hands joined together at the finger tips.

"A most nettlesome fellow, your principal violinist," he commented, opening his eyes at last. "You will not mind my saying so, but it is not such a bad thing after all, that he is gone."

"Yes, well he must be found," Haydn replied irritably. He was not surprised that Bartó's departure had not caused anyone a moment's regret. But surely the theft of valuable Esterházy property was a matter of some urgency and should elicit greater concern. "The Prince may not object to the theft of the violin, costly though it is. But surely you can see the music must be restored."

The Bürgermeister shifted his bulk in his chair, and exchanged an uneasy look with the barber-surgeon.

"But why trouble the Police Commissioner with this matter, Herr Haydn? If as you surmise, your principal violinist is still in the neighborhood, it will not be too difficult to find him, don't you agree?"

Haydn was somewhat affronted at the soothing tone the Bürgermeister had chosen to adopt with him as though he was in a pother over nothing. The theft of the music was no small matter, after all.

"Bartó must be found before he has an opportunity to sell the music, Herr Groer. The Police Commissioner has resources at his disposal, and men trained to discover and appropriate criminals."

Johann leaned forward to rest his arms upon the table, and looked at the Bürgermeister and the barber-surgeon in turn. "The music would be worth its weight in gold to any printer or publisher who got his hands on it. These are the very latest of my brother's compositions. Only consider, what disrespect to Her Majesty if the music composed in her honor should be published for all and sundry before she has even heard it!"

The Bürgermeister looked crestfallen. "To be sure, that is a grave problem indeed, Master Johann." His eyes drifted toward the barber-surgeon again. "But still, you must consider my position..."

The barber-surgeon turned toward Haydn with a mild cough. "Herr Groer has no authority in this affair. It pertains to the castle, you see."

So that was it! The town authorities had no intention of treading on the Estates Director's toes. Even the suspicions Haydn had voiced had been met with a blank stare.

"Besides, given your violinist's contentious views, the Police Commissioner might be inclined to look upon his disappearance with even greater suspicion—"

"Contentious views! What contentious views did Bartó hold?" Haydn's voice crossed Herr Groer's, and rose above it like an unruly line of harmony gradually extending to and taking over the main melodic line.

The Bürgermeister passed his hand through the air dismissively. "No more or less extreme, in all likelihood, than those of the rest of his countrymen. But still, his open rancor toward the Empress and his vitriolic outbursts against Hungarians loyal to the crown may not have escaped the Police Commissioner's attention.

"Surely you cannot have been unaware of his views, Herr Haydn?" He exchanged a glance with the barber-surgeon.

Haydn pursed his lips. How could he have been aware of them? Bartó had never voiced any such views in his presence. He had only allowed his resentment to show when he had made his demand for money, and Haydn had thought nothing of it.

"And with all this talk of an insurrection, your violinist's disappearance could well provide the tipping point for the Police Commissioner to advise the Empress to cancel her visit," the barber-surgeon took up the Bürgermeister's theme.

"An insurrection!" The word drove all thoughts of his violinist and stolen music from Haydn's mind. "I have heard no talk of an insurrection." He turned toward the Bürgermeister. They had spoken just this morning, and no mention had been made of any such thing.

"Of course, you have not." The Bürgermeister seemed to have trouble meeting the Kapellmeister's gaze. "A composer such as yourself has no time for such matters," he said quickly in a blandly reassuring tone.

A hot flush spread over Haydn's cheeks. He supposed he had been somewhat preoccupied with the Empress's visit. But how could he not be? "But this morning, you said it was all mere talk."

"It may still be mere talk," the barber-surgeon put in before the Bürgermeister could respond. "But with the Police Commissioner's visit to the castle this morning, and then the Prince himself setting out in all haste for Vienna. Who knows, there may be more to the rumors."

Haydn sank back in his chair, spent from the tide of opposition he had encountered. "Then I can expect no help from you in this matter?"

The Bürgermeister shifted uncomfortably under Haydn's steady gaze, his rosy cheeks deepening to a bright red. "I will have some of the townspeople keep a watch for your violinist. But let us keep this matter quiet for the time being. For all we know, the Police Commissioner may have already taken steps to cancel the imperial visit."

"Did the Prince say nothing to you regarding the Police Commissioner's visit this morning?" the Bürgermeister asked as they emerged from the arched wooden door of the Town Hall into the afternoon sun.

Haydn shaded his eyes from the bright glare of the sun. "Not a word. He merely asked after the entertainment being prepared for the imperial visit, saying he would be out of town on business for a few days." He stopped outside the door. "How can you be so sure he has gone to Vienna, Herr Groer?"

"I heard him call out to the coachman." The Bürgermeister shook his head. "What could it be other than a summons from Count Pergen? There must be some trouble brewing."

CHAPTER NINE

Haydn contemplated the Bürgermeister's large form traveling down the road in the direction of the town. The Prince had made no mention of Vienna that morning. His Serene Highness disliked the city intensely, and only the most dire circumstances would have compelled him to consider journeying to the capital. Could there be anything at all to this talk of insurgency?

Out of the corner of his eyes, Haydn could see Johann standing under the round oriel window on the left, in earnest conversation with the barber-surgeon. His younger brother was having as much trouble believing the news as he was.

"The Hungarians have espoused Her Majesty's cause since she first came to the throne as a young woman. Why do they turn against her now?"

The barber-surgeon hesitated. "The dying embers of a long-borne grudge can always be fanned into a raging fire, Master Johann," he said at last. "The Hungarian magnates may support the Empress, but even they baulk at her taxes."

Johann nodded. "Ah yes! The Prince has long sought to change Her Majesty's mind on the subject, to little avail. He says the magnates will have no recourse but to shift the burden onto the peasants if she pushes them for more."

Haydn was vaguely aware of the two men approaching him as they conversed. Nevertheless, the barber-surgeon's mild cough before he addressed a remark to him took him by surprise.

"Herr Kapellmeister, you will pardon my saying so, but your suspicions of the Estates Director do not become you. Herr Rahier is a difficult man to be sure, but he is not entirely without integrity. Your violinist, on the other hand, needed no incentive to escape his responsibilities. Nor any incitement to steal."

Haydn studied the barber-surgeon, his attention caught by Herr Hipfl's reference to Bartó's responsibilities. This was the second time someone had suggested to him that Bartó was eager to escape his obligations.

Before he could respond, however, his younger brother said, "My brother would be the last to deny Bartó had his faults, but neither one of us had taken him for a thief. Stealing the music seems an unnecessarily petty act."

"But understandable in the light of his insistent demand for money, would you not say?" The barber-surgeon looked eagerly from Johann to the Kapellmeister.

The unsettling tidings of the past few hours had obliterated Bartó's demand for money from Haydn's mind. Something stirred in his memory.

"We had surmised Bartó was in debt to Gerhard, the tavern-keeper," he said slowly. "There was some quarrel between the two, was there not?"

The barber-surgeon stared at Haydn, his grey eyes widening as though he had been given a revelation. But the gleam of illumination that had lightened his irises was just as quickly veiled. "It is unlikely Bartó had any unpaid debts at the tavern. Gerhard is quite good at ensuring he is owed no money, Herr Kapellmeister."

"Ach so," Haydn murmured, but he was most perplexed. He had assumed Bartó's financial obligations were common knowledge. But if Bartó had no debts at the tavern, what obligations did he have? Besides, how had Herr Hipfl known of his demand for money. Maria Anna's words from the previous evening returned to his mind.

"Bartó demanded money from you, did he not, Herr Hipfl. But why?"

The barber-surgeon was not much taller than Haydn, but he stiffened at this question, and drew himself up to his full height. "Why? Because your principal violinist is a scoundrel, Herr Kapellmeister. Although you seem unwilling to face the truth."

With a stiff bow, the barber-surgeon turned on his heels before either Haydn or Johann could say a word. They heard him muttering to himself as he stalked off: "I have nothing to be ashamed of!"

"You appear to have ruffled our good barber-surgeon's feathers, brother," Johann commented, his eyes fixed on Herr Hipfl's retreating back.

By the time Rosalie brought her brother and his violin up to the second floor of the West Wing, the Kapellmeister and Johann had already left. She turned from the window overlooking the inner courtyard, and led Sándor to an ornately carved wooden seat. It was one of many in the wide carpeted area outside the Music and Rehearsal Rooms; each one upholstered in white satin sumptuously embroidered with a design of pale pink cherry blossoms.

"Herr Haydn and Master Johann must have gone to see the Police Commissioner," she said, lowering herself onto the plump cushioned seat. "Why Herr Haydn thinks Master Lorenzo had anything to do with this affair, I cannot imagine. He was not the only one who disliked Master Bartó, you know." She twisted around to gaze out the window.

"If you ask me, if anyone had anything to do with Master Bartó's disappearance, it was the man who came to see him some days ago," she declared, turning back toward Sándor. "Master Bartó was none too pleased to see him, you know."

Sándor murmured a vague response. Rosalie could tell he was not listening to her. The sound of the orchestra practicing a violin concerto carried across the hallway, and Sándor's head was tilted in the direction of the Rehearsal Room, an expression of intense concentration on his face.

"How many times will they play those same measures?" he muttered to himself, as the solo violin stopped for the fifth time in the middle of a phrase gone wrong.

"As many times as they need to." Rosalie drew her brother down beside her, and directed an earnest look at him. "You must be sure to impress upon Herr Haydn that you will be diligent, Sanyi. You have no reference. Your manner alone will have to commend you."

There was an amused glint in Sándor's dark blue eyes when he looked down at her. He drew forth a packet from within his coat. "Never fear, sister, I have something more than my manner to show Herr Haydn."

Under Rosalie's inquisitive eyes, Sándor opened the packet. "See here, sister, a letter from Count Nádasdy, and"—he held out a large gold ring set with an enormous emerald—"a small token of his appreciation for my music."

The size of the emerald took Rosalie's breath away. She had never seen anything quite so large or lustrous. And the name her brother had so casually dropped! Why, Count Nádasdy was as influential at the imperial court as His Serene Highness. She took the ring from her brother.

"It is every bit as large as Master Bartó's ruby ring, Sanyi!"

She looked up, eyes wide with admiration. His Lordship's generous patronage had made the career of many a musician. What heights might Sanyi not achieve with his support?

"Count Nádasdy treats Herr Haydn like a friend, you know. Greta said he couldn't have been more disappointed to find Herr Haydn out when he came by a few weeks ago. He seemed pleased enough to see Master Bartó, though. Greta said she couldn't believe how cordially His Lordship greeted the old sourpuss!"

Rosalie sniffed, recalling the principal violinist's peremptory manner toward the palace maids. "I hope having friends in high places will not turn you into just such a coxcomb as Master Bartó, Sanyi." She reached forward, and took her brother's hand in both of hers. "Now tell me, how did you win the Count's support?"

"He came by Antal's shop one day, and heard me perform a piece at sight from the folio of compositions we were printing for one of his friends. You can imagine my horror when I looked up from the music to see the Count and his friend standing by the doorway. I thought I was in trouble."

Sándor looked down at his sister sheepishly. "We are not supposed to read what we print, Antal is quite clear on the subject. I needn't have worried, though. Far from offending them, I had amazed them with my ability to play at sight!"

Rosalie pressed her brother's hand, and smiled warmly up at him. "I do believe Mama and Papa can be won over to your new calling if they think it was Count Nádasdy who encouraged you in your aspirations, Sanyi."

"That he did, sister. Besides recommending that I seek out, if I could, Herr Haydn's tutelage to learn the art of composition."

Sándor's eyes had wandered toward the window as he spoke. They froze now, rooted on some object outside. Rosalie was about to look over her shoulder to see what it was when he relaxed. A slow grin spread across his face.

"Ah, I see I shall have to compete for this position."

———∿∿———

The barber-surgeon had long left, but Haydn continued to stare down the road. He felt Johann touch his sleeve, and turned around.

"I don't like to think Herr Hipfl may have something to hide." Haydn forced himself to move forward. Numerous responsibilities awaited him at the castle. If it were only as easy to tear his mind away. "What could Bartó have known about him? It must be bad indeed for him to be willing to part with money to keep it quiet."

"We do not know that he did so," Johann pointed out.

Haydn nodded. True, the barber-surgeon had seemed more angry than intimidated. Of course, with his violinist missing, Herr Hipfl was in no further danger. There would be no more threats to reveal his secret and no further attempts to extract money. This last thought made his stomach turn.

"What manner of man extorts money from another?" he burst out, stopping in the middle of the road. "How could our brother have been so mistaken in Bartó's character?"

It seemed to take Johann more than a few beats to voice a response.

"To be fair, we were deceived as well, brother."

Haydn turned to face him. Was his own brother going to accuse him of being oblivious to all that went on around him?

Johann met his gaze squarely. "Bartó appears to have been greatly adept at concealing his true nature from anyone who mattered. Either that, or his own desperate need gave him cause." He turned away with a slight frown. "Although, I cannot imagine why he was in need now that it appears he owed no debts."

They resumed their slow walk westward toward the castle, weighed down by the disturbing revelations of the past hour. The wind from the morning had died down, but the warmth of the afternoon sun did little to dispel the cold the storm had ushered in. Haydn drew his overcoat around him, his eyes on the ground. The few patches of snow that had not been swept to the side of the road had hardened into ice, making the path slippery.

Maria Anna's cryptic remarks regarding Bartó some nights ago returned to him. He stopped mid-stride, putting a hand on his brother's arm to halt his progress.

"Do you recall Maria Anna mentioning a dispute of some sort between Gerhard and Bartó?" At Johann's nod he went on. "Herr Hipfl did not deny it."

"But he said it was not about money."

"No. Although he did not deny Bartó's need for money either. Nor that he had obligations he was eager to avoid. Although if it had nothing to do with money..." He turned to face Johann. "What does the barber-surgeon know?"

"Whatever it was, he will not tell us, brother. The fact troubles me as well"—Johann directed a quick glance at the castle—"but dwelling on it will not reveal the matter to us. Sister-in-law may—"

Haydn shook his head. "If she knows anything at all, I doubt we will hear of it. She delights in speaking in riddles."

They walked on, almost at the castle now. A wide moat separated the castle grounds from the rest of the town. Haydn paused at the drawbridge extending from the town to the outer courtyard of the castle, and gazed down at the brittle film of snow-flecked ice that covered the dark waters of the moat.

"We shall have to conduct our own investigation into this affair, Johann, if we hope to recover the violin and, more importantly, my music. The town authorities appear to have more reason than just the possibility of an insurrection to stall any inquiries into Bartó's disappearance. I would go to the Police Commissioner..."

Johann nodded. "But if there is anything to these rumors of rebellion, your doing so could precipitate disastrous consequences."

He stepped onto the drawbridge. Haydn followed after a moment's hesitation.

They had almost crossed the drawbridge when Johann said: "I must confess your suspicions begin to make more sense, brother. Bartó may have intended to leave, but something must have occurred to trigger his departure in the middle of a snowstorm."

Haydn nodded, eyes still upon the icy ground. "His obligations became more onerous, no doubt." He raised his head. "We shall have to discover what they were, Johann"—his eyes drifted toward the castle looming in the background—"and no doubt we shall also discover Rahier had some hand in this whole affair."

He caught a glimpse of the guards who had ridden down from the castle to relieve the men standing watch at the castle gates since dawn.

"The evening guards are taking over duty. One among them must have seen Bartó leave, and may be able to tell us more."

Only one man from the night watch had seen anything.

"Came charging down the courtyard like an elephant in heat, he did, snarling at me to pull the drawbridge down!"

The guard's swarthy features darkened at the recollection. "I told him it was no hour for the drawbridge to be down nor for any man to be out and about in that storm neither. But would he listen? Just grabbed hold of my collar, and threatened to slit my throat if I didn't do as he said." His voice rose, his large, hooked nose almost seeming to quiver in indignation.

Haydn nodded absently, as he gazed down at the cobblestoned courtyard. He was not surprised by Bartó's belligerent response. His principal violinist's brusque exterior barely concealed the aggressiveness that seemed to constantly simmer within. It took very little to bring it to the surface.

The guard continued to rumble on. "I had half a mind, I did, to put in a complaint to the Estates Director." He directed a sly glance at Haydn. "But out of respect to yourself, Herr Kapellmeister, I let it go."

"Then the Estates Director was still here when Bartó left?" Now that was odd. At Johann's urgent nudge, Haydn dug into his pocket for a few gulden to compensate the guard.

The man's disgruntled expression faded at the sight of the money. He held out an eager palm, his eyes fastened greedily on the coins Haydn dropped into it.

"Ach no. Herr Rahier had been long gone by then. But he always asks us, he does, whether we have anything to report. *Anything at all untoward.* Takes an especial interest in your musicians, too, that he does. Wanting to know if their conduct is seemly and suchlike."

Haydn felt his face grow hot. Herr Rahier must be very eager, indeed, to see him in trouble. And the barber-surgeon wondered why he was suspicious of the Estates Director! The Kapellmeister gripped the stone parapet, having trouble swallowing his ire.

Johann stepped forward. "And did Master Bartó tell you why he needed to go into town so urgently at that hour?" he probed gently.

The guard stared at Johann for a moment. Then, seeming to recall himself, he withdrew his gaze. "No, that he did not. Just growled that he *had* to go."

"Well, it is no more than what we had surmised, Johann." Haydn had recovered his equanimity by this time. He handed over a few more coins to the guard, who looked as though he could scarcely believe his good fortune.

CHAPTER TEN

The ornate wooden doors at the West Wing entrance, Haydn was surprised to see, were thrown wide open. Who had failed to close the doors against the cold? He strode across the inner courtyard toward the wide stone steps that formed a terraced approach up to the building. The curved line of a charcoal grey object was visible just beyond the door. Was that a violin case?

He was hurrying toward it when his motion was arrested, his toes curling from the intense pain he felt. He looked down with a grimace at the stair he had walked into. His leather shoes and stockings had done little to lessen the impact of the stone riser.

He heard Johann come up behind him. "That is surely not—"

"No, no." Haydn shook his head as a white gloved hand came into view. "It is not Bartó. But the case..."

He climbed up the steps. Had the missing Stadlmann been recovered?

"Ah, Herr Haydn." A tall, slim figure swung around to greet him. "I have been waiting for you."

"Albert!" The Kapellmeister was barely able to keep the dismay out of his voice. He had not expected the Estates Director's nephew to present himself with such alacrity. Words failed him as he took in the young man who stood before him. Albert was but a younger version of Rahier; the same strands of gleaming blond hair slicked back close to the scalp. The same pale, blue eyes, albeit lacking the Estates Director's cold gaze.

A furrow appeared on Albert's smooth, white forehead. "Surely, my uncle informed you of my impending arrival." He swung his violin case. As it twisted around, the emblem embroidered on it came into view.

90

"You still have need of a violinist, do you not?"

Haydn's eyes were on the emblem. Bartó's violin case had been embroidered with an emblem, too, had it not? Hearing Johann's mild cough, he forced himself to turn his attention to Albert.

"Yes, yes, your uncle did..." Haydn adjusted his wig, still at a loss for words. His eyes were drawn toward the violin case again. Could there be two such cases, so very similar in appearance? He motioned toward it.

"That violin case. Where did you find it?"

"Find it!" Albert hefted the case up. He inspected it closely, as though attempting to discover what attraction it held for the Kapellmeister. "You will have to ask my uncle where he had it made. It was a gift from him along with this fine Stadlmann." Albert opened the case to reveal just such a beautiful honey-colored instrument as Bartó had possessed.

"A fine instrument, indeed." Haydn cleared his throat. "It looks very like the one my violinist appears to have made off with"—His eyes went briefly toward Johann—"And it was a gift from your uncle, you say?"

"In honor of my appointment to the orchestra." Albert beamed. "I know you must be disappointed to find your principal violinist gone, Herr Haydn. Count Nádasdy spoke quite highly of his talents, saying he was surprised the Archbishop of Salzburg had allowed him to leave. But all will be well. You will not find me wanting, I promise you."

Haydn forced himself to remain impassive. He would find Albert wanting, he knew, in every musical skill. And as to the Archbishop's willingness to let a virtuoso leave; a close acquaintance with Bartó's temperament had forced him to the conclusion that his brother Michael's employer had been only too glad to allow the violinist to seek his fortunes elsewhere.

But Albert's reference to Count Nádasdy had taken him by surprise. It was unlike the Count to take an interest in any but the most accomplished musicians.

"You know the Count?"

Albert puffed out his chest. "We met briefly when he came by here a month or two ago. He was gracious enough to hear me play, and to comment on my grasp of the notes. Did my uncle not mention any of this to you? Not finding you here, the Count asked my uncle to convey his regards to you."

"No, your uncle said nothing." Haydn led the way to the staircase. "It must have been his modesty that prevented him from conveying any part of this to me," he commented dryly.

―――――

They had no sooner gained the upper floor when they encountered Rosalie and her brother.

The young man rose from his seat, and came forward, his arms outstretched in greeting.

"Master Johann! Herr Haydn! The *Wienerisches Diarium* has been abuzz with excitement these past few months about your program for the Empress. I would be greatly honored to number among the performers."

To Haydn's surprise, Albert sniffed disparagingly. "That paper does nothing but pander to the imperial court," Haydn thought he heard him mutter under his breath. "It contains nothing of relevance to the people. Small wonder Hungary is at the end of its tether!"

Sándor must have heard the words, too, for he cast an amused glance at Albert. Then with a slight shrug, he returned his gaze to Haydn. "I am at your service, if you still have need of me, Herr Kapellmeister." His eyes moved toward Albert's violin case.

Haydn shuddered, recalling the last time he had been condemned to hear Albert perform. "As it happens, we may well have use for your skills, if"—Haydn gave the younger man an appraising stare—"if you are as gifted as Johann avers."

He led the way toward the Music Room. "Come with me gentlemen. We have much to do, and not a moment to waste."

Setting his leather case on the fortepiano, Haydn strode toward the closet, but stopped mid-stride, clapping his hand to his forehead. "Ach, I had forgotten we lack the master copy for the chamber music!"

"It is here, brother." Johann gestured toward a stack of scores on the Kapellmeister's desk. "I had the original set sent over from your study at home."

Haydn beamed. "Excellent!" Struck by an idea, he turned toward Sándor. "Rosalie informs us you have a fine hand. Do you suppose your penmanship will be up to the task of making a few copies of all our chamber music?"

A smile spread gradually over the young man's face. "I will let you be the judge of my calligraphy, Herr Kapellmeister." He picked up a blank sheet of music paper and a pen from Haydn's desk. Deftly drawing a treble clef sign, he wrote in eight measures of music and handed the sheet to the Kapellmeister.

"A fine hand, indeed," Haydn remarked, glancing down at the sheet. But what he saw, made him draw it closer to his eyes. "Why, that is the part for solo violin in the concerto in D!"

Haydn had rarely seen anything like it. Sándor had reproduced not merely the notes, but the expression, articulation, and dynamics for the first eight measures perfectly.

Sándor's shrug, when Haydn looked up at him, was deprecating. "I heard the orchestra practicing the piece. Your soloist seemed to be having trouble with the phrasing. I myself thought it should be played like this—" He brought out his violin, and played through the entire piece.

"Your ear is exceptional!" The young man was even more gifted than Johann had led Haydn to believe. Not even Bartó had been able to bring out the emotions in the piece quite so expressively.

"Yes, but can he read music?" Albert drew out his violin, and selected a score from the Kapellmeister's desk.

Haydn winced at the first shrill sounds the Stadlmann emitted as Albert's fingers grabbed at the strings on the soundboard, sliding on, long after they had landed, in an effort to find the right note.

He leaned over toward his brother. "The Count was right. I have never heard anyone grasp quite so desperately at every note. "

"And his grasp is such, one loses all sense of the music," Johann whispered back, as Albert continued to play valiantly through the piece.

The Estates Director's nephew had a tendency to emphasize the first beat in every measure. His slight pause at the end of each measure interrupted the phrasing, making the music sounded like a senseless stream of notes in triple time.

"Not a bad attempt, you will admit," Albert said proudly, "for a first performance. One has to practice the piece, of course, for a more effective rendition."

Haydn knew not what to say, but was saved the trouble of responding by Sándor.

"No, not a bad attempt at all, my young friend. May I try?" Sándor reached out for the music.

"But you have heard me play already," Albert protested. "You will merely reproduce what I have just played. Choose your own piece!"

Sándor glanced at the Kapellmeister, then turned back to Albert. There was a twinkle in his eyes. "Well, I hope I can be more original than that! But if it pleases you, I will perform at sight any piece the Kapellmeister selects for me."

Haydn had already begun leafing through the stack of scores in search of a violin sonata he wanted Sándor to play.

"Ah, here it is!" He handed the score to Sándor. "The last two phrases of the first theme and the ones beginning the next will suffice. I am more interested in your ability to improvise. He pointed to the prolonged rest in the score allowing the violinist free rein.

Sándor placed the score on the silver music stand near the fortepiano.

"A beautiful piece," he remarked, apparently having scanned it to his satisfaction while the Kapellmeister had been speaking. "I hope I may do it justice."

He began to play the phrases Haydn had indicated, capturing the sense of loss and its acceptance that marked the first theme. His cadenza began a gradual crescendo into the second theme, and drew forth a gasp of admiration from his listeners.

"Bravo!" The word erupted spontaneously out of Haydn's mouth. Sándor's cadenza, unlike Bartó's, was more than just a dazzling display of technical skill. The extemporized section connected the two themes of the piece; moving from quiet anguish and resignation to a resounding sense of resurrection.

Albert sank down onto the bench at the fortepiano, digging his bow into the floor in a huff. "Improvisation is not my forte! And Uncle said nothing about it. I thought all I had to do was read the music."

Haydn suppressed a shudder. "Never fear, Albert. It was never my intention to call upon you to improvise. Sándor, if he is willing, can take over those parts."

"You mean to hire both men, I take it?" Johann turned from the window to cast a discreet glance at the two young men deep in conversation near the fortepiano. Sándor was helping Albert learn a piece while the Kapellmeister sat at his desk writing up temporary contracts for each man.

Haydn followed his gaze. "I have no choice but to hire the Estates Director's nephew." His eyes fell on Albert's violin case. "Besides, it would be as well to keep him close for the time being."

Johann pursed his lips. "The color and design are common enough that one might regard it as a coincidence, and yet..."

Haydn nodded, glad his brother saw nothing untoward in his suspicions. "And yet it is an odd fact. Fortunately, we lose nothing by keeping him on. His own recognition of his inability to improvise gives me the excuse I need not to give him Bartó's parts."

"And what of Lorenzo?" Johann enquired, his voice reflecting the Kapellmeister's own qualms on the matter. "He will not take too kindly to Sándor being given Bartó's parts, I fear."

Haydn sighed. "No, he will not. But it is all Sándor is being given." He looked up at Johann. "Lorenzo will remain Konzertmeister, and will be able to attend to his duties without the additional burden of learning Bartó's parts. At any rate, I hope he will see it that way."

The Kapellmeister dipped his pen into a silver inkwell and signed the contracts. He was about to put his pen away when his gaze fell on the correspondence he had neglected to read. He thought he recognized the writing on an envelope peering out from the bundle stacked neatly against a penholder inlaid with lapis lazuli. But the postmark... He pulled the envelope out.

"Michael is in Vienna?" His voice nearly hit the treble notes far beyond his reach since he had lost his singing voice. He handed the envelope to Johann. "Whatever can he be doing there?"

Few things had the power to overset his younger brother, but Michael's letter, Haydn saw, seemed to have done it. Johann stared down at the letter, turning it over as though expecting to discover something more, and then handed it back.

"Whatever it is, it does not bode well for us," he said. "The news of his protégé's disappearance will most likely catapult a visit to Eisenstadt." The corners of his mouth puckered up as though filled with the sharp tartness of an unripe cherry.

His eyes swiveled toward the two young men at the fortepiano. "We had best conclude our business here first. Have them sign their contracts. I will take them to the Rehearsal Room."

<hr />

It was nearly a quarter of an hour later when Johann returned to the Music Room. Haydn was already seated near the window, letter in hand, waiting impatiently for his brother. As soon as Johann had settled into the armchair opposite him, Haydn tore into the letter, and began reading.

"*I am, as you will see from the postmark on this letter, in Vienna,*" Michael began in his usual abrupt fashion. "*It was fortunate for me that the Archbishop, having a hankering to spend some months in the capital, insisted on the entire musical troupe accompanying him. (Leopold Mozart is in town to show off the talents of his two unusual children, and the Archbishop, undoubtedly, feels the need to remind his Kapellmeister and everyone at the imperial court of his own hand in nurturing the children's gift.)*"

"Well, at least, there is no great mystery to his being in Vienna." Johann sounded relieved. Their middle brother was difficult enough to exhaust even Johann's infinite resources of tact and patience. "Improbable though it is, I had feared it might have something to do with Bartó."

"It does have everything to do with Bartó, I am afraid," Haydn said, perusing the rest of the letter. He began to read the next portion aloud.

"*At any rate, it has saved me the enormous inconvenience of having to beg a leave of absence to travel to your obscure, little Hungarian town. Bartó's wife has come to me several times since her husband left to serve your Prince with complaints that she has received neither word nor money from the man since he left. Nor any summons to join him.*"

"Then, he did have a family!" Haydn had barely finished reading when the words spouted out of Johann's lips. "But we knew nothing of it until he made his demand for money."

Haydn nodded, more than a little perplexed himself. Why had Bartó never mentioned his family until that moment? "He said he could not support a family on what he made, as though..." Haydn gazed out the window, attempting to recall the incident. "As though, the thought of supporting one had not been a consideration until fairly recently. Yet"— he tapped the letter—"he left a wife and children in Salzburg."

96

He turned toward Johann. Pensive lines ran across his brother's forehead.

"Besides," Johann began slowly, "his income of two hundred gulden could amply provide for a family. Even if he had only recently acquired one. What was he spending his money on that he needed more?"

It was a question to which Haydn had no answer. After a moment's silence, he picked up the letter and resumed his reading.

"Frau Daboczi's fears for her husband are many. And to tell you the truth, Joseph, I myself am quite concerned. It is not like Bartó to be so neglectful of his wife and children. If, however, he is, as she greatly fears, involved with some other woman, you must urge him to desist. It is your duty as a Kapellmeister."

Haydn found this last sentence most galling. It was just like Michael to suggest he meddle in his musicians' personal affairs! But he chose not to comment on it, merely glancing up to exchange a wry smile with Johann before he read on.

"Is there anything at all to these rumors of Hungarian unrest? They seem to have made the hiring of a coach more difficult and more expensive than usual. But I shall come as soon as I am able."

The mention of Hungary made Johann sit up in his chair. "There must be more to the rumors if they have reached all the way to Vienna. I considered the Bürgermeister to be overly concerned about the Police Commissioner's visit to the castle this morning. But it appears his fears were not so unreasonable after all.

"Still, all this talk may well serve our purpose. It may keep Michael at bay for a little longer, and give us more time to discover what has become of Bartó."

But Haydn, contemplating the undulating landscape beyond the castle grounds, barely heard what his brother said. Something was stirring in his brain. And it was some moments before he turned away from the window.

"I wonder what Maria Anna will make of all this. You must be sure to bring up the topic of Bartó's wife during our evening meal, Johann. We may learn much to our advantage," he explained in response to his brother's uncomprehending stare.

CHAPTER ELEVEN

Maria Anna was not surprised to hear Bartó had left.

"You will recall, I did warn you that something of the sort might happen," she said with some relish. "It grieves me to say it," she continued, showing no evidence of any grief that Haydn could see, "but it is not to be wondered at, at all."

She began clearing the table, shaking her head and muttering disapprovingly as she gathered up plates, forks, and knives and carried them to the kitchen sink. Turning toward the cabinet, she reached up for some clean dessert plates and forks, and brought them to the table with a pot of coffee.

She poured out their coffee, and then went toward the oven, saying: "Some men are all too likely to prove undependable no matter what promises they make."

It was just the cue Haydn had been waiting for. He mouthed a signal to Johann, hoping his brother would understand. Johann nodded, waiting until Maria Anna had returned to the table with her kuchen before saying in a loud voice: "Yes, he has left his wife quite bereft. But apparently, in coming here, he had already abandoned her to her fate. Michael says he has not sent her any word or money since he left Salzburg."

Maria Anna had been about to set her cake pan down on the kitchen table. But, at Johann's words, it slipped from her fingers, and hit the table with a resounding clack.

"A wife! Your principal violinist has a wife?" Her eyes went accusingly toward Haydn. "Why, that makes his behavior all the worse!"

Haydn glared sternly back. It was as he had surmised. "Yes, it does, although I do not imagine you can afford to throw stones."

Maria Anna turned red, but said nothing. Johann turned blankly from his brother to his sister-in-law, his face registering first confusion, then disbelief.

"What knowledge do you have of this matter, Maria Anna? Do you know who Bartó was involved with? You must tell me who it is."

Maria Anna seemed to have found her tongue. "Why?" she demanded with her hands on her hips. "So, you can pester her with your questions? You never see beyond your nose, husband. Until it is too late." With these words, she stalked out of the kitchen.

Johann turned to his brother. "This woman Bartó was involved with..." he faltered. "You cannot suspect...you cannot think it was my sister-in-law?"

Haydn wiped his hand over his face. It felt as though the skin were stretched tightly over it. "No, it was not Maria Anna. She has had just the one indiscretion, and it was some years back."

He turned toward his brother. Johann looked profoundly shocked.

"It is a matter best forgotten now." Haydn strove to keep his tone even. At the time, the realization that they could never have children had been far worse than Maria Anna's vain attempt to prove herself fertile. And their own desperate attempts to bear a child had ruined all semblance of harmony even before the incident. "We have more important things to consider."

Johann nodded, seeming to turn his mind with some difficulty back to their current problems. "If we could but find the woman Bartó seduced. She may have some clue of his whereabouts. Will your musicians know of her? Your principal cellist, perhaps?"

"It is a possibility," Haydn conceded. He brought his coffee cup to his lips, and took a long sip before setting the cup down. "I would be willing to wager, though, that she is connected in some way with Gerhard, the tavern-keeper. What other explanation could there be for the bad blood between the two men?"

The wine wagon from Kleinhöflein was late. Rosalie had been waiting for it all morning, running down the narrow corridor behind the kitchen to the back door every few minutes watching for its arrival. She was about to return to the kitchen yet again when she finally heard its wooden wheels rumbling slowly over the cobblestones to come to a halt in front of the wine cellar.

She opened the door and poked her head out. A covered wooden wagon, a good deal taller and sturdier than the rack-wagons the peasants used to transport goods to the market, stood outside. But the young delivery boy she was accustomed to dealing with was nowhere to be seen. Instead, Rosalie saw a tall, muscular man with a thick head of chestnut hair jump down from the wagon.

She took a quick step back.

Was that Master Bartó's friend again? What was he doing here?

"Oh!" she said, putting her hand to her cheek, as she realized her mistake. "You must be—"

"Gerhard," the man supplied in a booming voice. He sighed, his blue eyes travelling swiftly down her form before returning to her eyes. "I suppose I shall have to carry these wooden chests down to the cellar myself, then. Can't expect a little thing like you to give me a hand.

"Better get on with it, then," he continued, hefting a wooden crate packed with round, dark wine bottles carefully nestled amidst thick piles of straw. He set the crate down on the cobblestones. "I should have sent the boy down yesterday. But what with one thing and another..." He shook his head.

Rosalie regarded the man with open curiosity. So, this was Gerhard. She had overheard the musicians gossiping some months back, and had pictured the tavern-keeper as an older, plain-featured man. But Gerhard was...Quite good-looking! And certainly not much over thirty. Could there be any truth to the rumors? It seemed quite beyond belief that any woman could prefer the hard-featured Master Bartó over this man!

"Just as well that you left it till this morning," she commented, following him to the wagon. She gripped a crate.

"I am strong enough for this," she said in response to Gerhard's warning glance. She heaved the crate off the cart and onto the ground in one vigorous sweep, reeling slightly against its weight.

"There was quite a to-do here." She paused to take breath, and then returned to the wagon for another crate. "What with Master Bartó leaving, you know—"

"About time the Kapellmeister got rid of that scoundrel," Gerhard grunted. His features had darkened.

Rosalie drew a crate toward her, and turned around to gaze at the tavern-keeper. "Herr Haydn didn't get rid of him. Master Bartó left on his own. Just vanished, or so it would seem—"

"Disappeared, has he?" Gerhard lifted a crate off the wagon, sounding quite satisfied at the news. "It is no more than what one would expect of that swine."

Rosalie dragged her crate off the wagon, supporting it briefly on her knee before lowering it to the ground. "He had threatened to leave, but Herr Haydn is sure something is amiss. He suspects someone or other had a hand in Master Bartó's departure."

She looked up to see Gerhard apparently frozen beside the wagon, the crate still in his arms. He stared at her.

"Why?" he croaked at last. "What reason has Herr Haydn to suspect any harm may have come to his violinist?"

Rosalie wiped her nose with the back of her hand. "Master Bartó's travel trunk is still in his room in the Musicians' Quarters. I thought that strange myself."

The wine bottles clinked dangerously when Gerhard eventually put the crate down. His blue eyes were cold when he straightened up again. "Then he must have been in a great hurry to leave town."

Gerhard returned to the wagon. He unloaded the remainder of the wine crates in silence, then trudged down the wooden cellar-steps carrying one crate at a time, his lips clamped into a thin line the whole while.

He was ready to leave, gathering up his reins and prodding his mare into a gentle amble, when he turned to face Rosalie.

"Your Kapellmeister is wasting his time with his suspicions. Be sure to tell him that."

***

Haydn was approaching the castle when he saw the covered wagon roll out of the castle grounds, and turn west. He slowed down. The wine wagon that made deliveries from the Esterházy vineyards in Kleinhöflein was a familiar sight in Eisenstadt. But...

Its driver was not.

Although the wagon had made its turn much too quickly, Haydn thought he had discerned Gerhard at the reins. He stood in the middle of the path, squinting after the wagon long after it had disappeared into the distance. Why had Gerhard come to the castle? Was it to remind Bartó of his obligations?

It was likely, he supposed, that news of his principal violinist's disappearance had yet to make its way to Kleinhöflein. But the small, wine-producing village lay only a short distance to the west of Eisenstadt.

Then again, if he had already heard the news, what had brought Gerhard here?

Haydn walked slowly into the castle grounds, pensively chewing at his lower lip. Rosalie was still in the courtyard, and struck by a sudden thought he hailed out to her.

"Did you meet the wine wagon, Rosalie?"

Rosalie nodded, wiping her hands on her apron as she approached the Kapellmeister.

"Was it Gerhard who made the delivery this morning? I suppose he asked to see Master Bartó," Haydn continued when the maid nodded a second time.

Rosalie shook her head, clearly taken aback by the suggestion that the tavern-keeper might have wanted to meet the violinist. "I don't think he liked Master Bartó well enough to want to see him, Herr Haydn...I—eh..." She cleared her throat—rather abruptly, the Kapellmeister thought.

He directed a penetrating stare at her. A tide of information seemed to be swelling at the tip of her tongue. What held her back from divulging it? His mind turned over her words, his gaze drifting toward the arch leading to the outer courtyard.

"No, I don't suppose Gerhard did like Bartó," he said to himself. "Still, I would have thought he would want to see him—Unless..." He looked down at Rosalie. "Did he know Master Bartó was missing? Did he ask to see anyone at all?"

Rosalie shook her head again, peering up at the Kapellmeister as though he stood on the other side of an impenetrable fog.

"Gerhard didn't know Master Bartó was gone until I mentioned it to him, Herr Haydn. And then, he wasn't surprised to hear it. Said it was no more than he expected. He seemed glad, almost, but..." The sound of her voice dimmed. She lowered her eyes.

Haydn saw her fingers nervously twisting her apron. He waited a few minutes.

"What was it that Gerhard said, Rosalie?"

Rosalie twisted her head up so slowly one might have thought a heavy weight rested upon her neck. "He wanted me to tell you that you were wasting your time with your suspicions."

"Ach so!" murmured Haydn. He waited for her to continue.

She fidgeted with her apron for a few more minutes, and then blurted out: "Your thinking that Master Bartó might have been harmed gave him quite a turn, Herr Haydn."

Oh! Haydn's eyebrows went up at this. Had Gerhard been so certain, then, that Bartó would flee his obligations at the first available opportunity?

"Wasting my time with my suspicions," he repeated. "I would have thought that he, at least, would want to know what has become of Bartó. If not have him found."

Rosalie bit down on her lip. "I don't think it would make him all that happy if Master Bartó were to be found."

Haydn nodded, although the words she uttered made as much impression on his mind as a hand pressed into stone. He turned away, the groove in his forehead deepening. He had barely taken a few steps when he stopped again.

"Master Bartó's visitor last week," he began, turning around. "Was it Gerhard?"

"Oh no, Herr Haydn." Rosalie shook her head so emphatically, a wavy lock of her hair escaped from its pins, and dangled over her eyes. She pushed it back. "Of course, they do look quite similar. Why this morning, I thought—"

"You are sure it was not Gerhard," Haydn insisted. "You have seen Gerhard often enough to be certain?"

Rosalie hesitated. "I have never seen Gerhard before today, but I am quite sure it was not him. Master Bartó's visitor looked like a nobleman in peasant's clothing—"

"I see. Thank you, Rosalie," Haydn replied. But as he turned away he reflected that he was beginning to see less than he had supposed. Bartó had asked for money on the very day he had met his mysterious visitor. The snippet Haydn had overheard made it seem quite likely that his principal violinist's visitor had some claims on him. There was only one man in Eisenstadt, or so Haydn had supposed, who could make any claims on Bartó. And yet Rosalie had said...

He brought his hand up to his forehead, and pressed his temples. Was he utterly wrong in his conjecture, then, that the woman Bartó had seduced was in some way connected with Gerhard?

CHAPTER TWELVE

The orchestra had already begun rehearsing by the time Haydn made his way up to the Rehearsal Room. He stood by the stairs, debating the wisdom of drawing his principal cellist out of rehearsal. Bartó had not grated on Niklas's nerves to quite the extent he had the rest of his colleagues. If there was any information of value to be had, his principal cellist might be just the person to have it. And be the most willing, no doubt, to share it.

The symphony the orchestra was practicing had no solo part for cello. It was unlikely Niklas would be missed. Besides, the christening service for his son would serve as a suitable pretext to call him out.

His mind made up, Haydn made his way toward the Rehearsal Room, walking past the small chamber in which the two newest members of the orchestra had established themselves. Albert's raised voice rang out from within.

"What can your sister possibly know of the matter? Come to harm, indeed! It is just as well my uncle refused to call in the Police Commissioner. After last night, it is become quite clear, Herr Haydn's former violinist deliberately walked away from his position."

Haydn stopped, his attention arrested by this reference to Bartó. What was Rahier's nephew on about? What *had* happened the previous night?

He turned back toward the chamber, and thrust his head around the door. Sándor was sitting at a small desk equipped with ink, pens, and music paper, diligently copying out a score. Albert's slim figure stood before him, leaning against a chair, his violin tucked under his arm.

"Rosalie was merely repeating what she has overheard," Sándor responded, his head still bent over his work. He dipped his pen into an inkwell. "Why should the Kapellmeister's speculations on the subject trouble you? It matters not why his former violinist left. The fact remains, he is gone."

Albert's form still quivered with indignation. "Yes, but—"

"What is it you know regarding my principal violinist's disappearance, gentlemen?" Haydn's voice broke in sternly upon the conversation.

Albert started violently as though a jolt of lightning had run through his frame. He straightened up and turned around.

"Judging by his reappearance last night, he seems to be unharmed and well, Herr Kapellmeister." Albert's pale blue eyes regarded Haydn steadily.

"Have you seen him?" Haydn demanded, his eyes moving toward Sándor.

Sándor shook his head. "Neither one of us has seen him, but it is the only conclusion that can be drawn." He cast an amused glance at the Estates Director's nephew. "Albert here spent a restless night, and was awoken by a noise in the room next to his. It belonged apparently to your former violinist."

"It was the sound of something being dragged across the floor— something relatively heavy." Albert jutted his chin out as though defying anyone to contradict him. "I saw nothing when I went in to investigate. But this morning..." He looked down at Sándor. "Well, you said it yourself, his travel trunk was gone."

Sándor raised his shoulders in a brief shrug. "And, so it was, although you needn't have aroused me so early in the day to inspect his room!" He turned to face Haydn. "My sister said the man left without his belongings. He must have returned to retrieve them. The closet door was open, and the closet itself was empty."

"It is of a piece with what we have learned thus far," Johann pointed out when he heard the news. "Something precipitated your violinist's departure. His brief return only confirms it. If only we knew what it was."

"Could Niklas shed no light on the matter?" he asked, as they walked side by side toward the Music Room.

"Ach!" Haydn ground his heel into the carpet. How could he have forgotten? "I was on my way to speak with him when I heard Albert mention Bartó."

There would be time enough to do it later, he thought, taking the last few paces toward the Music Room. He pushed the door open. He had still more to tell Johann. "His return is not the only strange incident of the day. Gerhard, apparently, is not as eager as we surmised that Bartó stay on to take care of his mistress."

"And yet that makes no sense," he said after recounting all that Rosalie had told him that morning.

"No, it does not. Unless..." Johann ran his thumb over the polished surface of the fortepiano. He brought his head up. "There may be one other possibility—"

A sharp rap on the door startled the brothers. The door opened to admit Rosalie into the room.

"An urgent message for you, Herr Haydn." She held a note out to the Kapellmeister. "I believe it is from the Bürgermeister."

Haydn waited until the maid had left before tearing the letter open. He quickly perused the untidy sprawling hand that covered the entire sheet of paper, and then handed it to his brother.

"Herr Groer says his men have found Bartó's violin. Left in an abandoned abbey in the woods of Kleinhöflein."

Johann read through the note. "It will not be long before he is found, then. It would be quite unlike Bartó to stray too far from his beloved Stadlmann." He glanced down at the note again. "To think that all this while we have been looking for him, your principal violinist was hiding in the woods in Kleinhöflein!"

"Yes, but from what? And why?" Haydn began to pace the floor as he was wont to in moments of stress. "It cannot have been from Gerhard. He was not displeased to find Bartó gone."

Johann watched in silence, and then said: "Could Gerhard have been in love with the woman Bartó seduced? It would explain his reaction to the news. But then, surely the poor woman's family would have demanded that Bartó abide by her."

"Possibly. But could their demands have been strenuous enough to compel Bartó to disappear when he did? In the middle of a snowstorm? I find it hard to believe." Haydn paused in his perambulation.

"The Estates Director, then..." Johann ventured after a while.

Haydn nodded. "That is a strong possibility. But..." He shook his head, trying to clear his thoughts. "What could Bartó have been so afraid of?" he wondered softly.

He scrutinized the carpet for a few moments, and then straightened up. "I will meet the Bürgermeister in the woods as he asks, and recover the violin. Question Niklas, if you will, Johann. We must find out what we can of the woman Bartó seduced."

He strode toward the door, but looked over his shoulder just as he was about to open it. "If he seems reluctant to divulge any information, ask him if the name Marlene means anything to him."

"*Marlene!*" Johann repeated. But Haydn had already left.

The wooded area where the Bürgermeister had found Bartó's violin skirted St. Vitus Street on its left, and ran all the way up the hill to the Parish Church of Kleinhöflein. Haydn found the Bürgermeister waiting for him at the edge of the woods just below the church.

"Remembering that your principal violinist often frequented these woods, I began my search here." The Bürgermeister indicated the woods behind him. "Although I hardly know what business he could have had here," he continued, glancing around at the ancient, grey-brown tree trunks as they entered the woods.

Haydn, having nothing to say, squelched after the Bürgermeister wordlessly, his head bent to avoid the canopy of thickly entwined overhanging branches bowed down with its weight of snow.

"There is nothing in these woods, but the ruins of the old Cistercian abbey. He must have taken shelter from the storm there," the Bürgermeister said as they emerged from the damp leaf-covered forest floor into a small clearing.

Haydn followed the Bürgermeister's pointing finger toward an aged, yellowing stone structure standing amidst patches of snow and dried gray grass.

"And it is there that you found the violin, Bartó's Stadlmann?" Haydn asked, wondering why Bartó would have risked exposing his beloved violin to the dampness of the elements. Why had Bartó even come here?

"Oh, all violins look alike to me, Herr Haydn." The Bürgermeister led Haydn into a large hall with a ceiling formed of successive arches; the only part of the twelfth century monastery to have survived the ravages of time. "But his name was on the case, so it must be his. Here!" he said, coming to a standstill beside a stone bench.

Haydn stared at the battered, black violin case on the bench. "That is not Bartó's violin case, Herr Groer" he said. The color was different, he was quite sure of it. Besides, Bartó's case had been as immaculately kept as the violin it housed.

"But it has his name on it." The Bürgermeister opened the case, and jabbed at the words "Bartó Daboczi" engraved on the underside of the lid.

"And that is not his violin, either." Haydn was adamant. He lifted the violin out from its case. "It is a Stadlmann, but of an older make than the one Bartó possessed. The varnish is chipped, as you can see, and the strings need to be tightened. The case has protected it well, but it was not entirely able to prevent some damage.

"I will take it with me." He expelled a heavy breath as he turned to look at the pillars supporting the vaulted ceiling and the puddles of water on the cracked stone floor. Could Bartó have owned more than one violin? And if he had, why had he left the older instrument here, uncared for?

"Are any of his other belongings here?"

"Only that writing case." The Bürgermeister picked up a wooden box inlaid with lapis lazuli. "It must belong to your violinist. I have frequently seen him enter these woods with it. And yet when I asked him if he was going for his usual walk in the woods, he accused me of spying on him!" He puffed his pink cheeks out.

"He must have been up to some mischief," Haydn murmured, taking the writing case. "Although I cannot imagine what it was." He looked around him again. "If he has been hiding here, where is his travel trunk? Bartó returned for it last night, apparently," he explained in response to Herr Groer's stare of utter bewilderment.

The Bürgermeister shrugged his ample shoulders. "I know not of any trunk. My men found these, and I called for you as soon as I heard."

"Bartó must still be in the vicinity," Haydn murmured. "Although what he can be doing here is a mystery." He turned toward the Bürgermeister. "Would it be possible for your men to keep watch here, Herr Groer? Just in case Bartó returns."

Herr Groer bit his lip, looking unhappy at this request. "I will do what I can, Herr Haydn, but if the Police Commissioner should get wind of this..."

CHAPTER THIRTEEN

Shortly after Haydn set out for Kleinhöflein, Johann was about to leave the Music Room in search of Niklas, when the door was brusquely thrust open to admit Lorenzo and the principal cellist.

"Is it true, Master Johann?" Lorenzo demanded, looming over Johann. "Has that sw— Bartó—" he quickly amended upon receiving a sharp nudge from Niklas. "Has Bartó been found?"

Lorenzo held his arms rigidly by his side, clenching and unclenching his fists. What was making him so nervous, Johann wondered. And how had the musicians heard of Bartó's return? He turned toward the principal cellist.

Niklas must have read the question in his eyes. "The new men—" he began.

"Why was the Kapellmeister even looking for him?" Lorenzo interrupted, still standing over Johann with a lowering expression on his face.

The question was most inappropriate. Worthy of a reprimand, even. Worse still, it gave his brother's suspicions cause. But if Johann wanted to draw the man out, it would not to do to acknowledge it.

He chose his next words with care. "It would appear Bartó never left. Although no one seems to have seen him." He led the way toward the window, lowered himself into an armchair, and with a wave of his hand invited the musicians to sit down.

"The property he has stolen must be recovered, gentlemen. I am sure you understand that." Johann kept his features amiable as he met Lorenzo's eyes. Would to God, there was nothing more to the second violinist's anger than mere jealousy. "It has also, apparently, been some time since he contacted his family. My brother in Salzburg says it is not like Bartó to—"

"Ach, his parents!" Niklas glanced at Lorenzo, then turned back to Johann. "If they are still living, they must rely upon Bartó to provide for them. He has younger brothers and sisters, too, I think. I thought they were somewhere in Hungary. Not Salzburg. I could be mistaken, mind you. He doesn't often speak of them."

Lorenzo snorted. "That he does not. Other than to boast once in a while that *his* efforts have rescued them from extreme poverty."

Johann had no trouble believing they had. "Due to his extraordinary talents, no doubt, and the patronage they have earned him from men like His Serene Highness. Many a gifted man has been able to rise up in the world with such generous support."

His own brothers—sons of a humble wheelwright and his wife, a cook—had been so favored. Brother Joseph was known throughout the Empire. And brother Michael had acquired a reputation for being one of the finest composers of sacred works. Neither of their parents, God rest their souls, could have foretold such success.

"Ach no, Master Johann!" Lorenzo shifted impatiently in his chair. "You may depend upon it, that oaf bears the Prince no gratitude for his success."

"Once at the tavern, he said—" Niklas broke off, a hot blush of embarrassment suffusing his cheeks. "That it was no thanks to any of the Hungarian nobility that his family had survived," the cellist continued in response to Johann's questioning gaze.

"Ach, there is no need to mince words, Niklas!" Lorenzo retorted, his tone brusque. "That clod had nothing but the utmost contempt for the Prince.

"*A servile lackey to the Empress.* That is how he referred to His Serene Highness. As though the patents of nobility he bragged about procuring for his family placed him above his betters! But how he bowed and scraped when Count Nádasdy came here."

"Patents of nobility?" It was the first Johann had heard of this. Had Bartó not referred to himself as a humble peasant?

"Purchased to exempt oneself from taxation," Niklas explained, misunderstanding the reason for Johann's surprise. "Whoever heard of such a foolish practice?" He shook his head. "The Hungarian nobility not content with paying no taxes themselves, seem eager to dispense that benefit to anyone with the means to secure a title! It is a wonder the country still stands."

Lorenzo barked out a derisive laugh. "Small wonder they have no money for their insurrection. Your new man—the one who worked in a printer's shop—has been regaling us with tales of Hungarian foolishness."

"Sándor," Johann murmured, only half-listening to the exchange between the two musicians. He roused himself. "And what of his wife? Did he never speak of her?" Brother Michael had made no mention of either parents or siblings. Only a wife and children.

"But he has not married her yet," Niklas said in some confusion. "He *did* make her an offer. Or so he said."

"Made her an offer?" Johann sputtered. But Bartó already had a wife. To whom had he offered marriage, then? His mistress? What could the man have been thinking?

Niklas nodded. "He could hardly do any less under the circumstances," he enunciated carefully, as though speaking to a dim-witted child. He stared hard at Johann all the while.

"*Ach*, it was all talk with that scoundrel!" Lorenzo grunted. He leant back in his chair, and thrust out his arm. "He takes care of his parents, he says. They rely solely upon him. Well, what of them now that he has thrown up a perfectly good position? He promises to marry the woman he gets with child, only to leave so he doesn't have to."

"*She* is with child?" Johann felt as though the air had been sucked out of him. What would brother Michael say when he heard! Despite brother Joseph's suspicions, he himself had not supposed things had gone quite this far. His mind turned toward the woman Haydn had named. "Marlene—"

"Yes, Master Johann. Marlene is with child." Lorenzo's interruption was curt. "Bartó's child."

"But gentlemen, Bartó left a wife and children in Salzburg. Did he never mention them?" Johann leaned forward, his eyes darting from Lorenzo to Niklas. Could brother Michael have been so mistaken in his protégé's character?

"Married!" Niklas exploded, half-rising from his chair. He turned toward Lorenzo. "Gerhard must have known it. Why else would he try to keep them apart?"

Lorenzo shrugged. "What difference does it make? You think Bartó would stoop to marry a mere barmaid?"

———✦———

Johann was still sitting by the window, chin cupped in his hand, mulling over the musicians' words when Rosalie entered the room, followed by Greta.

"Herr Haydn recovered these from the woods, Master Johann," Rosalie said. "The cart he sent on ahead of him has just arrived, and the driver says Herr Haydn will be here shortly."

Johann nodded, too preoccupied to attend to her words. He saw the maid gesturing behind her with the wooden writing case she held in her hands. His eyes absently followed along. A second maid, buxom and blond, staggered into the room, panting heavily under the weight of a shabby violin case she half-dragged, half-carried across the floor.

"Stand it against the fortepiano," Rosalie instructed Greta.

"To think, Master Bartó felt the need to hide his writing case in the woods!" She approached Johann's armchair, and handed the case to him. "As though Greta or I, or any of the other maids, would rifle through his belongings!"

Both maids left the room, only to return again. Count Nádasdy and his companion had come calling. Johann roused himself with difficulty. It was the worst possible time for a visit, but he could hardly turn His Lordship away. He forced himself to smile as he came forward to greet the tall, good-looking man in his forties who entered the room.

"Haydn is not out, is he?" the Count enquired in a loud baritone as he strode into the middle of the room. He looked over his shoulder at his companion, an even taller man with a thick mane of brown hair and a sharp, piercing gaze of surprising intensity. "We seem to have missed him yet again, Leopold."

"It is most unfortunate," he continued, addressing Johann. "Leopold here is something of a composer, and is quite eager to have Haydn look over his efforts."

"My brother will return shortly, if you would care to wait, Your Lordship." Johann cleared his throat, not sure how much of the circumstances to reveal. Still, it might be best to allude to them. Brother Joseph had enough on his hands without being tasked with nurturing the talents of yet another man, however well-connected. He uttered a mild cough. "Our principal violinist—"

"Has left his position. I know. Your Estates Director mentioned it to me. I am sorry to hear it." The Count's eyes swept the room in a wide arc before coming to rest on Johann's face. "He seems to think his nephew will make a good replacement." The Count sounded amused.

Johann returned the smile, but forbore to comment on this veiled reference to Albert's lack of skill. "We were fortunate in hiring another young man. Sándor Szabó. You know him, I believe."

The Count was pulling his gloves off, but paused when he heard the name, and gazed vacantly ahead.

Johann held his breath. Had young Sanyi been boasting of a connection he didn't have?

"The name sounds familiar," His Lordship said at last, turning toward his companion.

"It is the young man from the printer's shop in Pressburg," the other replied. "An excellent replacement, if I may say so," he continued with a smile at Johann.

"Ah, Sándor!" The Count's face cleared. "Leopold is right. He is exceptionally talented. More so, dare I say it, than the man he replaces."

This testimonial did much to ease Johann's anxiety. He felt his shoulders, hunched up until now, begin to subside. His gaze shifted toward the porcelain clock. When would brother Joseph return? The Count was making little effort to conceal his impatience. He had already declined Johann's offer of a seat. Now he paced about the room in a restive manner, glancing every so often at a gold timepiece.

"A matter of some urgency awaits us in Pressburg," he said after a while, coming to a standstill beside the fortepiano. "We must on with our journey." He walked toward his companion, and held out his hand. "Your leather case, if you please, Leopold!"

"Thank you. Perhaps, Johann will be so good as to show these to Haydn. These are six of Leopold's finest string quartets. "

"Yes, of course." Johann repressed a sigh as he took the proffered case. His hint appeared to have fallen on deaf ears. He cast about for a way to speak more clearly without going so far as to refuse His Lordship. But before he could so much as fashion a response, the Count turned on his heels and swept out of the room. His companion, bowing his head, followed suit.

———

The Count's unexpected visit had driven all thoughts of Bartó and his writing case from Rosalie's mind. He and his friend had inclined their heads toward Greta and herself in so cordial a manner, they might have been old acquaintances. Was it on account of the Count's affable manner that she felt such a sense of familiarity in his presence?

"Although who knows, but he may have been a frequent visitor to Rohrau," she said to Greta as she polished a gilded silver coffee pot. "It is a small town, but our Count Harrach is just as influential at the imperial court as His Lordship." She paused to inspect the coffee pot's gleaming surface.

Master Johann had been so startled to see his guests he had quite forgotten to ask for any coffee or refreshments for them. But Rosalie had decided to take a tray up to the Music Room all the same.

"You can be quite sure he has," Greta hovered over the stove, watching the first coffee bubbles erupt ever-rapidly from the hot fluid. "He was telling Herr Rahier the last time he came that he is well-acquainted with the finest families, and their musicians, from every part of Austria. As far as Salzburg and Innsbruck, too, if you can believe it."

She took the coffee, bubbling now, off the stove. It would be a few minutes before the grounds settled to the bottom. Her face was flushed from the cloud of aromatic steam that rose from the pot when she turned to Rosalie.

"Herr Rahier was sounding His Lordship out about a job for his precious nephew. But I don't think His Lordship was inclined to bite." Her face broke into a mischievous grin.

Rosalie grinned back. They worked together in companionable silence. When the tray was ready, Rosalie lifted it, and edged past the kitchen door that Greta held open for her into the hallway. She was about to climb the stairs when the Count and his companion rushed down. Rosalie blinked and took a quick step back as they whirled past her toward the entrance, their cloaks flying behind them.

"Left!" Greta exclaimed, when Rosalie returned to the kitchen with the tray. "But they have only just arrived."

Rosalie put the tray down on the kitchen table. "They were in a great hurry, too. I cannot imagine why! They flew past me."

"Who flew past you, sister?" Sándor enquired, his tone mildly curious. He strolled into the kitchen followed by Albert.

"It was only Count Nádasdy and his companion." Noticing her brother's gaze fixed on the tray of sandwiches and cherry kuchen, she added: "Are you hungry?"

"We missed our mid-day meal, and Albert here—"

"Count Nádasdy!" Albert cried, his hunger apparently forgotten. He looked wildly around him as though expecting the Count to emerge from amongst the gleaming pots and pans that surrounded them. "He was here? Why did no one tell me? Did he not ask after me?" He pondered the question with a frown, then shrugged, and reached out for a sandwich. "He must have had urgent business in Pressburg to attend to."

"I wonder why he drives past Eisenstadt, then." Rosalie put a sandwich and a slice of kuchen on a plate for Sándor. "It must be quite out of his way. Eisenstadt is not on the postal route."

Albert's blue eyes pivoted toward the ceiling. "Men such as the Count do not travel by the stage coach, my dear girl. Besides, he has friends in Eisenstadt. My uncle, for one. Herr Haydn, too, of course." He tilted his head to regard the maids. "I am only surprised he did not ask after me. Are you certain—"

"Still, you must admit it is strange." Greta withdrew her mouth from the kuchen she had been about to bite into. "He was in an enormous rush the last time he came as well. Didn't wait more than a few minutes for the Kapellmeister before he hurried away. He was on his way to Pressburg at the time, too."

She took a large bite of her kuchen, and chewed thoughtfully. "It could all be on account of the dissidents, you know," she said, after she had swallowed. She looked at each of her listeners in turn, then leaned forward, and continued in a lowered voice. "I have heard some talk—"

Sándor glanced up at Rosalie from under his eyebrows. There was an amused twinkle in his eyes.

"There is no need to fear the dissidents, my fair Greta," he said lightly as he turned toward the maid. "They pose no threat. From the little I know, all they can think to do is cower behind the petticoats of a foreign power. Now, if only they could decide whether to hide behind the Turks or the French, we might have reason to fear.

"But the Turks are a spent force. And as to the French—"

Albert's spine had stiffened while Sándor spoke. He rose now. "That is not how it is!" he cried out. "They have no recourse but to turn to another power. Thanks to the Empress and her family, Hungary has neither the money nor the strength to fight for what is her own.

"You appall me. These are your countrymen. Yet you have nothing but contempt for their plight!" He leapt up, and stalked out of the kitchen.

Sándor's jaw dropped open at this outburst. He stared after Albert, then turned slowly toward Rosalie, his eyes wide with consternation. "But I meant nothing by it. I was only repeating what the Count himself has said on numerous occasions. I hope—"

"That Albert is not one of the dissidents," Greta gasped before Rosalie could say a word. "But what if he is?" She stared round-eyed at the kitchen door.

CHAPTER FOURTEEN

Haydn walked down the hill, emerging out of Kleinhöflein into Eisenstadt in a pensive mood. The violin the Bürgermeister's men had found only raised more questions. Where was the infernal Bartó, and what was he playing at? Walking with his head bent to the ground, he was barely aware of the imposing black carriage that rolled past him and lurched to a sudden stop.

"Haydn! Haydn!...Haydn!"

The voice calling out his name in a booming baritone jolted him out of his thoughts. The loud, somewhat imperious tone was so familiar, it brought his head up in a sudden, sharp movement. He briefly attempted to place the voice before turning slowly around.

"Count Nádasdy!" he cried, recognizing the handsome features and the nose, with its imperious tilt, of a man who was pleased to call the Kapellmeister friend.

"My dear fellow, it has been long since I last enjoyed your company. Do you recall those pleasant little soirées we enjoyed in Vienna? You and I at the violin, Albrechtsberger at the cello, and Pfarrer Martin at the bass!"

The memory brought a smile to Haydn's face. He may have had to contend with poverty, but how much simpler his life was in those days. "I do indeed, Your Lordship. It was your desire for a little something for four strings that provided the impetus for my quartets."

The Count raised a languid hand. "Well, I suppose I may take credit for the genesis of the form. Its popularity, though, is entirely due to your musical genius, my dear Haydn. Why, every would-be composer these days attempts to earn his Grand Cross by way of a set of string quartets!"

Haydn's smile broadened. It was just like His Lordship to exaggerate his humble achievements to the status of a military accomplishment. The Grand Cross was the highest honor of the Empress's Military Order. Even His Serene Highness, despite his years of service, had yet to receive it.

"Leopold here"—the Count leaned back to allow Haydn a view of a tall young man, who inclined his head at the Kapellmeister—"has just completed a set. I left the manuscript with your brother. Your opinion of it would be of enormous benefit to him, I am sure."

"Yes, of course. But why did Your Lordship not entrust the manuscript to the postal coach? Surely, that would have been more convenient than such a long trip."

The Count grimaced. "It was not so far out of our way. Matters of state, I fear, will take us more frequently than I could wish to Pressburg. It was only the thought of seeing you again, my old friend, that reconciled me to the journey."

"Matters of state?" Haydn pressed with a slight frown. Was the ever-simmering resentment of the Hungarians about to flare up into something more violent?

The Count stared ahead of him impassively for a few moments, drumming his long fingers on the carriage window. Then with a heavy sigh, he turned a troubled gazed toward Haydn.

"There is some talk—faint murmurings, really, but significant nevertheless—of an impending attack on the Empire."

"War!" This was worse than Haydn had expected. "It has been barely three years since the last one. What reason could there be for yet another so shortly after that?"

The Count hesitated a while, contemplating the side of the carriage as he drummed his fingers agitatedly against its side. He sighed again. "It is nonetheless true. My sources say the threat comes from France."

"But that is impossible, Your Lordship. France was our ally in the last war."

"Not any more, apparently." The Count's features hardened. He shook his head as though weary of the demands of state.

It was a feeling Haydn understood, although his own troubles must pale in comparison with the crises of state men such as His Lordship were forced to contend with. He waited for the Count to speak, eager for more information. His Lordship must surely know he could count on his discretion.

"But that is not all," the Count said at last. "The dissidents in Hungary grow more clamorous in their demands for independence. I fear that both threats might flank the Empire simultaneously, leaving us unprepared to deal with the chaos that must ensue.

"And Esterházy isn't helping matters at all."

Haydn raised his head sharply. Now, that could not be true.

"His Serene Highness is staunchly loyal to the Empress, Your Lordship. Surely that cannot be in doubt."

The Count shook his head. "Not his loyalty. Merely the wisdom of his advice. But you have troubles of your own, I hear," he continued with a sympathetic glance at the Kapellmeister. "So, I will cease to bother you with these more remote affairs."

The Kapellmeister, in truth, could have wished to hear more. But His Lordship was clearly not in the mood for any further disclosures. No doubt, he had already revealed more than wisdom dictated. Signaling to his coachman to gather up his reins, the Count drew his head back into the carriage.

Johann knelt on the floor examining the battered violin case retrieved from the woods when Haydn eventually returned. He stood up the moment the Kapellmeister walked into the Music Room.

"This is not the case Bartó brought with him, brother. I remember it well. It was charcoal gray with an emblem of some kind embroidered on the lid." He stood the case up against the fortepiano.

"But you were right about the woman he seduced. Her name is indeed Marlene. Bartó, if you can credit the tale, intended to marry her." Johann recounted his conversation with the musicians.

Haydn went to the closet to hang his coat up, and then stood quietly by the window listening to his brother. "Intended to marry her, did he?" he said over his shoulder when Johann had finished. Why did he have no trouble believing that?

"Or so he said. The musicians think it an empty promise. And I find myself inclined to agree, brother. How can a man who fails to honor the vows he made to his wife be trusted to honor a promise made to a mere mistress?"

"And yet..." Haydn's mind returned to the day Bartó had made his desperate demand for money. His principal violinist's anguish had been quite genuine. The Kapellmeister would lay his life on that. Was it on behalf of Marlene? Or for some other reason? He seemed to have no consideration for the family he had left behind in Salzburg.

He gazed sightlessly out the window. "I am quite sure it was not his mistress who compelled his sudden departure, Johann."

He turned to face his brother. "Bartó's need for money, his extreme agitation, and his theft of the music must all be related in some manner. Taken together, they must have some significance that explains his sudden departure."

"Perhaps," Johann conceded. "But what? No other explanation fits the facts so conveniently."

"Then we shall have to find one that does."

Haydn's eyes meandered away from his brother's earnest, somewhat anxious regard. They could ill-afford to take on any additional tasks, he knew. But one of his men was gone. And no one appeared to care. Were it not for the thefts, not to mention the Empress's impending visit, he himself would have been tempted to let the matter go.

Worse still, Bartó's disappearance might cost them the imperial visit. The thought made him shudder. Their duty, under the circumstances, was all the greater. His gaze alighted on the writing case sitting on the black lacquer table before him.

"That does belong to Bartó," Johann supplied before Haydn could ask the question. "Rosalie recalls seeing it in his room. He was loath to let it out of his sight, apparently, and took exception to the maids touching it."

Haydn approached the table, and bent over the case. "Its contents might bear examination," he said, raising his head. "I am inclined to believe Bartó is still in the vicinity. He may not have wanted to keep his old violin. But if he guarded that writing case so jealously, he would be averse to letting it go."

He sat down, picked up the cedar wood case, and peered closely at it. Brass hinges attached the lid, an eight by five inch rectangle, to the case. The case itself was no more than six inches deep. The swirls on the sides and the bird in mid-flight on the lid had been inlaid with lapis lazuli. A tiny brass latch attached to the lid hooked on to the fastener on the front edge.

"It is unlocked!" he said, not expecting the latch to yield so easily to his efforts. A stack of sheets covered in a sloping hand lay neatly folded within. He turned some of them over and flicked his eye down each page. "Letters. But they are addressed to no one." He handed the papers to Johann, who was now sitting opposite him.

"They *are* all signed, though." Johann held one of the pages up to his eyes. "Lipót György. It is a Hungarian name. A friend of Bartó's, no doubt."

Haydn, already perusing the pages in his hand, felt his stomach churn. "The insurrection, Johann. It is more than just idle talk." The nut-brown color of his cheeks faded to a dull grey.

"Something is being planned." He waved the sheets of paper in his agitation. "Some effort to restore the lost son of Ferenc Rákóczi, whoever he may be, to the throne of Transylvania.

"*Royal Hungary, Transylvania, and the Turkish holdings in between must be re-united into one strong Hungary.*"

"What can they be planning?" Johann leaned forward. "Sándor says the Hungarians have no money, and rely on support from the Turks, the French, even Austria to fulfill their dream of independence."

"The letters make no mention of anything specific. But—" Haydn peered closer at the page, his eye caught by a single phrase.

"*Hungary needs you, István!* Who is István?"

"It would appear to be Bartó himself." Johann's voice sounded flat. He leaned across the table, and turned the pages in his hand toward Haydn. "See here"—he pointed to a sentence on the topmost sheet—"*Recall how your parents suffered under the crippling burden of Habsburg taxes.*

"That is clearly a reference to Bartó. He holds the nobility responsible for the suffering his parents endured. And this—*Can a silly barmaid be closer to your heart than your country? —*must refer to—"

"Marlene." Haydn sat back in his armchair. A welter of thoughts eddied around in his mind. How long had Michael known Bartó? Had Bartó obtained his position in Salzburg under a false name?

"If there is no such person as Bartó Daboczi, his marriage to Frau Daboczi may not even be binding," he murmured.

Johann, studying the letters as Haydn spoke, now peered anxiously up at his brother. "Do you suppose Bartó has succumbed to the conspirators' demands? It would explain why he stole the music. He could sell it, and so obtain the funds his treacherous band of friends are in such desperate need of."

"It would also explain why he continues to lurk in the vicinity." Haydn felt the silken threads of the embroidered design on his armrests cutting into his palms.

Johann stared at him incomprehensibly. "The Empress?" he ventured at last, his tone horrified. "But surely..." he faltered when Haydn nodded.

Johann's gaze dropped to the letters he held, and lingered on the closely-written pages. When he looked up, it was to say with some decision: "I will visit Herr Weisenstein in Weiner Neustadt tomorrow. There may be more news to be had of this affair there."

Haydn pushed himself forward. "We shall have to do more than that if a crisis is to be averted. If any harm should befall Her Majesty during her stay here, the political consequences to the Prince do not bear thinking about." His fingers clenched tightly around his armrests at the thought.

"The Police Commissioner..." Johann began.

Haydn over-ruled the suggestion with an emphatic shake of his head. "It will only confirm his suspicions, and result in the imperial visit being cancelled. That is not a step I can take without consulting His Serene Highness. His hopes of securing his influence at the Archduke Joseph's imperial court ride upon Her Majesty's visit.

"No, Bartó must be found before that."

"That may not prove to be such a difficult task, after all, brother." Johann's smile was confident. " It occurred to me that Marlene may know something of her lover's whereabouts. And I do know where she is to be found."

"Have you, at least, informed Marlene that the father of her child is a married man?" Maria Anna seemed to have no recollection of her earlier objection to Haydn *pestering* Bartó's mistress with his questions. She pushed a plate of crusty bread and cheese across the kitchen table to him. "The news will take away from the sting of his abandoning her."

"How could I have when I have only just learned her name and her whereabouts?" Haydn demanded. It had been a trying day, and Maria Anna's question galled him no end.

"Brother Joseph intends to visit her on the morrow, sister-in-law," Johann explained. "It is a drive of six miles or more. By the time we learnt where she could be found, it was much too late to set out."

Maria Anna sniffed. "I could have told you where she was if you had only asked me." She deftly sliced her loaf of bread.

"And so I did, last night!" Haydn reminded her. "But you refused to even divulge her name."

Maria Anna sniffed again. "It is as I have said before, husband. You never see beyond your nose until it is too late." She rose from her chair and went toward the stove, busying herself with the coffee pot.

"Gerhard, I suppose, is quite pleased your violinist is gone," she remarked when she returned to the table.

"He seems to have exhibited no signs of concern at the news. No one has, of course. But why should *he* be more pleased than anybody else?" Johann's eyes, like Haydn's were riveted on Maria Anna's features.

She sat back, a smug smile on her lips. "Well," she said at last," I suppose I ought to tell you if only to save you the trouble of spending an entire day"—she rolled her eyes—"making enquiries.

"It is plain for all to see that Gerhard is in love with Marlene. He was quite put out when she chose that violinist over him. Then, when your violinist almost struck her when she told him she was with child, Gerhard hoped she would come back to her senses, and return to him."

"Gerhard was willing to take her back even though she was carrying another man's child?" Haydn could scarcely believe his ears.

Maria Anna pursed her lips. "When you are in love with a woman, husband, it matters not whom she has been with. Although I cannot tell whether that is something *you* would know much about."

The words were like a slap in Haydn's face. He turned his attention to his food. He had never been in love with Maria Anna, it was true. But when he had given into the Keller family's insistence that he marry their older daughter instead of the younger, who was already promised to the Lord, he had every intention of being a good husband. He would have been no more forgiving of Therese had she betrayed him the way Maria Anna had.

"Bartó struck Marlene?" Johann's voice broke the uneasy silence that had fallen over the kitchen table at 82 Klostergasse.

"That was his intent, but Gerhard prevented the blow from falling on her." Maria Anna rose to the diversion, but continued to glare at her husband. "To do your violinist credit, he did regret the action almost immediately. Although by that time, he'd been thrown out of the tavern, forbidden ever to return, while Gerhard proceeded to whisk Marlene away."

She rose from the table and went toward the coffee pot standing near the stove. She took off the lid, and scrutinized the contents. Apparently satisfied with what she saw, she brought the pot back to the table.

"It couldn't have been any more difficult for your violinist to discover where Marlene was than it was for you. Gerhard was more than a little vexed when it came out Marlene had accepted the man's offer of marriage."

Maria Anna returned to the cabinet above the stove to bring out cups and dessert plates. "He must be hoping she'll accept his offer of marriage now."

CHAPTER FIFTEEN

Marlene could be found in the village of Mörbisch am See in the care of Gerhard's mother, Frau Heindl. The next morning, after seeing Johann off to Wiener Neustadt, Haydn determined to travel down to the widowed midwife's farmhouse. He started out earlier than usual for the castle, wanting to leave instructions for the orchestra before he set out for the little village, about six miles distant from Eisenstadt on the reed-overgrown banks of Lake Neusiedl.

He was almost at the West Wing when the sound of voices raised in argument reached his ears. He recognized the icy tones of the Estates Director's voice. The other, a stentorian voice, so overbearing as to be almost strident, could not possibly belong to...

He climbed up the steps with growing trepidation. A short, stoutly built, pompous individual stood with his hands on his hips glaring up at Herr Rahier.

Michael! God in Heaven, he had not expected to encounter his middle brother so soon.

"Left! What do you mean, he has left?" Michael was demanding of the Estates Director.

For a brief moment, Haydn was tempted to turn around and leave, but the Estates Director caught his gaze, pinning him in place like the butterflies he collected. A dangerous glint appeared in Herr Rahier's eyes.

"I will let the Kapellmeister explain this unfortunate matter to you, Herr Haydn. He is right behind you," he said with a bow. There was a faint smile on his lips as he turned on his heels to leave.

"What is the meaning of this Joseph?" Michael whirled around to face the Kapellmeister. "How long has Bartó been missing? Why was I not informed of this occurrence? I entrust a good musician to your care, and what must you do, but lose him!"

Haydn sighed. His middle brother, he knew, would not take kindly to the news that his protégé's abilities extended beyond music to theft and treason.

He sighed again. "Bartó left his position of his own volition, Michael. He does appear to be still in town. As it happens, I was just about to visit his mistress. She may—"

"His mistress!" Michael expostulated. "What was Bartó doing cavorting around with another woman? And what were you thinking, Joseph, to permit a married man to behave in so reprehensible a fashion?"

Vaguely aware that the palace maids were gathered around them listening to their interchange with rapt attention, Haydn bit down the retort that had sprung to his lips.

"Master Bartó was married?" Rosalie blurted out the question while Haydn fought down his ire. She looked at the other maids for support. "But he had no wedding ring!"

"Nonsense, child!" Michael exclaimed, but his eyes had narrowed, and he directed an accusing stare at Haydn.

"It's true," Greta insisted, coming to her friend's support. "I am sure I would have noticed a wedding ring. The only ring Master Bartó wore was a large, ugly one set with a ruby that he flashed at everyone."

"Yes, yes! The ring Count Nádasdy gave him, no doubt. But he had a wedding ring as well. What was he doing without it, Joseph? Good kapellmeisters—"

"Are not responsible for their men's souls!" Haydn snapped, goaded beyond measure at Michael's words. He gestured toward the staircase. "We have recovered some of his things. Come up to the Music Room, and I will tell you what Johann and I have learned. And then"—he glanced at his timepiece—"we must be on our way if we are to find the man."

He was heartily regretting having sent Johann to Wiener Neustadt.

<center>~~~</center>

Johann was at that moment leaning groggily out of the carriage window. He took a deep breath of the chill morning air. It revived his somnolent senses. The early hour at which he had set out coupled with the steady clip-clop of the horses' hooves and the dull rumble of the carriage wheels rolling westward had put him into an uneasy slumber from which he had just awoken.

He turned his head from one side to the other, trying to determine his surroundings. The sky was a brilliant azure free of snow-clouds. The roads were in good repair. They must have crossed the River Leitha into Austria. He turned up the collar of his gray, wool coat and sat back in his seat, his mind going over the letters brother Joseph had recovered the previous afternoon.

Could the Empress really be in danger? She would be well-protected during her stay. Was it possible for anyone to approach close enough to harm her person? Her Majesty's affable nature, it was true, made her wont to shake off her guards to greet peasant and nobility alike in person. But whoever did the dastardly deed would be immediately apprehended. And how would that bring the dissidents any closer to their goal?

He stared stone-faced out the window. They were approaching Wiener Neustadt. He could only hope brother Joseph was mistaken in his speculations. Would to God, the bookseller's information would prove them all wrong, and set their minds at rest. Perhaps, there was a far simpler explanation for Bartó's departure.

The stone walls of the old Babenberg fortress that now housed the Empress's military academy came into view. Then the carriage rolled past the Cistercian Abbey and the beautiful Neukloster Church, and turned left to enter the town square. But instead of driving through the square, it lurched to an abrupt halt, almost throwing Johann out of his seat. His fingers still gripping the edge of the window, Johann pulled himself upright and leaned out of the window. Whatever was going on? All of Wiener Neustadt seemed to be crowded into the town square. Men carrying small children on their shoulders and women with their shopping baskets jostled shoulders around the town hall, shouting and shaking their fists.

Amidst the hubbub, Johann could hear calls for the Bürgermeister to come out of the town hall. He strained his ears. He could barely make out a word. Was that...

Rákóczi?

"Ferenc Rákóczi!"

There was that name again. Johann shivered, feeling a sudden chill as he recognized the name from the letters in Bartó's writing case.

"I will walk to Herr Weisenstein's bookstore," he announced to the coachman, as he climbed down from the carriage.

"Is that wise, Master Johann?" The coachman hopped down from his post, and looked worriedly at the crowd before them. "We can drive around to Marktplatz."

Johann shook his head, prepared to brave the crowd if there was news of any value to be had from it. "I will be quite all right, Hans. Here take this," he added, dropping a handful of florins into the coachman's hands. "Get yourself some food and the horses some hay, and then meet me in the market square at the bookstore."

Johann pushed his way slowly into the crowd, straining to hear the snatches of conversation that reached his ear.

A large woman backed into him. "Do watch where you're going!" she cried angrily.

The man next to her looked suspiciously up and down Johann's form, taking in his well-cut attire. "An official from Vienna? Well, it's about time!"

Johann shook his head, thankful he had had the good sense to wear an ordinary suit instead of the livery he usually wore. He would have looked even more like an official in his court uniform.

"No, just a musician from a little town on the Leitha," he replied. "What is going on over here?" he began to ask, but the two had already turned away.

"How can Rákóczi have escaped?" the woman asked her neighbor. "I thought he had died in the tower."

The man next to her shook his head. "He escaped, and joined forces with the Turks."

"The Turks!" the woman gasped. "Why then, there is no hope for us. Those heathens were almost at Vienna's door once. They will conquer us in no time."

Johann walked on. The rumors of impending war could not be quite as faint as Count Nádasdy had supposed if the townspeople of Wiener Neustadt were bandying the word about. But the Count had referred to the French as the source of the threat? Herr Weisenstein, he hoped, would be able to throw some light on this affair.

"It is almost as though we speak of two different men." Michael sat stiffly in the carriage, and stared out the window at the wintry landscape beyond. "I could well believe it, if I had not seen Bartó's violin."

"The violin is his, then?" Haydn ventured, unsure of Michael's response. His brother had been more than a little peeved at Haydn's speculations regarding his missing violinist. "You are quite certain of it?"

"Of course, I am, Joseph," Michael snapped. "It is somewhat the worse for wear, and I have no explanation for its being left exposed to the elements. But I have known the man long enough to recognize the instrument he plays."

They sat in silence watching the countryside drift by. Vineyards with their bare brown vines twisted around heavy trellises. Wine taverns with their cheerful branches and red ribbons. Farmhouses with thatched roofs.

"What made him leave the Archbishop's employ?" Haydn broke the silence a few minutes later. "Did you not wonder at his desire to leave? He was doing well enough in Salzburg."

Michael shifted around in his seat and stared at his brother, his features gathered into a disgruntled expression.

"It was Count Nádasdy who put the idea into his head. And I encouraged it. Bartó has a talent for composition. And I happened to agree with the Count that it might be best nurtured under your tutelage."

"Ach so!" Haydn was rendered speechless, having no conception Michael thought quite so highly of his musical abilities.

"Surely, you must have noticed Bartó's aptitude in that direction, Joseph?"

"He did seem to have a great many opinions on the subject," Haydn replied in as neutral a tone as he could manage. Bartó, to his mind, had a greater flair for argument than anything else.

He watched Michael fidgeting with his leather gloves, pulling them on and off his hands repeatedly. His face when he eventually turned toward Haydn was troubled.

"What am I to tell Frau Daboczi, Joseph? I would not have expected Bartó to desert his family in this fashion. He has always been an exemplary husband and father. But I suppose even the best of men may waver from their devotion when set upon by a strumpet such as this Marlene appears to be."

"I do not think—" Haydn began, but was interrupted before he could continue.

130

"But it is inconceivable that he should turn against his country in this treacherous manner, Joseph. Why, the man had no more affiliation to Hungary than you or I. He was born and bred in Salzburg."

"So, he claimed to you. All you know of the man is what he himself has told you."

"And, why would he lie about so trivial a matter?" Michael rejoined. He shook his head emphatically. "No, I am convinced that on that count, at least, you and Johann have allowed yourselves to concoct the wildest conjectures. Besides, the letters were addressed to some individual going by the name of István."

"The references to Bartó were quite clear. The little we know of his family, his childhood in Hungary, the poverty his family endured, the titles he bought for them, are from his own babblings. Revealed for the most part when he was in his cups."

"The man has deceived you in every way, Michael, even to the point of giving you a false name!"

"I am not quite so easily deceived, Joseph," Michael declared, crossing his arms huffily. "Mark my words, if what you say is true," he said a moment later, "if Bartó has in fact been led astray, it is the doing of that trollop of a barmaid he has been consorting with."

He leaned back in his seat, a determined expression settling itself upon his features. "I shall have much to say to the hussy when we meet."

Herr Weisenstein, bookseller and printer, rummaged through the contents of a rather untidy drawer. He was a portly gentlemen with thinning gray hair, a gray beard, and round glasses that sat on his nose.

"This Rákóczi the townspeople are so agitated about is long dead, Master Johann."

The bookseller pushed his glasses up with one hand while he sifted through old receipts and stacks of paper with the other. "There was a manuscript here," he muttered. He paused in his task to look up at Johann. "I should be most grateful for your brother's opinion of it, Master Johann. It is a selection of the most unusual pieces. If I could but find it," he muttered again, turning over the contents of the drawer.

"But the townspeople said Rákóczi was imprisoned in the fortress, and had escaped?" Johann persisted, watching the bookseller comb

131

through the drawer in fascination. Although if the man were truly dead, maybe there was nothing to these rumors of an insurrection.

"He was imprisoned Master Johann," Herr Weisenstein replied without pausing in his task. "Some sixty years ago for attempting to organize a revolt against Her Majesty's grandfather, the Emperor Leopold. It was nipped in the bud when his letters seeking the French King's support were intercepted.

"And he did escape, only to organize yet another unsuccessful attempt. When that failed, he fled to Paris and then sought refuge with the Turks. He is said to have died there, still claiming his right hand man, who had negotiated a peace treaty with the Emperor, had betrayed him. But even if he were alive, he would be an old man now."

"Ach so," Johann murmured. He stared vacantly at the bookseller, who was still combing through his drawer. How could a man long dead stir up so much strife? What manner of man was he? Bartó's letters had been quite vague on the subject of Rákóczi's identity. Only that he had a son.

A heavy, sinking sensation erupted in the pit of his stomach at the thought. How had he forgotten that?

"This Rákóczi," he said aloud. "Who was he?"

"A nobleman elected Prince of Transylvania, Master Johann. Had he been successful in his attempts, he would most likely have sat on the throne of a re-united Hungary."

"The Hungarian throne. So, that is what his son is after," Johann said to himself. "And he is of noble blood?" The knot in his stomach hardened. What hope did two musicians such as his brother and himself have of averting the designs of a man such as this?

He must have spoken aloud, for the bookseller looked up sharply. "You have heard talk of a son, too, then, Master Johann? I fear, if there is any danger, it will come from that quarter."

"What have you heard?" Johann leaned forward over the counter-top separating him from Herr Weisenstein. Any information might prove useful in thwarting the man.

The bookseller pushed his glasses up. "There is, apparently, a son other than the two who were raised in Austria. He claims to be the firstborn child and heir of Ferenc Rákóczi, and vows to take up and finish his father's cause." He began emptying the contents of the drawer in his search of the elusive manuscript. "And he may well succeed, if he is anything like his father."

"*Anything like his father*? What do you mean?"

"If, like his father, he can unite the nobility with the peasants, Master Johann," the bookseller explained. "It was only the protracted nature of the struggle that wore Ferenc Rákóczi's men down. And now even more of the Hungarian nobility are disgruntled..."

"The issue of taxes. Yes I know."Johann nodded. If the nobility had been won over there was very little hope. "The Prince himself is not too happy about it"—An unhappy thought stirred in his brain. He pushed it resolutely away—"and he is steadfastly loyal to Her Majesty."

The bookseller shook his head gravely. "The Empress herself still worn out from grief and tired of warfare..." He sighed. "The poor Bürgermeister has no information to allay the concerns of the townspeople. The Police Commissioner keeps him in the dark..."

"It is just the same in Eisenstadt," Johann said with a faint smile, recalling Herr Groer's frequent complaints on the subject.

"And whenever any of the nobility travel through the town, they assure us there is nothing to worry about. But there are more officers than usual at the military academy. *More* than you would need to train a college-full of young men. So, something must be afoot."

Johann lifted his chin from where it was resting on the back of his palm. "But where did you get your information from, Herr Weisenstein?" Was the bookseller merely repeating gossip and rumors? Would to God that were the case.

But the bookseller said nothing. He was closely scrutinizing a sheaf of papers he had retrieved from the bottom of his drawer. "Ah, this is it!"

What in the name of God was that? Johann drew back as the bookseller thrust the manuscript at him.

"I mean to venture into music publishing, Master Johann," he said. "If Herr Haydn considers the work to have any merit at all, I shall, with its publication, be able to launch myself as Austria's first music publisher."

"Yes, yes, of course." Johann was too preoccupied to cast more than a fleeting glance at the manuscript. "But have you any more information about this troublemaker?" He kept his tone light, forcing himself to swallow his impatience.

The bookseller shook his head. "The little I know, Master Johann, is from an itinerant printer who was traveling through town from Pressburg to Vienna. He claimed to have seen this son of Rákóczi—a man of some thirty years, tall, with a mane of chestnut hair and a piercing gaze. He said he had printed some pamphlets for the man. They had a picture of a raven tearing out the throat of a double-headed imperial eagle—"

"The emblem of the House of Austria!" Johann leaned forward. Brother Joseph had been right after all. The Empress *was* in danger. "What did the pamphlets say?"

"The words were rather cryptic, Master Johann. *Let the Eagle beware the mark of the Raven!*"

CHAPTER SIXTEEN

The carriage conveying the Kapellmeister and his brother to Mörbisch am See pulled up at last outside the Widow Heindl's farmhouse. Haydn, leaning out of the window, saw a sandstone structure with a thick covering of snow on its roof shingles. The solid wooden door opened a crack just as the carriage rolled to a stop, and a pair of sharp, blue eyes peered out.

The door opened a little wider, revealing a plump, rosy-cheeked face in the doorway. The midwife, herself, no doubt, Haydn concluded, noticing the gray curls straggling loose from under her red scarf.

"You are musicians?" Frau Heindl's gaze traveled curiously over the gold embroidery on Haydn's court uniform. "From the castle"—her eyes came to rest on Haydn's face—"Bartó—"

"Yes, where *is* Bartó?" Michael demanded, regarding the widow with an expression of extreme distrust on his face.

"He is *not* here. Why should he be?" A flicker of annoyance crossed Frau Heindl's pleasant features as Michael stood on tiptoe, craning his neck to see over her shoulder into her courtyard.

Michael had opened his mouth to respond, but closed it when Haydn directed a quelling glance at him.

The widow turned toward Haydn with a frown. "It is true, then, Bartó has left his post?"

Haydn nodded. "It is true he has left, but—"

"Ach, poor child! I had hoped it was Gerhard's envy speaking when he said Bartó was gone. Marlene, poor child, refuses to believe he has abandoned her. But, it has been three days since he has come by to see her..."

Michael had turned a deep shade of purple at the mention of Marlene. He would have spoken but for the urgent glare Haydn directed at him. His middle brother had all the tact of a bugle in the hunting field; his abrasive manner as offensive as the piercing call of that brass instrument sounding next to an unsuspecting eardrum.

"That is when Bartó left—about three days ago." Haydn pronounced his words with care, still glaring at Michael, who was sputtering indignantly. He turned toward the widow "When was the last time you saw him?"

Frau Heindl squinted as she considered the question. "It must have been a day or two before the snowstorm," she said finally. "We had not expected him on the day of the storm, of course. Still, when there was a knock on the door, poor Marlene could hardly contain herself." The widow shook her head at the memory. "But it was only a stranger seeking shelter from the storm.

"Bartó left three days ago, you say?" If the widow was aware of Michael glowering at her, she gave no sign of it.

"He has deserted his position, but he appears to be in the vicinity, still." Haydn allowed his eyes to drift toward a window to the left of the door. The bedchamber was usually in the front in farmhouses such as this one. "We were hoping Marlene might have some knowledge of his whereabouts."

The widow had been listening closely to Haydn. "That she might," she said, stepping aside from the door. "She is adamant Bartó has gone into hiding—" She broke off as Michael thrust his portly frame impatiently into the courtyard.

"Where is the young wench, then? In here?" He turned toward the first door.

"Wait!" Frau Heindl rushed toward the door, reaching out with her hand to grasp at Michael's sleeve. But he had already pushed the door open, and strode in dragging the widow, still clutching at his sleeve, behind him.

Haydn closed his eyes, bringing his hand up to his forehead in despair. He should never have suggested that his brother accompany him. He entered the room to find Michael glowering down at a pretty, fair-haired woman reclining against a quantity of soft pillows in her bed.

"So, you are Marlene?" Michael's voice rang out accusingly.

Marlene turned a startled face toward her visitors. "Yes, but who—"

"Never you mind, who I am! You should be ashamed of yourself, you little minx, seducing a married man. What were you thinking?"

"*God in Heaven*, Michael! The poor girl is with child," Haydn remonstrated.

The widow's cry drowned out his voice. "You're the one who should be ashamed of yourself, my good sir. Barging into my house uninvited!" She folded her arms, her patience clearly having run out. "Besides, what married man has Marlene seduced? Bartó has no wife." She turned toward Haydn.

Haydn sighed. What an unholy mess his violinist's thoughtless actions had caused! "Bartó *is* married. He has a wife and children in Salzburg." He sighed again, suddenly feeling very weary. "His colleagues and I could not have been more surprised to hear the news. We were all under the impression he was unmarried."

"And he is," Marlene declared, tossing her hair back defiantly. "But only for a little while longer. See here"—she thrust out her hand, showing them a slim, plain, band of silver on her finger—"We shall be married as soon as Frau Heindl considers me strong enough to be up and about." She smiled proudly, resting her right hand on her gently protruding belly.

Michael gave a contemptuous harrumph. "Not if I have anything to say about it! Bartó already has a wife."

"And that is not the worst of it." Haydn could barely look at Marlene, poor deluded child. His face as he turned toward Frau Heindl was grave. "Bartó has deceived us all, his wife, even my brother here. Bartó is not even the man's real name. His name is—"

"István!" Marlene cried out. "He never kept me in the dark as to his true identity."

The Kapellmeister's attention snapped back to her. What else did she know? "Has he also told you of his affiliation with the dissidents?" His expression was stern. "Where is he, Marlene? If you have any information about his whereabouts, you must tell us."

"He would not have had to go into hiding if you had only listened to his pleas for help. He—ohh..." To Haydn's dismay Marlene's face contorted in pain as she clutched at her belly.

He stared down at her open-mouthed, feet rooted to the spot until a rough hand propelled him toward the door.

"You had best be going, gentlemen." The widow hustled her guests out of the room.

"You must send word to the castle if Bartó should come here, Frau Heindl," Haydn insisted as the widow pushed them out the farmhouse door.

Let the Eagle beware the mark of the Raven!

The words from the pamphlet Herr Weisenstein had described rang in Johann's mind. The double-headed eagle represented the House of Austria. There could be no doubt about that. It would give brother Joseph no joy to learn that he had been right to fear for the Empress. But what did the raven signify?

Johann turned his head to look out the carriage window, his fingers tightening their hold on the window's edge. The carriage had rolled out of the market square, and was now turning into the town square. The crowd had largely dispersed, he noted as he listened idly to the clatter of the horses' hooves on the cobblestones.

A fleeting impression stirred in his memory, but it was gone before he could catch it. With a sigh, he turned his attention to the music the bookseller had pressed upon him. Were it not for their current troubles, Johann would have looked forward to the prospect of sharing his acquisitions with the Kapellmeister.

The bookseller had outdone himself this time, managing to procure the latest works of some of the greatest composers of the Italian style of comic opera. Why, Galuppi's *Witty Waitress* had premiered in Milan in October. And it was just last month that Jomelli's *Marriage Contest* and Gassman's *Ridiculous Traveler* had been performed! His Serene Highness would be quite delighted with these additions to his music library.

The thought of the Prince brought back to his mind the disquieting confirmation of his brother's suspicions. The letters the mysterious Lipót György had written to Bartó had made it seem as though the dissidents were a band of discontent peasants. But the danger was worse than they had imagined, if Ferenc Rákóczi and his son, rather than being mere peasants with designs on the Hungarian throne, were of the nobility.

Johann shifted uneasily in his seat. The conspiracy must go fairly deep if the nobility were involved. If anything should happen to the Empress while she was in Eisenstadt...

The Prince's own loyalty would come into question!

Johann sat upright, his back rigid with shock. Suspicion, would most likely, fall on the Prince for—he shook his head, not wanting to voice the thought—*for orchestrating the attempt?*

He had picked up a mass penned by Leopold Mozart's boy. But now he rifled through the pages so quickly, he barely read a note other than the title: *Kyrie in F Major*. His eyes glazed over as he stared down at the title. The Prince himself was not without detractors, his fealty to the Empress being a sore subject with those who considered Austria to be the source of all of Hungary's woes. But the double-headed eagle...

Johann shook his head. There was little point to these speculations. He could only hope brother Joseph, having met Bartó's mistress, was closer to finding him. He himself might be better occupied in trying to lighten his brother's load as best he could.

He set aside little Wolferl's *Kyrie*, and picked up the manuscript Herr Weisenstein had entrusted to him. There was little likelihood of brother Joseph having the time to look over this manuscript as well as the string quartets Count Nádasdy had left behind.

Silence prevailed within the carriage on the journey back to Eisenstadt, and it was some time before either the Kapellmeister or his brother spoke. Michael stared at the landscape rolling past, apparently lost in thought; while Haydn kept his gaze on the carriage floor, much too aggravated by his brother's behavior to say a word.

Were it not for Michael's unfeeling manner toward Marlene, he thought irritably, they might have learned something of Bartó's whereabouts. Haydn could only hope Johann was faring better with his enquiries in Wiener Neustadt.

"What pleas for help?" Michael broke the silence at last. He twisted around to look at Haydn. "What did the lass mean by that? I cannot recall your making mention of any such thing, Joseph."

"We might have had an opportunity to discover more had you not grated on the poor girl's nerves, agitating her so," Haydn retorted, still put out at his brother. "Could you not see how frail she is? Her condition seems to have taken a toll on her health."

"She would not be in that condition had she acted with greater restraint!" Michael crossed his arms belligerently, indignation making his chest heave. "And, what of Frau Daboczi's condition? She is heavy with child herself, and has several more to support, besides."

"Frau Daboczi is with child?" Haydn repeated, when Michael paused to catch his breath. Michael nodded. He sat back, appearing to relent at last.

"I suppose Bartó has treated both women shamefully."

"He has." Haydn agreed, resting his chin on his hand, although he suspected it was his violinist's wife, not his mistress, who would be forced to bear the brunt of his philandering. "Still, his affection for Marlene seems quite genuine. I do not expect he will be able to stay away from her for too long," he mused.

He turned toward his brother. "I shall have the Bürgermeister post some of his men outside Frau Heindl's farmhouse. He cannot but agree to do so. Bartó's letters, recovered from the woods, contain a clear warning of some awful occurrence. It would be foolish to ignore the threat."

Johann's eyes roved curiously over the manuscript Herr Weisenstein hoped to publish. Its pages were dog-eared and covered in stains. The grey impression of a large hand was imprinted on the first page. A number of smaller hand prints appeared throughout the work as though several small, grubby hands had pawed through the entire manuscript.

The pages in the middle felt damp and limp. Had someone left the manuscript out in the snow, and then attempted to dry it by a small fire? The notes, in many places, had been smudged over into the adjoining staves. And what were these dark, red stains on the back? He hoped he would be able to read enough of it to make a recommendation to the bookseller.

"If this manuscript proves to have any merit, I will need to have a fresh copy made for Herr Weisenstein," Johann murmured to himself. "At least, the composer, whoever he may be, had the sense to hire a professional copyist."

He examined the writing closely. There was something familiar about it: the slight flourish to the eighth notes, the twirl of the treble clef, the somewhat ornate font used for the time signature at the beginning of each piece.

Out of force of habit, Johann began sight singing from the score. The lively tempo of the works and their melodic motifs would appeal to brother Joseph. He turned the page, and abruptly stopped singing. The music on the next page belonged to an entirely different piece! Whoever had gone through this manuscript had left the pages in disarray.

Johann set to work re-ordering the pages. He hoped none were missing. In their present predicament, they could hardly take on the task of improvising any missing sections. Although at any other time, it would have been no trouble at all, the composer's style being so remarkably similar to his brother's.

He sighed as he encountered his first section of missing music. Well, he supposed, he could fill in the missing notes himself. Here, for instance, there was only one way the melody could develop. In a neat hand, Johann began writing out the missing section. He had almost finished, when his pen came to an abrupt halt, jabbing a little tear into the paper.

But how had...?

Johann hurriedly turned over the pages, perusing each one carefully. Despite the missing pages, it was clear that the manuscript did not constitute an opus of works of a single genre. The compositions that made up these pages were much too diverse. Symphonies followed divertimentos and concertos intermingled with sonatas in a seemingly random outpouring of genius.

Would any composer, however inexperienced, parcel together such an assortment of works for a publication? A faint suspicion stirred in his brain.

He inspected the writing again. It bore a remarkable resemblance to the hand of J. Koeller, a hired copyist who, until recently, had worked at the Esterházy court. Koeller had left for Vienna only a fortnight ago. He peered closer. *God in Heaven*, it was Koeller's hand! There was no mistaking it.

His head sank back against the seat. It hardly seemed possible, yet it was. He glanced down at the sheaf of papers clutched in his fingers. No. There was no other explanation for it. Small wonder, he had been able to fill in the missing notes and phrases. The author of these works was no unknown virtuoso!

But who had delivered the manuscript to Herr Weisenstein? *If they could but discover the person's identity...* Johann thrust his head out of the carriage, the import of his discovery dawning upon him.

"Hans! Hans!" He rapped his knuckles furiously against the carriage to attract the coachman's attention. "We must turn back! Turn back at once!"

Pulling sharply on the horses' reins, Hans brought the coach to an abrupt halt. "What is the matter, Master Johann?" He was clearly alarmed at Johann's agitated tone. "What's got you so upset?"

"We have not a moment to lose, Hans! We must return to Herr Weisenstein's store." Noticing the look of concern mingled with curiosity on the coachman's features, Johann added, "It is only a small matter, but it could cause a great deal of trouble if... Oh, there is no time for explanations! Be a good fellow, and turn around."

CHAPTER SEVENTEEN

The Bürgermeister was nowhere to be found in Eisenstadt. Haydn, although disappointed, was not entirely surprised.

"I expect Herr Groer is with his men in the woods of Kleinhöflein, keeping watch for Bartó, as I had requested," he remarked to Michael after instructing the coachman to drive them to the castle. He would have preferred to walk the short distance back to the castle, but Michael, he knew, would be loath to leave the comfort of the carriage on this chilly day.

He heard Michael grunt beside him as he leant his head out the window for a whiff of the refreshingly cold air. "I cannot be persuaded Bartó has joined with the dissidents, Joseph."

The words were uttered with such quiet emphasis, Haydn wondered what knowledge his brother had to be so convinced of the fact. He turned to face Michael, noticing the deep creases that lined the corners of his mouth and his forehead.

"The lass was convinced he was in danger. It is far more likely he has fled to escape their efforts to turn him into a traitor."

Haydn was silent for a while. Marlene's words *had* struck a chord in his mind. He cast his mind back, but could recall nothing that shed light on the barmaid's strange assertion. Bartó's behavior had grown increasingly strange in the days prior to his departure. He had regarded his colleagues with suspicion, acting as though someone were dogging his heels. Yet all that was easily explained as the natural wariness of a man with treacherous intent.

He shook his head. "What little we know of his views suggests otherwise, I am afraid," he said at last. From the carriage window he saw a dark-haired boy with an impish face lounging near the drawbridge. The lad squinted at the carriage as it approached, and then began gesturing animatedly for it to stop. Haydn was about to call out to the coachman to stop, when the boy grabbed hold of the horses' reins.

"Hoy! Stop! Are you the Kapellmeister?" he demanded, ignoring the stream of invective the coachman was raining upon him.

Haydn inclined his head. "And who might you be, young man?" he gazed curiously down at the child. He could have been no more than twelve years old.

"Ludwig," the boy replied in a solemn tone. "I fetch and carry for Herr Heindl at the tavern and for his mother at the farmhouse." He fished out a note from his pocket, and handed it to Haydn. "But it was the Bürgermeister who sent me to find you. *Most urgent*, he said it was."

"Thank you, Ludwig." Haydn took the note, and dropped a few florins into the lad's palms.

He quickly perused the note, his face turning white at its contents. He sat still for a moment, and then looked down at the note again. Its contents seemed to galvanize him, for he thrust his head out the window to issue instructions to the coachman.

He turned at last to Michael, who sat watching him with ill-concealed impatience. "Bartó, it would appear, is not just a dissident. He is a murderer as well."

The Bürgermeister was waiting for them at the corner of Weinberggasse, a small alley off of St. Vitus Street. The woods lined St. Vitus Street on the right as it wound its way sharply uphill to the Kleinhöflein Parish Church. The church steeple, peeping over the snow-topped forest trees, overlooked the alley. The path up was so steep that had the Bürgermeister not hailed them, Haydn would have dismissed the carriage, and walked the rest of the way.

"Ah, there you are Herr Kapellmeister!" Herr Groer's eyes slid inquisitively beyond Haydn to Michael before returning to the Kapellmeister. He held the carriage door open for the brothers. "There is no need to go all the way up. Gerhard has taken a cart up to where the body was found. The barber-surgeon is with him."

"Found near the abbey ruins, I take it," Haydn said as he and Michael followed the Bürgermeister down the alley to Gerhard's wine tavern: a small structure of gray stone with a wreath of fig leaves on its arched wooden doors to announce the serving of newly made wine.

"Very close to it." The Bürgermeister was puffing slightly from the exertion of walking down the street. He reached out for the brass rings on the tavern door, turning over his shoulder to cast another curious glance at Michael.

"My brother from Salzburg," Haydn explained, noticing the Bürgermeister's gaze. "It was he who recommended Bartó to us."

"Ach so!" Herr Groer averted his eyes. The task of opening the solid wooden door seemed to require his utmost attention. Haydn was glad of the time it took, not at all looking forward to hearing of this matter. The Bürgermeister succeeded in opening the door at last. Ushering them into the warmth of the wine tavern, he led them to a rough wooden bench near the hearth.

"It was Gerhard, who found the body," he said as he lowered his bulk onto the bench. "He was taking wine up to the church for the christening ceremony—for your cellist's son," he added in response to Haydn's blank stare. "One of the farmers was helping him.

"They were accompanied by the farmer's boy, a frisky young lad, who suddenly darted into the woods. Gerhard gave chase, running after the boy until he stumbled upon a bank of snow-covered branches piled so loosely over a hollowed area they gave way under Gerhard's weight when he attempted to follow. It was as Gerhard was pushing aside the branches to pull himself and the boy out that they discovered the corpse."

"Yes, but what does any of this have to do with Bartó?" Michael's tone was belligerent. He had his hand on his thigh, and as he leaned forward his elbow jutted out, stabbing the air. "The body may have been found close to where his belongings were concealed, but it does not follow that he is the killer."

Michael's eyes bore into the Bürgermeister. "You must have a very low opinion of Bartó, indeed, Herr Groer, if you suspect him of the misdeed!"

Herr Groer drew back. "It was Gerhard who made that surmise," he said hastily. He turned toward Haydn. "He recognized the body, you see, despite the changes death appears to have wrought on the poor fellow. Herr Hipfl—our barber-surgeon"—he turned toward Michael—"seems to think they are natural occurrences, but that is neither here nor there," he conceded with an apologetic air when Michael uttered a tetchy grunt.

"Bartó and this fellow—a stranger to these parts, and a musician, too from what Gerhard says—got into a drunken brawl at the tavern a few months back. It got so ugly, Gerhard tossed them both out."

"How long ago was this?" Haydn was frowning. This was the first he had heard of Bartó getting into fisticuffs with anyone. Of course, given his violinist's aggressive tendencies, it was not difficult to believe.

"On the evening of the *Festlicher Almatrieb*. That is one of the reasons Gerhard remembers the incident so well. The cattle had been brought down and the festivities were almost over when they entered the tavern."

Haydn nodded, remembering. "It was in September that Bartó arrived at the castle." A few more details returned to his mind. "Now that I think about it, it *was* the day after the cattle drive."

The thought of the dead stranger made him feel sick. "It must have been a violent fight to have ended so badly for the poor man."

How had he been so oblivious to his violinist's vile deeds? He had hired a man he knew virtually nothing of. A heavy weight seemed to bear down on his shoulders. He could hardly deny his own culpability in this awful affair.

"An accident, of course! Still, it must have weighed heavily on his conscience, poor man." Michael's voice sounded gruff. "What was he even doing drinking? He has never been able to handle his liquor well."

"It was not Bartó who was drunk, gentlemen." The Bürgermeister seemed taken aback by the stunned look on Michael's face. "It was the other man who was unused to drinking. Bartó, despite all he had drunk, was in control of his faculties."

"Max Rosen?" Johann repeated, not sure he had heard the name right. He had returned to the bookstore in Wiener Neustadt some minutes before, opening the door with such force that the loud jangling of the bell above it had startled the portly bookseller into dropping the papers in his hands. But he had not expected to hear the name the bookseller had uttered in connection with the manuscript he had been given.

Herr Weisenstein nodded, still looking confused. His glasses slid down the bridge of his nose, sitting askew. But he ignored them, peering at Johann, his blue eyes shrouded in perplexity.

"The wine merchant? It was he who brought you the manuscript?" Johann could not prevent his voice rising, the news was so incredulous. "But where could he have come by it?"

Max Rosen, merchant and trader, dealt solely in fine wines. Johann had seen him a time or two at the castle. But the wine merchant only ever came on business, the Prince having granted him an exclusive license to market the Esterházy estate's wines in the wider world beyond Eisenstadt.

"It was brought to him, I believe," Herr Weisenstein replied, pushing his glasses up.

Johann was aware of the bemused manner in which the bookseller was staring at him. Herr Weisenstein had politely refrained from asking for an explanation when Johann had brusquely entered the bookstore and begun firing his questions at him. The bookseller's curiosity was clearly aroused, but Johann did not feel up to the task of providing a coherent explanation. His mind was much too clouded with the information he had been given.

"But what could he possibly hope to gain by its publication?" Johann blurted out the question without any forethought. Max Rosen was one of the wealthiest of the few hundred families residing on the upper and lower lanes of Judengasse in Unterberg, the Jewish Quarter in Eisenstadt.

Besides, the Jews of Eisenstadt had fared well under the Prince, and Max Rosen, in particular had benefited greatly from His Serene Highness. How could the wine merchant even consider engaging in an undertaking that, whatever little profit it might earn him, was likely to cause his benefactor great distress?

"He does not hope to gain anything by it, Master Johann." There was a mild note of reproof in the bookseller's voice. "It was to help a friend that Max brought me the manuscript."

"A friend! What friend?" Johann was liking the sound of this even less. Who had befriended the merchant and prevailed upon him to act as he had done?

The bookseller shrugged. "An acquaintance of long standing, is what he said. Someone in urgent need of money, I imagine. Max is a man of great influence. The composer of these works"—he tapped the manuscript that lay on the counter—"must, no doubt, be eager to sell his works.

Although..." Herr Weisenstein's voice trailed off. A pensive furrow creased his brow as he gazed into the distance.

"I wonder why the man didn't think to approach Herr Haydn?" The bookseller turned toward Johann. "And, for that matter, why didn't Max approach your brother?"

"Yes, it is a question greatly to be wondered at?" The thought had not occurred to Johann until Herr Weisenstein had voiced it, and now he was beginning to regret the blundering way in which he had asked his questions. Was it too much to hope that the bookseller had not realized his suspicions had been aroused by the wine merchant's behavior? He had, at least, succeeded in eliciting this much from Herr Weisenstein. Could he draw him out any further?

But the bookseller merely gave an apologetic shrug. "I did not question him too closely, Master Johann. Why should I? Max is a friend of mine and a good man. When he asked for my help..." He shrugged again.

"What can be taking them so long?" The Bürgermeister shifted uneasily on his bench as he broke the uncomfortable silence that had fallen upon them. He twisted around to look out the tavern window.

Haydn, following his gaze, caught a glimpse of a familiar blue silk skirt and black apron outside the tavern. Was that...

"*Maria Anna?*" he uttered as the tavern door opened to reveal his wife. Why in the name of heaven was she here?

Maria Anna stood in the doorway, adjusting the black shawl over her shoulders and shifting her basket from her left arm to her right. Her eyes, travelling over the nearly empty tavern, narrowed as they fell on Haydn sitting across from the Bürgermeister near the hearth.

"What can you be thinking of, husband, to be lounging around here all day?" she cried, rushing toward the hearth. Her basket came perilously close to hitting the Bürgermeister as she gestured wildly around the tavern. "The singers have been at the church well over an hour waiting for you to conduct the mass. But instead of being at the church, here you are guzzling down Gerhard's wine!"

"Mass?" Haydn repeated. Whatever was Maria Anna on about? What mass had he forgotten to conduct? He was about to say as much when there was a fortunate interjection.

"Ach, the Christening service!" the Bürgermeister murmured with a shake of his head.

"Yes, but that is not until—the day after tomorrow..." Haydn's voice trailed off as he recalled insisting some weeks ago on a rehearsal at the Parish Church a day or two before the Christening took place.

"But you knew I was going to Mörbisch am See this morning, Maria Anna. And it was you who insisted I go see Marlene. We have just returned." He indicated Michael with a slight wave of his hand.

"Brother-in-law." Maria Anna acknowledged Michael with a nod before turning toward Haydn. "I did not mean for you to take all day over the one thing, husband," she said huffily. She dropped down onto the wooden bench beside the Bürgermeister, grumbling: "The singers have all left now."

The Bürgermeister cleared his throat. "Ah, would it not be best for you to return home, Frau Haydn?" he suggested in a tentative tone.

"Why, Herr Groer? Why would it be best?" Maria Anna turned to stare at the Bürgermeister. She still sounded cross.

The Bürgermeister cleared his throat again, looked toward Haydn, apparently for support, before venturing again: "There has been an incident, you see—an untoward incident. It would be"—his eyes slid pleadingly toward Haydn—"most upsetting for you, I am sure, to see..."

"A corpse has been discovered in the woods, Maria Anna," Haydn said bluntly. "It would be best if you returned home as Herr Groer suggests."

The tavern door was pushed open before Maria Anna could respond. Gerhard wedged the door open with his weight as he slowly backed into the tavern carrying one end of a pallet. The barber-surgeon, his halo of gray hair rising in tufts around his face, followed him in, supporting the other end of the pallet. Breathing heavily from their exertions, they set the pallet down in the middle of the room.

Gerhard straightened up with a grunt. "Who would think a man could grow so heavy in death?"

Haydn felt sour bile welling up in his throat, nearly threatening to choke him, as his eyes followed Gerhard's finger and landed upon the darkened, bloated corpse that lay limply on the pallet. Even Maria Anna, he noticed had turned white. Her face was averted from the ghastly sight, her fingers closed tightly over a crumpled, white handkerchief.

"Look, even his hair and nails have grown," Gerhard was saying. Maria Anna uttered a brief cry at his words, and pressed her handkerchief to her mouth.

"Natural occurrences as the body turns to dust, my dear man," the barber-surgeon assured the tavern-keeper as he straightened up. "He was up there for some time, poor man," he continued, regarding the body speculatively. "Strangled from the looks of it, and left for dead."

The Bürgermeister came forward, his nose buried in his handkerchief, and turned toward Gerhard. "But you are still certain, this is—"

"Bartó!" Michael cried out in a strangulated tone. "It is him! It can be no other!" His voice rose in anguish as he turned a horrified gaze toward Haydn.

CHAPTER EIGHTEEN

"It is Bartó's doing all right!" Gerhard dragged the back of his arm wearily across his brow. "Haven't I been saying so all along, Herr Bürgermeister?" He stole a glance at Haydn as he spoke, but the Kapellmeister was gaping at his brother.

"But that"—Haydn turned toward the corpse and felt an immediate sense of revulsion rising up within him—"that is *not* Bartó. It is *not the man* I hired as my principal violinist..." His voice faltered.

Michael's face had turned a sickly shade of yellow-green, but he seemed to have recovered himself for he responded in his customary tetchy fashion. "I have known the man long enough in life, Joseph, to recognize him in death. Look"—he jabbed the air before him in the general direction of the body—"that is his wedding ring. I recognize it well."

Haydn forced himself to look down, and saw the thick gold band with a tiny ruby in the center that was clamped around the swollen, discolored finger of the corpse's left hand. He looked away again. "But—"

"Whom did you hire, Joseph?" Michael turned upon him. "Did it not occur to you to ask to see his papers? Can you be so lacking in sense that you accepted the word of the first man who presented himself to you as Bartó?"

The Bürgermeister, his head swiveling from Haydn to Michael, was following the brothers' conversation with a gaping mouth. "If this poor man, God rest his soul, is Bartó, then who is the other fellow?"

"How should I know?" Michael snapped, still looking shaken. "It was not I who hired him!" He glared at Haydn. "But this much is evident; it was no accident that killed poor Bartó." He looked at each man in turn,

151

the expression on his face defiant. "I cannot imagine why anyone would think so!"

"No, it was not," Haydn said in quiet agreement. "Bartó, that is to say, István," Haydn corrected himself when he noticed Michael's enraged look. "My principal violinist's name is István." He gave the Bürgermeister and the barber-surgeon a meaningful glance, willing them to staunch their questions until they were alone. He did not wish to speak of the letters he had discovered in his violinist's writing case in the presence of so many other people.

He turned toward his middle brother. "István must have incited a fight, no doubt plying your Bartó with drink, Michael."

"That is *exactly* how it happened, Herr Kapellmeister!" Gerhard declared with such force, it was clear he had made the suggestion many a time and had just as often been discounted. "And, what is worse"—a flicker of disgust crossed his features—"although Marlene refuses to believe it—spurred him on to make bawdy advances toward her.

"Then at each lewd gesture he incited the other to make, that two-faced wretch would turn around and apologize profusely to Marlene. She, poor, misguided lass, thought he was coming to her defense when things went too far."

Gerhard's handsome features were set into a stony expression. "I thought at the time that he must have some devilry planned. And then when I heard he was working at the castle, I was convinced the villain was up to something!"

The Bürgermeister exchanged a skeptical glance with the barber-surgeon. "But he could hardly have planned a murder on the spur of the moment? Besides, why would the man go to such lengths to obtain a position at the castle?"

Behind them Maria Anna sniffed. "Because he is Hungarian!" She gathered up her skirts and, averting her eyes from the corpse, rose to leave. "I knew all along he would be trouble, husband. But you have your nose buried in your music, and are blind to everything beyond the notes."

"What does that have to do with anything?" the barber-surgeon enquired of no one in particular as Maria Anna left the tavern. Her casual remark appeared to have stung him.

"Unfortunately everything," Haydn responded wryly. He had noticed the barber-surgeon's aggrieved air, and could not help wondering why

Maria Anna's insinuation that all Hungarians were troublemakers should have nettled him so.

———⁓———

The sudden arrival of the Kapellmeister's middle brother from Salzburg had so disrupted the morning, it was nearly noon by the time Rosalie and Greta set out to clean the Musicians' Quarters.

"Fancy Master Bartó being married!" Greta adjusted the handle of the silver pail with its long-handled brooms on her arm. "I suppose it is no surprise, he has vanished. I hear it was Gerhard's intended he was chasing after."

Rosalie nodded. She had heard the same rumors herself. They had left the outer courtyard, and were making their way up a broad, tree-lined path. Out of the corner of her eyes, she saw Greta taking in the bare-branched oaks and beeches on either side of them in a swift, furtive sweep before leaning closer toward her.

Her voice lowered to a conspiratorial whisper, Greta hissed: "She is apparently with child!"

"With child!' Rosalie stopped near an old Hungarian oak. A few, yellow-brown leaves were all that remained of its foliage. "Where did you hear this?" she asked, her eyes narrowing. She put her pail down. Greta was notorious for making up stories. But if it were true...

She stared at a low, curving branch of the oak tree, recalling Gerhard's strange reaction to the news of Master Bartó's disappearance and the Kapellmeister's suspicions. If Master Bartó had not returned to retrieve his travel trunk, she might have thought... She shook her head, and turned her attention to Greta.

"Were you even listening to a word I said?" Greta demanded. "I heard Master Lorenzo and Master Niklas talking about it the other day. Gerhard's barmaid is with child. Master Bartó promised to marry her before he disappeared!"

"Ach so!" Rosalie picked up her pail, and resumed her way up the small hill, motioning to Greta to follow her. "Gerhard was not at all surprised to hear Master Bartó was gone. I shouldn't wonder if he was behind Master Bartó's disappearance," she murmured more to herself than to Greta.

Even so, Greta's sharp ears caught the words. "I had the same thought myself," she declared, but her mind had already flitted on, alighting on another topic.

"Who would think Herr Michael was Herr Haydn's brother? What a lordly manner he has to be sure! Just like Master Bartó, I thought, when I saw him this morning raving and ranting at Herr Rahier..." Greta prattled on. Rosalie walked beside her barely listening to her chatter. The thought of Gerhard with his thick, chestnut brown wavy hair and his muscular form had reminded her of the man who had come calling on Master Bartó dressed in peasant's clothing.

The Kapellmeister had given her a look of utter disbelief when she had insisted it was not Gerhard who had come to see Master Bartó that day. But, although the two men were remarkably alike in form and coloring, there was really no mistaking one man for the other. Gerhard was a common tavern-keeper, while the other, despite his clothing, had seemed to be a man of some quality.

"Such soft, white hands!" Greta's voice broke in upon Rosalie's thoughts. "Herr Michael looks as though he has never done a day's work."

White hands! Rosalie slowed down. A vivid image of the stranger's hands on the tray she had almost dropped arose from the depths of her memory. They had been white and clean, the nails perfectly manicured with a pearly sheen. She glanced down at her own hands, work-roughened and brown in comparison, barely noticing that Greta had walked past her.

Gerhard was no farm-hand, but even his hands were rough and calloused, the nails chipped with dirt under them, his skin burnt by the sun.

"Whoever he was, he was no peasant!" she murmured. *But who was he?*

———

Shortly after Maria Anna left, Haydn persuaded Michael to ride back to the castle.

"I will do what needs to be done here, Michael," he said, gently ushering his brother to the carriage that awaited them outside the tavern. Michael, seeming uncharacteristically subdued, allowed himself to be helped into the carriage. The shock of finding his protégé murdered must have set in, Haydn thought, glancing down at his brother's deflated form.

"It would be as well if you were to stay for a day or two more. Herr Lichtenegger..." Haydn paused, his lips pursing at the unsavory thought that the Police Commissioner's discovery of his violinist's involvement in murder was unlikely to bode well for the imperial visit or the Prince's ambitions.

With a sigh, he turned back to Michael. "The Police Commissioner may wish to question you further on this matter. Besides," he added, noticing his brother's drooping features, "it would please Maria Anna, I am sure, if you were to conduct the mass for our godson's christening. It needs but a skilled conductor with your fine understanding of sacred music to infuse the work with the true spirit of God's grace."

Haydn's words brought a feeble smile of pride to Michael's lips. "I will peruse the music directly I arrive at the castle," he promised.

Haydn returned to the tavern to find Gerhard had already set out for the barber-surgeon's clinic, taking the pallet and its grisly burden with him. Finding himself alone with the Bürgermeister and the barber-surgeon, he decided to acquaint the two men with the recent discoveries he had made about his violinist.

Before he could say a word, however, the barber-surgeon turned to him with a frown.

"What did you mean, Herr Kapellmeister, when you said your violinist's nationality had everything to do with this unfortunate affair?"

"The writing case we discovered in the woods"—Haydn inclined his head toward the Bürgermeister—"contains clear evidence of my violinist's involvement with the dissidents." He recounted the contents of the letters.

"Lipót György," the barber-surgeon murmured to himself when Haydn had finished. "I have heard the name before, I am sure of it. If only I could recall the context."

"I myself suspect far worse," Haydn continued. "Do you recall, Herr Groer"—he turned toward the Bürgermeister—"how we surmised that Bartó—or István, to refer to him by his true identity—must still be in the neighborhood. The contents of the writing case are far too sensitive for a man of his wary nature to leave lying around?"

The Bürgermeister brought his head down in a slow, uncertain half-nod; the folds of his chin rested on his chest as he peered at Haydn from under his bushy, white eyebrows.

"His lingering in the area, I suspect after reading the letters, must signify that some drastic action is being planned—" Haydn paused. "Against Her Majesty's person, I have no doubt of it! Those are most likely the rumors that took His Serene Highness all the way to Vienna.

"And this"—Haydn thrust his hand out to indicate the area where the corpse had recently lain—"is but confirmation of my suspicions. With the real Bartó out of the way, István was able to take on his identity and infiltrate the castle as a spy."

"Yes, but…" The Bürgermeister's voice trailed off, dissatisfied. He looked over at the barber-surgeon, a doubtful expression on his features. "How would the dissidents know when your brother's protégé would be arriving or even what he looked like? Who besides yourself and the Prince could have known of his arrival, Herr Haydn?"

"Herr Rahier," Haydn muttered under his breath, thinking of the Estates Director's strenuous objection to Bartó's arrival. But the Estates Director had wanted the position for his nephew. Why would he hire a man to kill Bartó only to have the murderer impersonate the slain man? *Unless…*

Haydn straightened up, and stared blankly at the gray stones on the wall opposite him. He was recalling Albert's criticism of the court newspaper. He had taken no notice of it at the time, but now he wondered whether there was more to the young man's disparaging remark. How deep did Albert's sympathies for the Hungarian cause run?

Then there was the matter of Albert's violin. The instrument and its case were so remarkably similar to the one the imposter Bartó had been so loath to let out of his sight. In all likelihood, the very same. But the imposter was still alive. That could only mean…*that he had lent the instrument to a fellow dissident*!

Lost in thought, he was not aware of the tavern door opening.

"If we could but find the fellow," he said so loudly his listeners gave a start, "we might have a chance of learning enough to foil the plot."

CHAPTER NINETEEN

"It may take some time, brother, but I believe I have discovered the means to tracing our missing violinist." Johann closed the tavern door behind him, and approached the hearth.

Haydn looked up, startled. How had his brother known where to find him?

Johann must have read his mind. "I was almost at the castle gates when I met Michael. He directed me here."

He took a seat beside Haydn, inclining his head at the Bürgermeister and the barber-surgeon. "I take it we were deceived into harboring an imposter at the castle."

"What was it you learnt at Wiener Neustadt that prepared you for that revelation?" Haydn searched his brother's features. Johann's ready acceptance of the news was even more unexpected than his opening remark.

Johann glanced briefly at the Bürgermeister and the barber-surgeon before replying. "Your suspicions, I am afraid, proved all too accurate, brother." His tone was somber as he related all he had learned that morning. "I was unable to determine who Lipót György is," he said, as he brought his account to a close. "But, this much is clear, the dissidents seek to put their leader, the man claiming to be Ferenc Rákóczi's son, on the Hungarian throne, and—"

"Assassinating the Empress is, in all likelihood, the first step in their nefarious plan," Haydn finished for him. It was the only conclusion to be drawn. Why else had his violinist chosen to linger on in the region?

"Assassinating the Empress—if that is even possible, gentlemen—will bring the dissidents nothing but trouble." The barber-surgeon dismissed the idea with an emphatic shake of his gray curls. "The Archduke Joseph will then be Holy Roman Emperor in more than just name, and, with the vast network of spies Count Pergen has put in place for him, will quite easily crush any rebellion—"

"Not if they have French support," Haydn countered, recalling the information Count Nádasdy had given him.

But the barber-surgeon shook his head again. "They may seek it, but I doubt they have it. Besides, how many Habsburgs can the dissidents kill? The Empress has twelve other children apart from the Archduke Joseph. Then, there are her uncle's children and grandchildren. They would have to kill the entire line of Habsburgs to regain control of Hungary!"

"Maybe that is what they intend to do," Haydn murmured, thinking that the turbulence of war with France could quite easily lay waste to an entire dynasty.

The Bürgermeister shifted his girth uneasily on the wooden bench on which he was seated. "I would keep your suspicions to yourself, Herr Haydn. These are but speculations. I have no doubt the dissidents mean to disrupt the imperial visit in any way they can, but..."

"As far as we know," the barber-surgeon added, "your brother's protégé was accidentally killed in a drunken fight."

"Gerhard—" Haydn began, only to be interrupted.

"Will not want the Police Commissioner bothering Marlene with his questions, Herr Haydn." The Bürgermeister's voice was firm. "I will keep my men posted in these woods. We will find your violinist."

Haydn nodded. It would be as well, he realized, to say as little as could be said to the Police Commissioner about István's involvement in this dreadful affair until after the Prince's return. The slightest whiff of a conspiracy could have the most disastrous consequences. But the danger to the Empress was all too real, and his former violinist would have to be sniffed out.

"Very well, Herr Groer." Haydn rose to his feet. "I only ask that you also station some of your men near Frau Heindl's farmhouse. István will not be able to stay away from Marlene for too long."

Rosalie pushed the olive green linen chest against the foot of the bed, and straightened up to cast a critical eye over the room Master Bartó had occupied. The question of his friend's identity had so preoccupied her mind, she had almost forgotten to turn the carpet down in one room and had nearly neglected to change the bed linen in another. The feeling that she had seen the stranger before jostled uncomfortably in her head. If only she could remember *where*!

With a determined shake of her dark curls, she thrust the notion away from her, forcing herself to inspect her work. Her eyes swept over the room. The wooden floors were polished to a shine; there was not a speck of dust anywhere; and she had even remembered to put a fresh pot of ink and some writing paper on the small writing desk under the window.

A frown appeared on her forehead as her gaze fell on the windows on either side of the bed. The glass panes and frame were gleaming, but the branches of the weeping beech that stood behind the Musicians' Quarters had grown so long, they threatened to overrun the room. It had taken all her strength to open and close the windows with the branches thrusting up against the panes like that.

She went toward one of the windows for a closer look. Yes, she would have to get one of the gardeners to prune the branches. She was about to come away when a blur of red caught her eye. She unlatched the window, put her arms out to push the thin, silver beech branches out of the way, and swung the sash out.

What was that? Rosalie leaned over the sill, and spread the branches apart. The blob of silver-grey and red resolved itself into a recognizable shape, making her eyes widen. *A travel trunk!*

It was sitting in the hollow formed by two thick branches forking away from the main trunk. *Whatever was it doing there?*

She peered down at it, craning her neck to examine it as best she could. It looked like Master Bartó's trunk. In fact, she was quite sure it was his travel trunk! But who could have put it there? Surely not Master Bartó—

A sudden noise behind her jolted her out of her thoughts.

"Oh, it's you!" Rosalie gasped, turning around to see Albert at the door.

"Greta is waiting for you downstairs," Albert said, coming into the room. "What were you doing leaning out of the window like that?"

Rosalie ignored the question. "Have you just come in? Are any of the gardeners about? Master Bartó's trunk"—she pointed an urgent finger out of the window—"is down there, caught between the branches of the beech tree—"

"Nonsense!" Albert stared at her as though she had lost his mind.

"Come and look!" Rosalie insisted.

But Albert refused to budge. "Bartó's trunk? Really? Are you quite certain?"

Rosalie bobbed her head vigorously "We shall have to send for the head gardener," she said, but Albert appeared not to have heard her.

"This is certainly an interesting development," he was murmuring to himself. "Uncle will wish to be informed of it, I'll warrant."

Haydn blinked as he followed Johann out of Gerhard's wine tavern into the bright afternoon sunlight. He gently closed the tavern door behind him, and stood squinting up at the Kleinhöflein Parish Church steeple for a few minutes.

When he turned toward Johann, his mouth was set in a grim line. "The town authorities are all too inclined to dismiss this entire affair as an insignificant peasant flap, but if the nobility are involved..." he shook his head. "Somehow that does not surprise me," he murmured, deeply troubled to realize the news came as no shock to him.

What had occurred in the past few days, he wondered, to have prepared him for the disturbing fact that the peasants had powerful allies.

"There is worse, I am afraid, brother," Johann began as they set off down the alley toward St. Vitus Street. "It would appear the Jews are involved, too—or, at any rate, one extremely powerful and wealthy merchant," Johann explained when Haydn turned to stare at him.

A large rack-wagon laden with wine barrels made a slow left into the alley. The brothers stepped to the very edge of the path as the horses trotted in, muscles straining against the weight of the wagon. In the few minutes that it took the wagon to drive by, Johann recounted his discovery of the stolen master copy in Wiener Neustadt.

"Herr Weisenstein says Max Rosen brought the manuscript to him to help a friend of his—a man Rosen represented as the author of the manuscript. A man in urgent need of money, apparently."

"István, of course!" The path now clear, Haydn turned onto St. Vitus Street. "The Prince has often remarked upon Rosen's astute understanding of the affairs of commerce. The conspiracy must have a good chance of success for him to have joined the cause."

"With such a powerful ally, the dissidents cannot be lacking in funds." Johann hurried down the street after his brother. "Why steal your music, then? It seems such a purposeless, petty crime."

Haydn paused to consider the question. Had the wine merchant suggested the theft? It would explain his failure to approach the Kapellmeister for an evaluation of the manuscripts he had acquired. And arranging for the sale of the stolen music would, no doubt, serve to keep his own hands clean.

"Max Rosen is a man of business, Johann, and like any shrewd businessman, he wishes, no doubt, to hedge in even a sure thing. If caught in the endeavor, he was, ostensibly, merely helping a man in need, thus preserving his relations with the Prince. On the other hand, should the conspiracy succeed, his willingness to use his connections in the service of the cause will have earned him the good will of the dissidents."

A reluctant glimmer of appreciation appeared in Johann's eyes. "Ach so! A wise strategy, to be sure. But"—an expression of dismay crossed his features—"he will not be too likely to disclose much of our violinist's whereabouts, then, will he?"

"On the contrary." Haydn's tone was unrelenting. "The prospect of losing his license may well loosen his tongue."

"Why did you tell him about the trunk, Rosalie?" Greta demanded. Albert had decided to take charge of matters, and had sent them about their business. They were now back in the palace kitchen. "I don't trust him an inch! We should have waited until Herr Haydn or Master Johann returned."

She peeped out of the kitchen door. They had deliberately kept it ajar, and Greta had stationed herself near it, so they could keep an eye out for the Estates Director when he set out for the Musicians' Quarters.

"What can be taking them so long?" Greta wondered, impatiently brushing a lock of golden hair away from her face.

"What does it matter? It is not as though the trunk will disappear," Rosalie replied, carefully rinsing out the porcelain breakfast cups. But she was just as eager as Greta to learn more of this strange affair.

"Ah, here they come. Quick! Let us be off!" Greta turned around, beckoning Rosalie to the door. "Those dishes can wait."

They scurried out of the kitchen and down the hallway to the doors of the West Wing. The Estates Director followed by his nephew and the head gardener were already at the outer courtyard. Rosalie and Greta followed at a safe distance, taking care to keep near the shrubs and trees. Herr Rahier would send them scuttling back to the palace if he caught them following him.

A weeping hornbeam was planted near a marble figurine a few paces behind the Musicians' Quarters. Rosalie pulled Greta behind its densely spreading branches. From behind its drooping branches, they had an unobstructed view of Herr Rahier who, along with Albert and the head gardener, had come to a standstill beneath the beech tree.

An under-gardener had almost finished cutting down the long, thin beech branches with a pair of large pruning shears. The tree trunk with its two forking boughs was now clearly visible.

"Where is the travel trunk?" Greta hissed.

The same question must have occurred to the Estates Director, for he turned toward his nephew, a stern expression on his features. "Where is this travel trunk, then?"

The under-gardener looked over his shoulder. "There was nothing here, Mein Herr."

Albert shrugged. "I cannot say I saw it, either, but..." he turned his head.

Greta had chosen that very minute to poke her flaxen head out from behind the branches of the hornbeam. Albert must have spotted her, for he pointed an accusing finger at the maids.

"It was the maids who reported the matter to me," he said.

The Estates Director turned slowly around, and fixed his icy blue eyes on the two maids.

"Making mischief, as usual, I see," he commented before turning on his heels to stride down the path. Albert followed close behind, a strange expression in his eyes as he glanced briefly at the maids, and quickly looked away.

Greta made a rude face behind his back. "I am surprised the old stick had nothing more to say." She turned toward Rosalie. "You don't suppose he'll take another gulden out of our salary, do you?" The corners of her mouth turned down at the thought.

But Rosalie, staring after the Estates Director's retreating form, made no reply.

CHAPTER TWENTY

Walking at a brisk pace, the Kapellmeister and his brother found themselves a half hour later at the arched entrance into Unterberg, the Jewish Quarter of Eisenstadt. Some of the most powerful Jewish families of Europe resided here. The wine merchant, judging by his imposing mansion, was in all probability one of the most affluent of these.

A maid responded to their knock, and led them through a large tiled courtyard with a marble fountain at its center into a richly furnished study. A portrait of a beautiful woman, the lady of the house, Haydn surmised, hung on the wall behind the walnut wood desk.

"It is by Gottfried Auerbach!" Haydn said, recognizing the style of the artist who had painted a portrait of no less a personage than the Empress herself. The wine merchant must be well-connected indeed to have secured the services of so illustrious a painter.

"Musicians from the Esterházy Court!" said a quiet voice behind them.

The brothers turned to see a man of medium height with fine, ascetic features and a brown beard entering the room.

"What can I do for you, gentlemen?" Max Rosen surveyed his visitors through a pair of penetrating brown eyes. He gestured toward some armchairs upholstered in fine blue and gold silk that stood around a low table. "Let us make ourselves comfortable, gentlemen. And then you may state your business."

Haydn lowered himself into an armchair, and exchanged a glance with Johann. Max Rosen did not appear to be a man who could be easily discomfited.

"It is this manuscript"—Haydn took the sheaf of papers that Johann had brought out from within his overcoat and handed them to the wine merchant—"that a mutual acquaintance gave my brother that brings us to you, Herr Rosen."

Rosen glanced down at the scores, and laid them on the table before him. "Ah, Herr Weisenstein sought your opinion, did he? That was wisely done. Is it of any value, then?"

Haydn exchanged another glance with Johann. For a man who had just been caught out in an act of treason, the wine merchant seemed to be showing no signs of distress. Instead, his eyebrows raised slightly, Rosen swiveled his head from Haydn to Johann. The Kapellmeister found himself rendered speechless by the wine merchant's mildly expectant manner. It was Johann who broke the silence.

Forgive my asking the question, Herr Rosen, but why did you not approach my brother directly?"

The wine merchant spread his hands wide. "The man who brought it to me, gentlemen, wanted the manuscript sold. Being a man of integrity, albeit in dire straits, he would accept no money from me. What could I do, gentlemen, but ask Herr Weisenstein if, as a bookseller, it was worth anything to him?"

"The man who brought it to you had no idea of its value?"

His brother, Haydn noticed, made no effort to conceal his skepticism.

The wine merchant laughed. "How could he have, gentlemen? He is but a peasant. He barely knows his letters. How can one expect him to read and understand music?"

A peasant! Haydn leaned forward. "What did this peasant look like, Herr Rosen? Was he a harsh featured man, swarthy with dark hair, the faintest trace of a Hungarian accent in his voice? Or was he..." His voice trailed off. István's strange visitor had been a peasant, had he not? If only he had thought to ask Rosalie for a description of the man.

Rosen leaned back in his armchair, every trace of humor wiped from his features. "What is it about this manuscript, gentlemen, that gives rise to all these questions?"

Johann picked up the manuscript. "Do you have any notion who the author of this manuscript is, Herr Rosen? If it was brought to you by an unlettered peasant, why did you tell Herr Weisenstein it was the composer, himself, who brought these works to you?"

"But I said no such thing! The man I referred to was the peasant who brought me this manuscript. He had received it in payment, he said, in lieu of money. But what good is a manuscript, however valuable, to a peasant deep in debt and with hungry mouths to feed? I ask you again, gentlemen: what is it about this manuscript that elicits your questions?"

The wine merchant's calm exterior appeared to have cracked. He looked toward Haydn, in some agitation, for an explanation. But it was clear the truth of the matter was beginning to dawn upon him. "This is *your* music, is it not, Herr Haydn?"

Haydn nodded. "That manuscript contains all of the music composed for the forthcoming imperial visit. No one, except for myself and my musicians, not even the Prince, has seen the score or heard the music."

"Stolen, then!" The wine merchant dragged his hand through his dark hair.

Haydn nodded again. "We believe by one of my violinists, who—" He paused, unsure how much to reveal.

"But Helmut would not lie to me! I have known the man long enough, gentlemen. He would not steal to supply his own needs, much less help another."

"He was given the manuscript, you say. Did he tell you *who* gave it to him?"

Rosen shook his head. "Nor did I think to ask, gentlemen."

Haydn looked briefly in Johann's direction before continuing. "The musician who stole the music is missing. We have reason to believe he may have joined the dissidents. If, as you say—"

The wine merchant turned a deep shade of purple. "I have no reason to lie gentlemen. Nor reason to join in any conspiracy against His Serene Highness or Her Majesty. My own business would be deeply affected if there is truth to these rumors of unrest and war—"

"You have heard talk of an impending war, then?" Haydn was unaware that the rumors were so widespread.

"I have extensive connections at the imperial court, gentlemen, as well as in France. If, as seems likely, the Archduke Joseph should decide to strike against France, I will be ruined. I strongly hope His Serene Highness can persuade against that course of action. But that is neither here nor there." Rosen turned briskly toward his visitors. "You will want to meet

Helmut, no doubt. His brother delivers vegetables to my kitchen every morning. Come any morning, you like, and he will take you to Helmut."

"What did you make of that, brother?" Johann looked over his shoulder at the arched wooden door of Rosen's mansion being closed behind them. A key could be heard turning in the lock.

"I wish I knew what to think." Haydn began walking slowly toward the head of the lane. "His consternation at the manuscript being stolen seemed genuine enough."

But even as he uttered the words, it occurred to him that Rosen was a man of commerce, a man who consorted with the nobility. A man such as him was undoubtedly skilled in the art of dissembling. Could a mere musician such as himself fathom the complex machinations of the wine merchant's mind?

He nodded at the rabbi who, coming out of the synagogue a few paces down the road, gazed in open curiosity at them. "On the other hand, that may mean nothing at all. He may still be involved. Although after meeting him, I cannot but think he could never have endorsed the theft. It is too reckless an act for a man of his discreet nature."

Johann nodded, hastily stepping out of the way as a crowd of children spilled out from the school into the lane. "He acted in every way as a man who would seem to be innocent. Suitably indignant at the mere suggestion that he might be involved in the conspiracy, but he was not discomposed at all when you first showed him the manuscript. He played it off as having helped a friend just as you had surmised he would. I—"

He broke off, emitting a cough of mild disapproval, as two young boys chasing each other rushed headlong toward them. Almost without thought, he held out a hand as much to brace himself as to ward the boys off.

"I myself," he went on, having dismissed the lads with a few words of admonition, "am inclined to believe he deliberately misled Herr Weisenstein into believing the peasant was a close friend. And that is another thing! Why would a man as greatly in debt as this Helmut is accept a manuscript, however valuable, as payment for his work?"

167

Haydn stopped. "That struck me as odd, too. It occurred to me, at the time, that the peasant who visited István might have been the man to deliver the manuscript, but if Rosen says..."

"*A nobleman in peasant's clothes!*" he murmured aloud. He gazed down, startled to see two Jewish matrons with shopping baskets on their arms glowering at him. He looked around him. *Ach so!* He had stopped under the archway leading into Judengasse, and was standing right in the middle of the narrow entrance, blocking their path. He stepped aside with a brief apology.

"It is something Rosalie said about István's mysterious visitor," he explained in response to Johann's perplexed stare once the women had walked past. "I wish I had questioned her further when she made the remark, but"—he shrugged again, throwing his hands up—"we were so convinced at the time that István's disappearance had to do with his quarrel with Gerhard..."

Johann was silent, apparently digesting this bit of information. "Two different men, then. I don't suppose a man as poor as Helmut could be mistaken for anything other than a peasant. He must have been threatened or bribed into doing the conspirators' bidding. Rosen would hardly risk directing us to a man not involved in this matter."

His expression when he turned toward Haydn was worried. "If that is the case, Helmut is unlikely to reveal anything of István's whereabouts. That is yet another person the Bürgermeister will need to keep a watch on."

"The thought had occurred to me," Haydn conceded with a slight nod. The peasant, he knew, had little reason to be forthcoming no matter what the reason for his involvement. Even as he made arrangements with Rosen to meet the man, he had held out little hope of learning much that was useful. "But it is another matter altogether that has been troubling me."

The Kapellmeister stopped near the apothecary run by the Brothers of Mercy. "To tell you the truth, I was not at all surprised to hear that the nobility might be involved in the conspiracy, Johann. A mere peasant uprising, however angry and violent, could never be quite as bold as the plot the dissidents have come up with.

"Michael's protégé was quite deliberately killed in order that István might take his place at the castle. But if Rosalie's impressions of István's friend are not mere fancy, then—"

"The visit was most likely connected with the dissidents' plan and has everything to do with his departure," Johann finished for him.

Haydn inclined his head in quiet assent. The town authorities might continue to shrug off his concerns, but his younger brother, he was glad to see, had at last been persuaded to his point of view.

"We shall have to question Rosalie when we return," Johann went on as they resumed their walk toward the castle. "What could she have seen that has her so convinced the man was in disguise?"

"Truth be told, I was barely listening when she reported the matter to me. At the time, her impression of the man came as no surprise to me. I had surmised as much myself from hearing his voice."

He shook his head ruefully. Maria Anna had been right all along. There was so much he had failed to see. And even now, an uneasy sense that he had been blind to yet another detail persisted. What was it? It seemed to be just beyond reach, hovering below the surface of his mind, resisting his attempt to grasp it. They were almost at the castle now, and despite his best efforts he could neither recall what it might be or shake off the feeling. The weight of it made him stop.

"There is something else about this entire affair that troubles me, Johann," he confided. "I only wish I could put my finger on it."

The Kapellmeister and Johann returned to find that Michael had taken over the Rehearsal Room, gathering the church singers in there to rehearse the mass for the Christening. A few members of the orchestra had been pressed into service as well. The remainder trooped down the stairs.

"To the concert hall, Herr Kapellmeister," Lorenzo explained when Haydn turned toward him for an explanation.

"An excellent notion," Haydn said, still plagued by the nagging sense that some small detail brought to his attention during the day was at odds with everything else they had hitherto uncovered. Was it something that Rosen had said? He leaned absently against the marble cherub that capped the newel post, and went over their conversation with the wine merchant.

Johann was already hurrying toward the Music Room. "I will ring for Rosalie at once, brother. The sooner we can"—he looked over his shoulder—"What is it?" he asked, turning back to where Haydn stood as though welded to the newel post.

"Did Rosen say it is the Archduke Joseph who plans to strike France?" His head pivoted in a slow half-turn toward his brother.

Johann nodded. "In preparation, no doubt, for an attack, should it ever come. Is that what was troubling you? Rosen cannot be too far off the mark. According to Herr Weisenstein, a large troop of soldiers has moved into the military academy—on a permanent basis, so it would seem. And each day brings more men to Wiener Neustadt."

"Yes, but Rosen said nothing about an *imminent* attack from France."

"No he did not!" Johann stood rooted to the carpet, and regarded Haydn. "*He* seems to think it is Austria that seeks to attack France. With all his connections in that country, how can he have heard no word of a strike against us!"

Haydn drummed his fingers on the marble cherub perched upon the newel post. "It *is* inexplicable. But can it signify anything? His anxiety on account of an impending war was not feigned. And it matters not how the war starts, it will surely affect his business."

He began to slowly make his way to the Music Room. Could this small detail really have caused him so much concern? It was the only inconsistency his mind had been able to unearth. Besides, what else could there have been?

"What seemingly insignificant aspect of this matter have we overlooked, I wonder." He dragged his hand through his wig, wishing he could rid himself of the unsettling notion that he had been blind to a crucial detail that could prove to be the key to the entire affair. He resolutely cast the thought from his mind. "It will come to me in good time, I suppose."

"I am sure it will, brother." Johann reached out in front of him to push open the Music Room door. "In the mean time, we had best send for—"

"Herr Haydn!" Rosalie's voice gave both men a start.

～

"You are quite certain it was Ist—eh...Master Bartó's trunk that you saw?" Haydn scrutinized Rosalie's features before turning toward Greta.

Best to still keep calling the imposter by his assumed name, he thought. Especially if the news was to be kept quiet.

Greta reddened under his scrutiny. "I didn't see anything. But I believe her," she added stoutly. "Rosalie wouldn't lie about such a thing."

"Hmm..." Haydn stroked his chin thoughtfully. If the maids were to be believed, this was the second time his violinist's travel trunk had disappeared. Who could have concealed it—amidst the branches of a tree, no less—only to haul it out of sight once its hiding place was discovered?

If it had been Greta who reported the matter to him, he would have had no trouble dismissing the entire story as a product of her overwrought imagination. But Rosalie was not one to tell improbable tales.

"And Albert, you say, was in the room?" he asked, recalling his earlier suspicions of the Estates Director's nephew.

Rosalie shook her head. "He came in afterward. But he refused to go to the window to look."

"And he chased us away almost immediately." Greta chimed in. "It was some time before he returned to the castle. If you ask me, he had plenty of time to make off with it."

Haydn nodded. He was coming to the same conclusion as Greta.

"It was Albert who said he had heard noises in the room late at night and discovered the travel trunk missing," he reminded Johann in a low voice. "And now that I think about it, the drawbridge is pulled up every night. How, then, did our violinist manage to penetrate the castle grounds to retrieve his trunk?"

The maids must have heard these last words for Greta brought her hand to her mouth and Rosalie stifled a gasp.

"Albert must have pushed the travel trunk out of the window," Rosalie said, "and then deliberately called Sanyi into the room early the next morning. He made it seem as though we had imagined the trunk was there to begin with!"

"He did the same thing this afternoon," Greta declared, hands going to her hips until she hastily recalled herself and brought them down again to hold them, tightly clasped, before her. "I knew we shouldn't have trusted him."

Haydn regarded Greta with interest. What had Albert done to earn her distrust?

"Has Albert ever said or done anything strange or"—he hesitated before pronouncing the word—"suspicious? Before this afternoon's incident, I mean?"

The maids' eyes were drawn toward each other, and an apprehensive glance passed between them. *What had they seen,* Haydn wondered, noticing it.

"He got all huffy, remember," Greta said, still looking at Rosalie, "when Sanyi made fun of the dissidents hiding behind foreign skirts? Didn't I say at the time he was one of them. And I was right! You don't suppose"—she turned toward Haydn, eyes wide with terror—"you don't suppose he killed Master Bartó for his position, do you?"

"No, our violinist is very much alive." Haydn was glad to be able to reassure them on that point. "But be wary. If we are right, Albert is not a man to be taken lightly." He stared hard at Greta to impress his next words upon her. "Say not one word of this afternoon's incident, or your suspicions, to anyone. Not even your brother," he said, turning to Rosalie. "He is much too close to Albert, and may inadvertently serve to put him on his guard."

Greta nodded, still round-eyed, and turned to leave. Rosalie was about to follow her, but hesitated a few minutes at the door before turning around.

"Albert let Herr Rahier think I was making up stories about the trunk, Herr Haydn. But Herr Rahier was not even all that annoyed..." She hesitated again, her fingers twisting the corners of her apron.

Haydn met Johann's eyes. Could Rahier be aware of his nephew's ardent support of the dissidents? Possibly even condone it?

CHAPTER TWENTY-ONE

Haydn regarded Rosalie as he pondered the information she had provided. It was the second time in about as many days that the Estates Director had conducted himself in a manner entirely inconsistent with his usual behavior. Rahier was wont to inflict a swift and harsh retribution for the most minor infractions. Yet he had been uncharacteristically unconcerned by his violinist's departure. And now he had let slip an opportunity to chastise the maids, in particular, the one the Kapellmeister had referred to the position.

His thoughts turned to his violinist's strange visitor. He would have recognized the Estates Director's voice had he heard it. And no disguise could conceal the man's haughty manner. Could it have been Rahier's nephew whom Rosalie had seen?

"The man who asked to see Ist...Master Bartó, Rosalie. Was it—"

"It was not Gerhard, Herr Haydn!" Rosalie burst out, too excited apparently to realize that she had interrupted the Kapellmeister mid-sentence. "It could not have been. Even though he had reason enough to hate Master Bartó, what with his intended carrying Master Bartó's child!"

"Marlene was promised to Gerhard before she took up with Bartó!" Johann's voice rose sharply. "Small wonder there was bad blood between those two. But what makes you so sure it was not him?"

"The man's hands, Master Johann. I remembered them just this afternoon—he almost bumped into me, and had he not reached out to grab the tray I carried, it would have dropped to the ground."

But the explanation meant as little to Haydn as her reference to the tavern-keeper's hands. "What is it about Gerhard's hands that are so distinctive?" Haydn's eyes drifted toward Johann. Gerhard's hands had been the least of his concerns earlier that afternoon, but surely even he would have noticed anything out of the ordinary? The bemused expression on his younger brother's face suggested Johann was equally at a loss.

"Not Gerhard's hands, Herr Haydn. They are as they ought to be, I am sure. It was the peasant's hands that were so peculiar. They were whiter and softer than my own." Rosalie held out her hands, holding the palms down for a moment before turning the palms up again. "The nails, far from being chipped or dirty, were pink and clean and well-cared for."

"Ach so!" The force of the revelation caused Haydn to straighten up. The lass was right. No peasant he had ever seen had such well-manicured hands. He met her eyes, his gaze keen. "Think carefully, Rosalie! Have you seen the man since—not in his peasant's garb, but dressed like a gentleman?"

The maid shook her head, dark curls bobbing vigorously. "Not since, Herr Haydn. But I have seen him before. I am quite sure of it. The chestnut brown hair, those blue eyes, the tall, well-built frame—they are all so familiar to me."

"Albert, perhaps?" Haydn suggested, trying to recall the precise shade of his hair. He had seen the young man without his wig, he was certain of it.

Rosalie looked doubtful. "I can't be certain. If only I could see him without his wig..."

"That can be arranged!" Haydn's gaze settled on the door as he recalled one of his schoolboy pranks. It had been a hat that he had plucked off a schoolfellow's head as the unsuspecting lad pushed open a door and crossed the threshold. Who knew, but the same trick might serve to separate Albert from his wig!

The corners of his mouth twitched slightly, and his eyes briefly lit up. It had been such a long time since he had played any pranks at all!

<center>~~~</center>

"We will know soon enough whether it was Albert in disguise," Haydn said after Rosalie had been dispatched with instructions to procure a stick, some stout string, and a small hook. "Even if it is not him, there is no doubt in my mind that Albert is in some way connected with István."

"I am inclined to agree, brother." Johann followed his brother's progress as he perambulated about the Music Room. "István would need help retrieving his travel trunk. He must have arranged to return for it once his accomplice succeeded in removing it from his room."

"And Albert did not count on its being discovered before István's arrival, I'll warrant." Haydn paused near the fortepiano. "What could that travel trunk contain that Albert needed to dispose of it in such haste?" His fingers rapped out a quick trill on the keys as he pondered the question.

"If its contents were so important, surely István would have sought the opportunity to return for it sometime these past couple of days. Unless..." Johann shifted uneasily in his armchair.

Haydn nodded. It took no great prescience to read his brother's mind. The self-same thought had occurred to him, and it made his stomach turn. Had he inadvertently abetted the dissidents by hiring Albert?

"Unless its contents are related to the dissidents' treacherous plans," he voiced the thought slowly. "In that case, it will remain here until the imperial visit."

A knock on the door put a stop to their speculations. Rosalie had returned with the materials Haydn had requested. She was accompanied by a footman, who, under Haydn's direction, attached the stick to the door casing. One end of the string was tied to the stick, the other around the hook. When the door swung open next, the stick would angle down from its horizontal position, lowering the hook and allowing it to latch onto the unsuspecting victim's wig.

The footman had just departed in search of Albert when the sound of voices from the grounds below drifted in through the open window.

"Yes, but a hasty strike against such a powerful nation—and an ally, beside—would be a foolhardy move," said an irritated voice that was easily identifiable as belonging to His Serene Highness.

"And not to strike would expose ourselves to the gravest danger," rumbled a second voice.

Hearing it, Haydn froze. "That is the voice I heard!" He rose from the piano bench, and in a single swift movement strode toward the window.

Rosalie followed on the Kapellmeister's heels, but Johann had already hurried to the window, and was now standing beside Haydn.

"Who is it, brother?" he asked, leaning over the window sill just as the tail end of a satin coat bordered with brocade whisked into the West Wing in a whirl of blue and gold.

175

Haydn turned back from the window, a strange expression on his face. "I only caught a glimpse of two figures as they passed under the portico. But the voice was oddly familiar to me. I remember having the same thought when I overheard István's conversation with his mysterious friend."

Haydn was still standing by the window when the door swung open. He heard Rosalie's loud gasp beside him almost as soon as he saw the stick attached to the door casing bend down. She must have recognized István's visitor. But it was not Albert whose wig remained suspended in the doorway, his mane of chestnut brown hair falling to his shoulders, as he crossed the threshold into the room.

Haydn blinked at the figure standing in the middle of the Music Room, having trouble recognizing his visitor without his wig. He was vaguely aware of the Prince frowning as he brushed aside the wig dangling in the doorway, and followed his companion into the room.

"What is the meaning of this, Haydn?" he demanded irritably at the same time as his companion said: "Haydn, my dear fellow, this is surely not the time for such schoolboy pranks!"

Haydn's mouth dropped open when he heard the voice.

Count Nádasdy! Surely, he was in error!

But the voice was unmistakable, and there was no doubt in his mind to whom it belonged. Yet, how could it be?

"The Police Commissioner has just given us the tragic news about your first violinist, Haydn. Nádasdy insisted on coming up to offer his condolences when he heard."

Haydn, still speechless, turned his head toward the Prince. But the Count had already come up to Haydn, clasping one of his hands in his own.

"I was never more shocked to hear the news, my dear Haydn. I knew the fellow well, and could hardly believe it when I heard he had left his post without a word. Who could have wanted to harm the man?"

"Yes, Your Lordship must have known him quite well indeed." Haydn enunciated the words slowly. "Michael said it was *you* who recommended he join the Esterházy Orchestra!" He had at last identified the small fact that had until now eluded him.

The Count nodded. "His talent needed fostering, and who better, I thought," he continued, retaining his grasp on Haydn's hand as he looked over his shoulder at the Prince, "to develop it than Haydn, here." He turned back toward the Kapellmeister. "Michael will be quite devastated to hear the awful news."

"It was Michael who identified the body, Your Lordship. He was, I believe, in shock."

"Your brother is here!" The color appeared to have drained from the Count's face.

"Your Lordship! I *thought* I heard your voice." Michael burst into the room. "Your Serene Highness!" he inclined his head at the Prince, and then turned toward the Count.

"Bartó—"

"The Count is well aware that Bartó is no more," Haydn interrupted. His eyes bore into the Count's. "When he saw his protégé lying dead on the tavern floor, Michael wanted to know how I could have been duped into hiring an imposter. Since seeing the poor man, I have asked myself the very same question."

"Imposter!" the Prince repeated, but Haydn continued to speak. His eyes never left the Count's features.

"But the imposter, Your Lordship, had come prepared with Bartó's papers and the letters of reference Michael sent him with. What is more, when the only man who knew him by face came into town, he said nothing to us of the deception. That man was you, Your Lordship! Small wonder, then, that we were so completely gulled!"

"Nonsense! Your violinist's untimely death seems to have addled your brains, my dear man." The Count attempted a contemptuous laugh, directing a quick, appraising glance at his host. "Surely, you cannot condone such a rude reception of one of your visitors, Esterházy!"

But the Prince's eyes had narrowed. He positioned his stout, richly clad frame between his guest and the doorway. "Explain yourself Nádasdy! Is it really all nonsense or is there any truth to what my Kapellmeister says?"

Johann stepped forward before the Count could respond. "The imposter was introduced to Your Lordship as Bartó Daboczi. I am told he fawned over you in the most slavish manner. Yet you said nothing! You even commended the imposter to the Estates Director. My brother was not here at the time, but all this can be vouched for."

The Count uttered a derisive snort. "I have been a generous patron to countless musicians, Master Johann. Do you suppose I remember them all by face—"

"But Your Lordship was well-acquainted with Bartó!" Michael cried out. "His countenance cannot have escaped your mind!" He looked around frantically, then stretched his arm unsteadily out, fingers clawing the air as they reached out toward the Count.

"It did not, Michael!" Haydn's voice, loud and firm, stalled his brother's movements. "It was the Count who had Bartó killed so that István—the imposter," he explained for the Prince's benefit, "might take his position in the castle. That was the only reason for recommending that Bartó come here, was it not, Your Lordship? How could we suspect a man that Michael had sent?"

His middle brother looked as though he could take no more, but the Kapellmeister forced himself to continue: "Your man in place, you came to see that all was going as planned. But how many times could you drive through Eisenstadt in your own person? So, you adopted a disguise. That is your peasant, is it not, Rosalie?" Haydn eyes remained fixed on the Count.

"It is, Herr Haydn. The very same!" Rosalie's dark curls bounced up and down with each nod. The Count stared down his nose at her. He would have spoken had Haydn given him an opportunity to utter a word.

"But clothes by themselves do not make a man, Your Lordship. It was your hands—much too clean and well-manicured, for a man of such humble origins—that gave you away. And your voice as you spoke with István. It has been such a long time since I last heard it, I could not place it at the time, although it seemed so familiar to me."

The Count's lips had curled into an angry sneer as Haydn spoke. His gaze now fell on Rosalie, still standing open-mouthed next to Haydn. "Ah, the pretty maid! So useful, but I might have known you would be trouble." He took a step forward, as though intending to lunge toward her.

"No!" barked the Prince. He must have rung for the footmen while Haydn had been speaking, for now, as he snapped his fingers, two strong, liveried servants burst forward and grasped hold of the Count.

"Take him down to the Police Commissioner!" The Prince looked his visitor up and down in disgust. "What earthly reason could have possessed you to get involved in this perfidious affair, Nádasdy? To think a member of my family, however distantly related, should be involved in treason! But whatever you and your treacherous friends have been playing at, you will not succeed!"

The Count gave a harsh, jeering laugh as the footmen dragged him away from the room. "Bah, ever the Austrian flunky, Esterházy! Take me where you will, but you cannot stop us. Not this time. Rest assured, Lipót György will take back Hungary! And he will restore to the Nádasdys the lands your grandfather stole from us."

CHAPTER TWENTY-TWO

The Kapellmeister stood beside Johann at the window of the Music Room, watching as the Police Commissioner pushed his richly-attired prisoner roughly before him. He and his brother were alone in the room, and it felt as though all the world had receded from them.

He gripped the edge of the sill hard. To think that he had gloried in the thought that he, a mere wheelwright's son, could name a personage such as His Lordship his friend. What a blind fool he had been! How could he have failed to see the Count for what he was—a cold-blooded, murderous traitor?

The image of Michael's pale face and shrunken cheeks at the revelation that the Count was responsible for his protégé's murder haunted him. His middle brother had returned to the Rehearsal Room, his shoulders drooping. Despite his self-important, blustering manner, Michael, Haydn realized, had little conception of the evil that existed in the world, nor the inner strength to confront it. They had never gotten on well, but the Kapellmeister would have done anything to spare his middle brother the rude awakening he had experienced that day.

He stared down at the Count with loathing. Why was he straining against his handcuffs and vehemently shaking his head like that? It looked for all the world as though he were signaling to someone. An accomplice, perhaps?

Haydn cast an eye around the grounds, but could see no one. Most likely, he thought, the black hood covering the Count's head and secured tightly at his neck was causing his skin to chafe.

He heard Johann's heavy sigh as his brother withdrew from the window. "What madness could have possessed His Lordship to join in with the dissidents?" Johann exclaimed. "Were it not for Michael's presence, his part in this matter would have remained undisclosed."

Haydn inclined his head, but his mind was elsewhere as he leaned over the window sill. A rapid clopping sound as of horses moving at a fast trot accompanied by the rumble of carriage wheels came to his ears. The Police Commissioner was just pushing his prisoner into his carriage. Whose carriage was it that he could hear, then? The Count's? Surely, it would not drive away without any instructions from its owner.

He drew away from the window, wondering what would become of the Count's conveyance. It was not an important question, but it played like an insistent basso continuo in the back of his mind.

"It was his oft-repeated assertion that he knew Bartó well that gave him away," he responded at last. "An oddly foolish mistake to make for one so astute."

"So, it was." Johann, already seated in the armchair by the window, tilted his head back to regard Haydn. "I cannot understand why he went to such lengths to assure us he knew the man well. I was at such pains to ward off those quartets he thrust upon us, I didn't notice it at the time. But when he was here last, he exhibited no sign of surprise, expressed no concern at all, at the disappearance of a man whose welfare he was apparently so interested in."

Haydn lowered himself slowly into the armchair opposite his brother. "I thought it curious—most curious, indeed—that the discovery of the corpse seemed to have left him so unperturbed." He was not sure why the thought bothered him, but it did.

Johann clearly saw no significance in that minor detail, however. "Well, he already knew Michael's protégé was dead—"

"Yes, but he was ostensibly reacting to the news of my violinist's untimely demise?" Haydn chewed at his under lip.

"Naturally, there was no need to worry about the imposter! He must be well aware the man is alive and well."

Haydn bit his lip, unable to refute the point, but still not satisfied. "Then who did he think was dead, I wonder," he murmured.

A knock on the door interrupted his thoughts. A servant entered to inform the Kapellmeister that he and his brother had been summoned by the Prince.

"A bad business, gentlemen! Very bad, indeed! And the sooner it is resolved, the better," the Prince declared as soon as Haydn and Johann had seated themselves in the gilded chairs opposite his own.

"The imperial visit, then—"

"Will take place as planned. Her Majesty remains undeterred in her intention. If anything, the news of the unrest fermenting here seems to have spurred her on. She is convinced her presence here will serve to calm things down. And such is her charm, it well may!" The Prince let out a deep breath, resting his hands on the silk sash covering his ample stomach.

"The intelligence Her Majesty's informants have gleaned is known only to a privileged few, gentlemen. But you appear to have discovered much more. No one at court could have foreseen Nádasdy's involvement. And were it not for your ingenious little trap, Haydn, who knows when we might have discovered the truth! What precisely do you know?"

Haydn felt the heat rise up in his nut-brown cheeks at the gleam of appreciation in the Prince's eyes. He had foreseen nothing. His discovery of the Count's treason had quite simply been a happy accident. He cleared his throat noisily.

"The trap, in truth, was set for someone else." It took some effort not to squirm under the Prince's steady regard as he made his confession. "Had the Count not walked into it, I might not have realized his involvement in this affair."

He quickly recounted what they had uncovered so far. The Prince interrupted with a question or two, but for the most part listened in silence.

"These letters written to your violinist, where are they?" the Prince wanted to know when Haydn had finished.

"In the Music Room, Your Serene Highness." Johann rose from his seat. "I will bring them down."

Silence prevailed in the room while Johann was gone. The Prince appeared to be lost in thought, his chin rested on his chest as he contemplated the green and gold patterned carpet. Haydn studied the gilt-edged frame around the portrait hanging behind the Prince.

Once the Prince shifted in his seat to glance over his shoulder at the portrait behind him of his grandfather, majestic in military uniform. "Nádasdy's defection should have come as no surprise to me, Haydn. Treason seems to run in some families. His great-uncle—mine as well, for my grandfather married one of the Nádasdy sisters—was led astray, too. By a Rákóczi, another family of perpetual troublemakers."

"That was when the Nádasdy lands were confiscated and granted to Your Serene Highness's grandfather!" Haydn recalled hearing the story. On such petty grounds, then, had the Count sought to whip the Hungarians into a fury, and bring ruination upon two nations! How depraved could any man get? He fought down his growing revulsion.

"Where did you meet the Count this afternoon, Your Serene Highness?" It was an insignificant detail, but Haydn wished to satisfy his own curiosity on the point. "He was here but yesterday, and claimed to be traveling to Pressburg on urgent business. And you yourself were in Vienna, were you not?"

The Prince nodded. "It was just outside the castle. He was on his way in to see you. To get your opinion, he said, on some quartets a protégé of his had composed."

"Indeed! Why, it was but yesterday that he left them behind. And he knew we were on the trail of a missing violinist." Haydn studied the carpet, attempting to divine the reason behind the Count's unexpected return to the Esterházy palace. "His coming to see me was but a pretext to meet his man here. But he knew István was not within the castle. Whom could he have wished to meet?"

The sound of the door opening interrupted his thoughts. Johann had returned with the writing case. He handed the case to the Prince, and resumed his seat beside his brother. The Prince began to pore over the letters. Haydn, watching him, tapped an impatient rhythm on the carpet.

Moments later, His Serene Highness read the last of the documents, and placed the bundle on the marble table between them. His mouth was set in a grim line.

"This Lipót György is a dangerous man, gentlemen. Our apprehension of Nádasdy means nothing if your violinist cannot be found—and quickly, at that. But I take it you have a means of finding him?" He searched Haydn's features.

Haydn bowed his head in assent. "We do, indeed, Your Serene Highness, although how much this peasant is likely to disclose of the dissidents' whereabouts remains to be seen. It would be as well if the Police Commissioner, along with some of his men, were to follow us at a safe distance on the morrow.

"István may well be lurking in the neighborhood, and his close contact with the leader of the conspiracy suggests he is equally dangerous." He leaned forward as he uttered his next question. "Lipót György is the leader of the band, is he not—the man who styles himself the son of Rákóczi, Your Serene Highness?"

He held his breath. Would His Serene Highness confirm his conjecture?

The Prince appeared to hesitate for a moment, before inclining his head briefly. "I would ordinarily not entrust information of so sensitive a nature to members of my household, but..." He gestured vaguely. "It is your perspicacity that has brought us this far."

Haydn's own nod was barely perceptible as he lowered his eyelids for a moment, acknowledging the unusual circumstances that impelled the Prince to take two of his musicians into his confidence.

"Briefly, then. Lipót György is a man we believe to be Comte St. Germain, a person of indeterminate nationality with a penchant for stirring up unrest wherever he goes. He escaped arrest in England for that very reason some decades ago, and fled to France. There he gained such an unfortunate hold over the French king that six years ago, there was an attempt to arrest him. But it was thwarted, so it is rumored, by the monarch himself, who helped him escape.

"Not too long ago, however, the Empress's spies began receiving reports of his appearance from diverse Hungarian towns. He is a charismatic man, and his claim of being Ferenc Rákóczi's long-lost eldest son appears to draw rich and poor alike to him." The Prince paused.

When he spoke next, his voice had taken on a wry tone. "He claims, moreover, to be supernatural. At any rate, he has resisted all our efforts to arrest him."

"Ach so!" Haydn stroked his chin. The affair was beginning to make a little more sense, now. "Close to the French King, is he? Then, he must be the source of these rumors of an impending attack from France."

The Prince looked down at his hands resting on his knees, his fingers tightening on the fabric of his satin breeches. A moment later, he raised his eyes. "I fear that might be true. Nádasdy has always refused to reveal his sources. And no one at court has received independent confirmation of a strike."

Haydn, finding himself at the edge of his chair, slid back. A few more pieces of the conspirators' plan were falling into place in his brain. "It is clearly a ruse," he said. "No doubt, to incite the Archduke Joseph into attacking an ally."

From the little he knew of the new Emperor, the conspirators could not have chosen a better ploy to bait him. The Empress's son and co-regent was rumored to be fascinated with the exploits of his mother's arch-enemy, Frederick of Prussia. In all likelihood, the Archduke had leapt with alacrity at a chance such as this to prove his own military prowess.

"A foolhardy move since the Hungarian Diet will not countenance another war. And without Hungarian support, any strike would be doomed."

"That is precisely what the dissidents are counting on, Your Serene Highness."

"Perhaps, so! But to what end?" The Prince threw his hands up with the air of one who has long wrestled with the question without coming any closer to a reasonable explanation. "How does it bring them any closer to their goal?"

Haydn brought his fingertips together, and stared at them before eventually responding. "You made reference once, Your Serene Highness, to a certain condition first introduced by the Emperor Leopold, and then reinforced by Her Majesty's father. What was it?"

"What can it matter Haydn," the Prince began. He brushed the air impatiently. "Well, if you must know, Hungary was to give up her right to elect her own king, accepting the Habsburgs as hereditary monarchs until the Habsburg line itself"—he paused, eyes widening at the revelation— "*ceased to exist!*" he finally said, enunciating the words in a slow, hushed voice.

He stared at Haydn. "It *is* a long shot, but—with the Archduke set on his disastrous strike—not impossible. And without the Empress to rein him in, who knows how long it will be before the Archduke launches a precipitous charge against the French? Your violinist—"

"We will find him, Your Serene Highness. But, unfortunately, he appears to have allies closer to home that we must beware of as well."

185

Haydn was beginning to have an idea whom the Count might have been coming to see that afternoon.

———

It was late in the evening by the time Haydn and Johann returned home to 82 Klostergasse. Maria Anna said nothing, but her displeasure was evident.

"Where is Michael?" she enquired, slapping down a bowl of stew on the table. A portion of the rich gravy sloshed out onto her table linen, the brown stain spreading over the pristine white cloth.

Haydn, hanging his wig and coat on the pegs behind the kitchen door, threw Johann a glance of desperation. But Johann could only shrug helplessly. Michael, declaring himself too distraught to be fit company for his sister-in-law, had clutched a little too readily at the use of Haydn's sleeping quarters within the castle.

He cast about in his mind for a suitable explanation.

"Michael has offered to conduct the mass for our godson's christening. Thinking it would be inconsiderate to keep you up late into the night until he finishes studying all the music—not to mention that he might risk waking you at the crack of dawn when he sets out to lead a rehearsal—he decided to make do with my rooms at the castle."

But Maria Anna refused to be so easily placated. "And what will you be doing, husband, while Michael takes over your duties?" She put her hands on her hips, and glared at her husband.

Haydn sat down at the table, and brought a spoonful of stew to his mouth. It was barely warm, and he grimaced slightly as he tasted a lump or two of congealed fat. He refrained, however, from making any comment. His wife was clearly in a disagreeable mood, and spoiling for a fight. He had no intentions of giving her any such cause.

Maria Anna must have seen his mouth pucker up, for without waiting for a response to her earlier question, she demanded: "Well, how long was I supposed to keep your dinner warm, husband? There are murderers roaming this small town, and rather than come home early to keep your wife safe, you go gallivanting around all night! I could have been lying here in my kitchen with my throat slit for all you care!"

Haydn stared into his bowl of cold stew, not knowing what to say. It was Johann who, as always, leapt into the fray.

"Never fear, sister-in-law! One of the principals involved in the affair has already been apprehended. In no small part due to brother Joseph's efforts. Tomorrow we go in search of our missing violinist. Once he is found, the danger will be over."

It was not enough.

"Tomorrow!" Maria Anna gave Haydn a dark look. "It is the day before our godchild's christening! Why must you go traipsing after that no-good violinist of yours tomorrow?"

Haydn forced himself to look up, swallowing the retort that sought to burst forth from his mouth. "Because the Prince has asked me to, Maria Anna! It is a matter of national security. The man is involved with the dissidents, as you well know. We cannot have him still on the loose when the Empress visits. Surely, even you can understand that."

"I thought you were a Kapellmeister not a Kapell-detective," Maria Anna muttered, but she seemed somewhat mollified for she took Haydn's bowl of stew with a—"Here, let me heat your dinner. I will have a warm bowl of stew for you as well, brother-in-law. Cold meat will not help you catch a murderer!"

187

CHAPTER TWENTY-THREE

"How will you obtain evidence of Albert's involvement in this affair, brother?" Johann carefully lifted a cup of coffee from the tray Maria Anna had brought up to Haydn's study and, setting it down on the table before him, began to stir it vigorously.

"I wish I knew!" Haydn took a cautious sip from his own cup. The brew was so hot, it threatened to burn his tongue. "Nothing Rosalie or you or I could say would convince His Serene Highness that Albert's suspicious behavior itself is sufficient evidence of his involvement in this matter. And he seems equally ill-disposed to hear any condemnation of the Estates Director."

Johann had been alternately blowing over his cup and fanning it with a stack of papers. His head still bent over his cup, he now directed a sympathetic glance up at his brother.

"We have no direct evidence against the Estates Director, it is true. But Albert's beliefs as much as his behavior should be considered suspicious enough." He brought the cup to his lips, nodding in appreciation as he tasted the brew. "Excellent!" he murmured, more to himself than to his brother. He set the cup down.

The brother's sat together in companionable silence.

"I wonder whether his father's family was involved in any of these past conspiracies against the Empress's grandfather," Johann began after a while. "Albert's strong convictions must come from somewhere, and they seem undiluted by any German influence he might have received from his mother."

Haydn took another sip of his coffee, before responding. "It is quite likely, I suppose. Although to blame a man's character on his parentage makes us seem as prejudiced as Maria Anna." He tapped thoughtfully on the rim of his coffee cup as Maria Anna's remark earlier that day surfaced from the depths of his memory.

"She said something of the sort at the tavern this afternoon, and elicited the most peculiar reaction from the barber-surgeon." He repeated what Maria Anna had said. "Herr Hipfl could not have been more offended if he were Hungarian himself."

Johann was prevented from responding by a knock at the door. "Who could that be at this late hour?" he wondered, walking over to the window to open it. He thrust his head out into the chill air, and peered down. "It is too dark to see." With a light shrug, he returned to his chair. "We shall know soon enough, I suppose. Sister-in-law must be letting the man in as we speak."

But Maria Anna had already come upstairs. She poked her head in at the study door. "Why must your friends come calling at all hours of the night, husband? It is not something I can approve of, if you must know!"

Nevertheless, she was clearly not averse to opening the door for she whisked her head out of the doorway and clattered loudly down the stairs, still grumbling to herself.

<hr>

"Herr Hipfl!" Haydn was surprised to see the barber-surgeon standing in the doorway. He had two thick books under his arm.

"It appears we were in error, Herr Haydn." The barber-surgeon wore a somewhat sheepish expression as he entered the study. "Herr Groer and I have just returned from the Police Commissioner's office."

The Bürgermeister followed him into the study. "He sent for us shortly after the...eh...arrest." Herr Groer lowered himself gingerly into a chair, looking as though he had been subjected to an extremely uncomfortable interrogation. "There is no further news of your violinist, I take it?"

"Nothing conclusive, I am afraid," Haydn replied, wondering what had brought the two men to his home at so late an hour. "Merely a few details that might help us get closer to him." He recounted the pertinent details from his conversation with the wine merchant.

"There is no doubt that he is somewhere in the area," Johann added. "He may well return to the castle, although it would be unwise to wait as long as that." He briefly narrated the peculiar reappearance and subsequent disappearance of the travel trunk, but made no mention of Albert. "Its contents, we fear, must be potent enough to make its discovery untenable for the dissidents."

"Ach so!" The Bürgermeister bent his head, and frowned down at his hands resting loosely interlocked over his stomach. "Well then...that points to an accomplice within the castle grounds, does it not?" he rumbled at last, raising his head to regard all three men in turn.

Haydn's eyes drifted briefly toward Johann before returning to the Bürgermeister's face. "It would seem to be the most likely explanation, but who it might be remains a mystery." He was reluctant to share his suspicions of Albert or his uncle without garnering some solid evidence against them both.

"Whoever it is must surely carry the sign of the raven," the barber-surgeon declared. He opened one of his books and laid it on the table, pointing to an illustration of a coat of arms. At the very center of the red shield was a smaller shield with a large raven within it. "It is the emblem of the fifteenth century Hungarian king, Matthias. That is what the mark of the raven refers to, Master Johann."

"Matthias Corvinus! The king who laid siege to Wiener Neustadt?" Haydn raised his eyes from the book. "There is a golden goblet displayed in the town hall there that he apparently presented the city in recognition of the brave fight she put up." He gestured toward his brother. "We have often seen it."

The barber-surgeon was nodding eagerly. "The very same. It is because of this emblem that he was called Corvinus."

"Well, I suppose it is fitting that the dissidents should have adopted his emblem as their standard." No king was more revered in Hungary, Haydn knew. He stared down at the illustration, convinced he had seen it somewhere. On István's violin case? It had an emblem, he was quite certain. *As did Albert's case!*

He leaned back in his chair. Could the emblem on Albert's violin case be a raven? He must remember to examine all the violin cases in the Rehearsal Room on the morrow. The uneasy sensation that he had managed somehow to hire yet another dissident took hold of him. He was still trying to shake it off when the barber-surgeon's voice penetrated through his thoughts.

"...and it was in connection with this very book that I recall hearing the name Lipót György—"

"We now know who he is, Herr Hipfl," Johann interrupted gently. "He claims to be the son of Ferenc Rákóczi, and is the leader of this treacherous band."

"Yes, the Police Commissioner did say something to that effect." The Bürgermeister stirred in his seat. "I suppose we had best be leaving then. Herr Haydn! Master Johann!" He nodded at each brother in turn, as he began to rise from his seat.

"A moment, if you please." Haydn sat up straighter. His eyes sought out the barber-surgeon's. "What precisely have you heard about Lipót György?"

"This book"—the barber-surgeon tapped the volume on the table—"is a history of Hungary commissioned by Matthias Corvinus himself. Every Hungarian household has a copy—"

"Indeed!" Haydn stared at the barber-surgeon, whose cheeks had flushed. Where, he wondered, had the barber-surgeon procured the book?

Recovering his equanimity, the barber-surgeon continued. "It is written in Latin, which few Hungarians can read any more. Lipót György, I have heard, was having German translations of these published and distributed in the streets along with the Hungarian Bible, also translated"—he held out a second volume that had been sitting on his lap—"and diverse other materials."

"What possible reason could you have for keeping those items in your house, Herr Hipfl?" the Bürgermeister grumbled at his friend. "Although I suppose it is fortunate you possess such an extensive knowledge of the country and its history."

The barber-surgeon said nothing, appearing to study the thick red rug covering the wooden panels of the study floor.

Haydn continued to stare at him, a few odd bits of conversation stirring in his memory. "I suppose you have some Hungarian blood—from your mother's side of the family, I would warrant. That is what my violinist discovered about you, did he not? And threatened to expose the fact unless you gave in to his demand for money?"

"There is no harm in being of Hungarian descent." The barber-surgeon looked up, a defiant expression in his eyes. "My father was German. A *Catholic,* at that. I take my nationality *and* my religion from him."

191

"Of course, you do." Haydn nodded. But the words the barber-surgeon had inflected had given him a clue as to the true source of his visitor's unease. For all her affable nature, the Empress tolerated Protestants less well than she tolerated the Jews, and Hungary had many of the former.

"Still, if the fact came out, there might be some enquiry made into whether or not you owe Her Majesty's government duties on the beef you import. And, while that may be easily resolved, if it was discovered that your mother was a Protestant, you would lose your official post as medical examiner for Eisenstadt."

The barber-surgeon rose. "I have nothing to be ashamed of, Herr Haydn. I told your violinist that." He turned toward the Bürgermeister. "If my mother's religion makes me unfit for my post, then so be it."

"Calm yourself, my dear friend!" The Bürgermeister reached out to grip his friend's arm. "It is your religion, not your mother's, that counts. But even if you were a Protestant, how would the Empress be any the wiser? Eisenstadt could have no better medical examiner than you. You shall have your post as long as you choose to keep it."

"I did not mean to cause you any distress, Herr Hipfl." Haydn rose to his feet as well. "I was merely trying to understand why my violinist attempted to extort money from you. Although the answer to that question has raised yet another. Why did he need money to begin with? With the nobility involved, surely there can be no dearth of funds within the conspiracy?"

The Bürgermeister shrugged. "Soldiers, even in such a cause, need to be paid, Herr Haydn. The nobility, however wealthy, are unlikely to dig into their own pockets to provide for the families of the poor peasants they have beguiled into joining their conspiracy."

"True enough," Haydn agreed as he escorted his visitors down the stairs to the door. But he could not keep the skepticism out of his voice. István's urgent need for money had come about much too suddenly to be explained away quite so simply.

"And it was so desperate," Haydn murmured as he closed the door behind his visitors, "as to seem almost personal." He turned to face Johann. "He owed no debts that we know of. Why, then, did he want funds?"

Dawn had barely broken when Haydn arose from his bed. Seeing Maria Anna fast asleep under the bed clothes, he tiptoed out of his room and crossed the hallway to his brother's room. He had spent an uneasy night, tossing and turning in a vain attempt to fall asleep. But repose being quite impossible now, he was determined to get an early start on their enquiries. Johann must have already awoken, for a light knock brought him, bleary-eyed, to the door.

Snatching a quick repast of some re-heated coffee and remnants from the previous evening's meal, the brothers set out.

"Herr Hipfl's talk of ravens has me more worried than I would care to admit," Haydn confessed, casting an anxious glance at the sky as they began walking toward the palace. It looked to be a gloomy day, gray and overcast with the threat of another bout of snow. "I feel sure I have seen the emblem he showed us—quite recently in fact."

Johann drew his overcoat around himself. "I had the same thought when Herr Weisenstein mentioned it to me."

"We must have seen it on István's violin case, and then noticed the same emblem on the case Albert brought with him." Haydn's strove to keep his voice from faltering. "That one of my musicians should be involved in this dreadful affair does not bear thinking of, and yet it is an inescapable conclusion!"

"It is small consolation, I know, but in Albert's case, your hand was forced, brother. Rahier gave you no choice but to hire him."

Haydn tightened his grip on his leather music case. "But we knew nothing of István's involvement, Johann. Now I cannot but wonder if any other of my musicians have been drawn into this miserable affair."

"I very much doubt it, brother." Johann's reassuring tone soothed Haydn somewhat.

"No, I suppose not. And brooding over the matter is hardly likely to help us." Haydn drew himself up and began to walk a little more briskly. "Besides, there is much to be done if we are to get to the bottom of this affair.

"This very morning, I will have Rosalie clean out all the instrument cases, giving her a pretext to examine every one of them." He rubbed his hands together, sounding a little more cheerful. "And once we have settled our business at the castle, Herr Rosen's man will drive us to see this peasant of his."

They walked on in silence. The drawbridge was being lowered over the moat as they neared the castle grounds.

"If only we had remembered to ask the Prince to have some of the gardeners look out for that travel trunk," Johann lamented while they waited. "Whatever Albert did with it, he cannot have taken it too far from where it was found."

"No, it cannot be too far from the Musicians' Quarters," Haydn agreed. "But it is just as well we said nothing to the Prince, Johann. Any arrangement for a search would have to be made through Rahier. And, if he is involved, as I suspect him to be, that would only give him warning of what we know. Under his direction, the trunk would never be found."

He glanced up at the sky again as he spoke. Despite the gray day, he had recovered his equanimity to a degree. They would avert the crisis, he was confident. Once he had secured proof of Albert's involvement, how could His Serene Highness fail to see the young man's culpability?

He rubbed his hands again. It was a chill day. "No, there is a better way. I will have Rosalie discreetly search the grounds near the Musicians' Quarters. Having at least seen the travel trunk, she and Greta will know what to look for. And be more likely to find it," he added darkly, as he set foot on the drawbridge.

CHAPTER TWENTY-FOUR

"Master Bartó is an agent of the dissidents?" Greta stopped in the middle of the tree-lined avenue leading to the Musicians' Quarters, and gaped at Rosalie. Her mouth had fallen open, rosy lips forming an enormous oval.

"Yes," Rosalie said. She nudged her friend on. "We had best get going."

Wrapping her arms around the heavy silver pail weighed down by brooms and mops, she trudged slowly past her friend up the path.

"It was Count Nádasdy who sent him to the palace," she called over her shoulder. "Although, if it was the dissidents who sent him, I can't say I know why he left his position? He can be of no use to them outside the castle!"

Greta giggled as she hurried up the path behind Rosalie. "The way he was chasing after Gerhard's intended, I cannot imagine he was of much use to them within the castle! They must be quite glad to have Albert take his place."

"He *is* one of them, I am sure. Herr Haydn must think so as well. He didn't deny it when I said as much yesterday."

They had almost reached the Musicians' Quarters. The weeping beech that had held Master Bartó's travel trunk was visible through the trees, looking rather pathetic now that it was shorn of its long, drooping branches. On the hill above it, a weeping hornbeam presided over a small waterfall that cascaded down a few wide, shallow stone steps to splash into an ice-encrusted pool below.

"I wonder how Herr Haydn can be so sure Master Bartó is still alive." Rosalie stared vacantly at the waterfall. The water was spraying out in every direction from under the branches of the hornbeam instead of gushing down, as it usually did, in a graceful stream.

Greta came huffing up the path behind her and, putting her pail down, leant against a trunk, panting heavily. "Herr Haydn must have seen him or had word of him—from the Police Commissioner, perhaps," she said after a while, having recovered her breath. "Why, you don't think Albert did him in, do you?"

She looked expectantly at her friend, but Rosalie's gaze was riveted on the waterfall. "But if they are both dissidents, Albert could have no reason for killing Master Bartó, could he?" Greta sounded almost disappointed.

A while later, she tugged at Rosalie's sleeve. "What if Master Bartó was so caught up in his dalliance, he was truly of no use to the dissidents? Herr Rahier was forever trying to get him dismissed. Why"—Greta lowered her voice to a conspiratorial whisper, and looked furtively around—"the very day before Master Bartó disappeared, I heard Herr Rahier telling Herr Haydn that nothing good would come of him keeping Master Bartó on!"

"*Oh!*" Rosalie swiveled her head sharply in Greta's direction. "Well, there is something odd going on!" She gave the cascading waters one final glance before she began to make her way up to the Musicians' Quarters. "Those gardeners will need to do something about that waterfall. Something must be blocking its head."

She had only taken a few steps when, struck by a sudden thought, she came to an abrupt halt in the middle of the path. Greta, following close on her heels, held out her hand with a little shriek to prevent herself from falling.

"What is it, Rosalie?" she asked, sounding annoyed.

"The travel trunk!" Rosalie cried. "I think I know where it is. Albert wouldn't have had enough time to take it very far from where it was. And he'll not have had the sense, I'll warrant, to remove it to a safer place from where he concealed it!"

❦

Within the palace all was quiet. Two solitary maids assisted by a footman went about their chores in hushed silence, careful not to make the slightest sound. Haydn, approaching the short, dark-haired maid dusting an enormous Chinese vase at the entrance to the West Wing, was informed that Rosalie had already set out for the Musicians' Quarters.

"She will have returned, no doubt, by the time we have attended to our business here," Haydn reflected as Johann and he made their way to the wide, carpeted staircase that swept up to the concert hall and the Music and Rehearsal Rooms above it.

He was about to set foot on the staircase when the Estates Director's raised voice broke the silence. The shriek it elicited from one of the maids nearly startled him into biting his tongue. Rahier seemed oblivious to who might hear him, for his voice thundered on unabated.

"How often have I told you to hold your tongue, boy? Your views, indeed! It is your constant spouting of your confounded views that will land us all in trouble!"

"He must be speaking to Albert," Haydn whispered to Johann. "What can that young man have done to so upset his uncle's composure?"

He stepped away from the staircase and, after a moment's hesitation, walked toward the Estates Director's door. "I think it would benefit us greatly, Johann, to hear some more of what is being said."

Aware of the maids and the footman in the hallway, he positioned himself near the marble figure of Hercules just before the Estates Director's office, and peered up as though studying the stone features, hewn from the finest Italian marble.

Rahier had by now lowered his voice, and Haydn had to strain his ears to the utmost to hear his next words.

"Mark my words, boy, this blatant airing of your views will do neither you nor your cause any good. The violinist you were fortunate enough to replace behaved in just such a foolish manner. It did him no good, I can tell you that."

What Albert said in response neither Haydn nor Johann could hear. That it was not to the Estates Director's liking was evident from the loud snort that was clearly audible through the solid, wooden door.

"The Prince has already..." Rahier's voice trailed off. "The Kapellmeister...trunk..." The Estates Director was evidently pacing the floor between his writing desk and the window for Haydn could only hear snatches of the conversation now.

Rahier seemed, in his perambulation, to have neared the door of his chamber for now Haydn heard: "You will lose your position if you continue on in this way, and what good can that do you?"

"We had best be gone." Haydn tugged urgently at his brother's sleeve. His ear had caught the muffled sound of a chair being scraped across the marble floor within, indicating that Albert was preparing to leave his uncle's presence.

They had barely reached the staircase when Albert swept out of his uncle's office, and stormed out of the palace. In his haste to leave, he left the doors wide open.

"Herr Rahier seems to be well aware of his nephew's views." Johann's gaze followed Albert as he raced down the steps to the courtyard.

"And to be oddly more troubled by his loose tongue than the views he espouses." Haydn stared out at the paved courtyard visible through the open doors of the West Wing. "*That*, apparently, will do Albert as little good as it has done István!" The remark they had overheard puzzled him.

He turned to Johann. "What in the name of heaven, do you think, he meant?"

<hr />

"There! Just as I thought." Rosalie held the branches of the weeping hornbeam aside, and looked triumphantly over her shoulder at Greta.

"Why, that sneaky little weasel!" Greta's eyes, following Rosalie's pointing finger, had widened as they alighted on a silver-colored travel trunk with a bright red clasp that sat in the middle of a rocky grotto, covering the source of the waterfall. "So, this is where he brought Master Bartó's trunk!"

"Oh, it is heavy!" she cried, tugging on one of the handles at the side.

"Here, let me help." Rosalie bent down and grasped the handle on the other side, and began to push.

"The water must have soaked into the wood." Greta was breathing heavily by the time they managed to push the trunk out of the grotto onto the surrounding grass. "It's a good thing we found it when we did. The damp would have rotted out the wood before long."

She dragged a moist hand across her forehead, and surveyed her sodden stockings and shoes in dismay. The water, released from its impediment, began to cascade down the stone steps into the pool below.

"I wish we had thought to take our shoes and stockings off first. We shall catch our deaths in this cold!"

"I don't think Albert meant to wait as long as that," Rosalie murmured, peering down through the branches at the tree-lined avenue below.

Greta moved toward her with a frown. "As long as—What!" she ended on a subdued shriek as Rosalie suddenly thrust her back behind the branches of the hornbeam with a hissed: "Stay back!"

"It is Albert coming up the path," Rosalie whispered, her hand still preventing Greta from coming forward. "To retrieve the trunk, I suppose." Her lips clamped shut as she caught sight of another figure behind the Estates Director's nephew. "And not content with making mischief on his own account, he must bring my brother along for company!"

"Well, what shall we do, then?" Greta stood on tiptoe, trying to see over Rosalie's shoulder.

Rosalie turned around, and the two girls studied each other for a minute before turning their heads slowly to survey their surroundings.

"Quick!" Rosalie pointed as Greta simultaneously cried, "The wheelbarrow!"

One of the under-gardeners had been trimming the hedgerows on the other side of the hill. He must have been called away for the large wheelbarrow filled with branches, leaves, and other diverse trimmings stood unattended near the hedges.

It was but the work of a minute to bring the wheelbarrow to the waterfall and empty it of its contents. Once again they grasped a handle on either side of the trunk and, grunting from the effort, swung it into the empty wheelbarrow.

"Now, let's toss the branches and leaves back on top of the trunk. And we can put our pails and brooms on top as well." Rosalie's voice came out in a breathless gasp. She began to pile the plant debris on top of the trunk.

"But where are we taking it?" Greta panted out as she grabbed a handful of dead leaves and twigs and tossed them into the wheelbarrow.

"To the wine cellar. And let us be quick about it! We must be gone before Albert sees us."

Their business at the palace concluded, Haydn and Johann emerged an hour later from the West Wing, and climbed down the wide stone steps that led away from the building. Pausing on the lowest step, Haydn brought out his silver timepiece from his coat pocket. Rosalie had still not returned from the Musicians' Quarters, but was expected back any moment.

They were so close to bringing this affair to a close, he could barely contain his impatience. He had overheard enough to be convinced he was right. But it would be foolhardy, he knew, to attempt to convince His Serene Highness on the basis of evidence he had garnered by listening in at Rahier's door. But if Rosalie were to succeed in her task...

He looked over his shoulder at Johann. "We may as well wait for her. We have a quarter of an hour left before our appointment with Max Rosen. And I would rather issue my instructions in person than leave a note, and risk it falling into the wrong hands."

Johann murmured a brief assent as he came down the steps behind his brother. A few moments elapsed; Haydn glanced every now and again at his timepiece, and was about to leave when a voice spoke behind him.

"Herr Haydn."

Haydn turned his head hesitantly in the direction of the voice. His name had been uttered in such hushed tones, he wondered whether it was really a voice that he had heard, or just the wind rustling through the bare branches of the trees in the inner courtyard.

There was no one behind him, but he heard the voice again: "Herr Haydn!" It sounded a little more urgent now. "Over here!"

"It is Rosalie, I believe. From the kitchen courtyard." Johann pointed toward the trellised archway thickly covered with climbing rose to the left of the West Wing building. Rosalie's dark curls could be seen poking out from behind the archway.

"The trunk, Herr Haydn! We have found it," she said as soon as Haydn and Johann followed her under the arch into the roughly cobblestoned kitchen courtyard. The appetizing aroma of roasting fowl and baking bread filled the air as they approached the rough-hewn wooden cellar door set into the wall.

"Down there, is it?" Haydn squinted down at the ladder that led into the depths of the cellar. The thought of dust and dirt sullying his immaculate blue and gold livery gave him a momentary twinge of misgiving, but he soon overcame it. His mother had cultivated an aversion to uncleanliness in all her children, and even in the days of his extreme poverty he had striven to abide by those childhood principles. Still, what was a little dirt in a matter of such consequence?

"Here—" He took off his coat and gloves, but looked around him, nevertheless, for a clean spot. His gaze fell on a clean wooden bench near the cellar door. "Ah! We may keep our things here." He laid the garments neatly on the bench, and waited for Johann to do the same before lowering himself onto the ladder.

Light from the windows close to the cellar ceiling fell on the travel trunk, which was resting on one of its shorter sides on a pile of old rags on the cellar floor. The maids had found some torn sacks to cover the wooden cellar floor, but had found the trunk much too heavy to do more than push it down the ladder.

With Johann assisting him, Haydn pulled the trunk down so it rested on its wide base, then knelt down to examine it. He wiggled at the red brass clasp, which seemed to be wedged against the drawbolt.

"It appears to be unlocked," he said in surprise, when the clasp suddenly yielded to his efforts and fell open. He carefully lifted the lid up. "And—"

"*It is empty!*" Johann peered over his brother's shoulders into the bare chest, his calm ruffled. He knelt down beside his brother, and reached into the trunk.

"Empty?" Rosalie and Greta exclaimed with one voice. They had by now clambered down the ladder into the cellar, and looked at each other. "But how can that be? It was heavy enough when we dragged it here."

They watched as Haydn and Johann patted the sides and bottom of the case, examining every corner of it.

"It is solidly made," Johann said, "and has no false bottoms or secret compartments that I can detect."

"But, why should Albert be concerned about an empty, old travel trunk, Herr Haydn?" Rosalie sounded perplexed. "There was no reason for him to be at the Musicians' Quarters at that hour this morning. He must have meant to retrieve the trunk from its hiding place."

But Haydn, stroking his chin as he regarded the trunk, had nothing to say. He was pondering the same question. What had Albert wanted with an empty trunk? Had he known it was empty?

It was Johann, who replied. "If Albert concealed the trunk to discredit you, Rosalie, he would have realized his initial hiding place would not serve for very long. He planned, no doubt, to dispose of the travel trunk more permanently. After all, if it were ever to be found, it would prove beyond any doubt that you were not lying."

201

"Besides, raising the additional question of why our former violinist was so eager to retrieve an empty travel trunk in the first place," Haydn murmured, as he rose slowly to his feet.

Johann stood up as well. "It may not have been empty at the time. Albert must have had the sense to remove its contents before he moved it out of sight."

"Yes, I suppose that is possible," Haydn conceded. It was a plausible enough explanation, but for some reason it failed to convince him. He knew not why.

CHAPTER TWENTY-FIVE

A thickset man with a morose expression awaited the Kapellmeister and his brother in the alley behind the wine merchant's mansion. He had evidently made his morning delivery of vegetables, for the sturdy rack-wagon against which he leant was empty save for a few baskets pushed to the back.

Max Rosen followed Haydn and Johann into the alley. "This is Helmut's brother, Klaus." He gestured toward the peasant. "I have instructed him to drive you to his brother's farmhouse in Mörbisch am See."

Haydn received the news of their destination without comment, but when the wine merchant returned to his house, he said in a low voice to Johann, "István seems to have a great number of friends in that small village." He climbed gingerly into the back of the wagon, sitting on the sacks the vegetable seller had spread on the floor.

"Then, that may be where he is hiding." Johann eyed the old nag harnessed to the wagon with some misgiving before climbing into the narrow space beside his brother.

The nag, gently prodded, began to move forward at a comfortable trot. They had barely turned out of the Jewish Quarter when a carriage began following them at a discreet distance.

"The Police Commissioner," Haydn observed with a satisfied nod.

In a carriage, the six mile drive to the village on the banks of Lake Neusiedl would have taken no more than an hour. In Klaus's rack-wagon, driving slowly on the icy roads, it took nearly two. Sitting squashed together in the wagon, the brothers felt the painful impact of every bump and jolt in the road.

It was with considerable relief that they descended from the wagon when it pulled up outside a small, ramshackle cottage not far from the swampy meadows and reedy banks of the lake. Klaus hurried in through the open door into the narrow courtyard, going toward a gaunt-featured man in the back. After a whispered consultation, the two men came forward.

"What is it you want to know, gentlemen?" Helmut gazed sullenly at his visitors.

"That manuscript that you brought to Herr Rosen—who gave it to you?" Haydn scrutinized the peasant's features, and then took in the courtyard in a quick glance. Could István be hiding in this little hovel?

"He was a musician from the palace"—Helmut's eyes traveled over Haydn's court uniform—"such as yourself." His eyes met Haydn's in a defiant stare.

"Did he tell you that?" Johann asked quietly.

"He didn't have to. I have seen him often enough"—a sly smile briefly replaced the surly expression on Helmut's features—"outside the Widow Heindl's house."

"What did he want you to do with it?" Haydn glanced at Johann as he asked the question. Helmut was proving to be even more uncommunicative than he had expected.

Helmut folded his arms. "I have already told Herr Rosen why your musician gave me the manuscript. It was as payment."

"Payment for what?" Haydn demanded, finding himself increasingly annoyed by the peasant's terse responses. His eyes drifted toward the three small, grubbily dressed boys, who were peeking out of the barn door at the back. He had caught a glimpse of a fawn-colored leather purse in their hands, and thought he recognized it.

"For giving him shelter from the storm. It was a windy and stormy night, you will recall. The snow was pelting down. Your musician asked for a night's shelter. He had no money with him, so..." Helmut lifted his shoulders as his voice broke off mid-sentence, as though he saw little need to even complete the thought.

Haydn regarded him for a space. The peasant had uttered his explanation in a flat monotone, and stood motionless and stiff before them as though he cared not at all whether his visitors believed his story or not. His attitude of disinterest grated on Haydn's nerves.

Just then, the boys ran out of the barn, dropping the leather pouch on the mud floor of the courtyard. Haydn's eyes were drawn toward it. He was certain he knew now whose it was. He glanced around his squalid surroundings, deliberately letting his mouth curl in disgust.

"A night in your farmhouse must be expensive, indeed, for my musician to have left not only a valuable manuscript, but"— he strode toward the barn, snatched up the pouch, and held it up—"his purse as well!"

He tossed the purse into Johann's hands.

"It is his. It has his name stitched on the inside," Johann said, drawing the mouth open to examine the interior. He looked up at his brother. "He *must* be here, then!"

Haydn peered into the barn, but saw nothing save for two pigs, a cow, and a few scrawny fowl. He turned toward the peasant. "Where is my musician, Helmut?"

He thought he detected a glimmer of fear in the peasant's eyes, but it was gone a moment later, lost in the surly expression that had descended upon his features.

"Why should he be here, gentlemen?" Helmut's voice sounded hoarse. "He stayed the night, and was gone at daybreak." He jutted his chin at the purse in Johann's hands. "He only left the purse because my children took a fancy to it."

"Did your children also take a fancy to his ring, then?" Johann, feeling around inside the purse, had drawn forth a large, ruby ring from it. He held it out in his hand.

The sight of the ring caused Haydn's eyes to widen. It was the selfsame ostentatious ornament that had graced his violinist's forefinger. He looked toward Helmut for an explanation, but the peasant's mouth was set into a stubborn line.

"Your musician is not here, gentlemen," he repeated. "I have nothing more to say."

Haydn's patience had at last worn thin. "I would to God, it had not come to this," he burst out, striding toward the farmhouse door. "But you leave me no choice. You will not find the Police Commissioner quite so accommodating as I. He will drag the truth out of you, come what may!"

"What can István have said to the man to so cow him into submission?" Haydn cried out on the ride home. The brothers had hired a carriage from a little inn in the village square after the Police Commissioner had led Helmut away in handcuffs. "I saw the fear in Helmut's eyes. It was brief, but unmistakable."

This endless chasing after his elusive violinist was getting as tiresome as an overused false reprise. Every fresh lead brought about a new development rather than bringing the affair to a close. How often had they thought they were close to finding István, only to find him just beyond reach?

"I would imagine it is more a question of what he has done—or threatened to do, more likely," Johann gently reminded him. "Our former violinist has already killed one man. What would stop him from killing another?"

Haydn nodded. His brother, he supposed, was right. The imposter seemed to have no compunctions in dispatching anyone who was in his way, and the peasant had young children to consider.

His eyes drifted toward the window. The carriage was driving through a narrow alley lined with a row of whitewashed farmhouses, sturdier, but no larger than the run-down dwelling they had just left. Was his violinist in one of them?

"He could find no better hiding place than this." He motioned toward the small structures passing them by. "Who would think to look for him in one of these farmhouses?"

"And yet there was no trace of him, other than these—" Johann lifted up the fawn-colored pouch with its ring from the seat beside him.

"No, there was not," Haydn agreed quietly. He took the purse from his brother. The Police Commissioner's men had combed through Helmut's tiny dwelling, but their search had yielded nothing. He held it up, regarding the soft leather pouch as it slowly twirled on its drawstrings.

"Suppose István had briefly left his hiding place to meet Marlene, perhaps, or on some other mission," he began slowly, "why would he leave this purse behind? True, the purse contains no money, but the ring itself is worth several hundred gulden. I cannot recall ever seeing him without it. So, why take it off now?"

Haydn glanced at his brother, his confidence shaken by the discoveries of the past few hours.

"If he had seen us and fled, he might in his haste have left the purse behind. But the ring..." Johann's voice trailed off, equally at a loss to fathom István's behavior. "Can he have bought Helmut's silence with it?" he ventured at last.

"A few gulden would have sufficed for that. Besides, if István needed money as desperately as he did, this ring—ugly, though it is—would have fetched a goodly sum." Haydn leant back in his seat as another disquieting thought occurred to him. "And if he stole the manuscript to meet his own need, why give it to Helmut?"

"That, at least, is easily explained, brother. He could hardly have approached the wine merchant or even Herr Weisenstein himself. He must have coerced Helmut to serve as a go-between."

"But why not attempt to sell the ring at the same time?" Haydn brought the ring out from its purse, and scrutinized it. "Only look at the size of the ruby, and the quantity of gold lavished on the design! It is worth three times as much as the manuscript—at the most conservative estimate, at that. And, I imagine, could be more easily and quickly sold, beside."

He rubbed his finger against the wide gold wings on either side of the ruby. "It is a singularly ugly ring to be sure. And there is some kind of blemish in the stone." He held the ring up against the window. The afternoon sun lit up the crimson jewel, revealing a dark, almost black, discoloration in the center of the stone.

As he turned the ring to the light, his finger accidentally slid against one of the wings. It gave way, taking his finger along with it. What was happening? Had the slight pressure from his touch caused the piece to break off? His finger slid further down, slipping off the edge to expose the wing tip. It was still attached to the ring, but now pointed downward. Almost immediately, a small needle sprang out of the gold bezel in which the stone was set.

The sudden movement caused Johann to draw back. His eyes slowly rose to meet Haydn's. "It was Count Nádasdy who gave this ring to our violinist. That can only mean one thing—"

"That this is the weapon with which they meant to do the vile deed." The carriage was not cold, and yet Haydn felt as though all the warmth had been driven out of his body. What diabolical mind had created a weapon such as this? He flicked the wing up, causing the needle to retract into the bezel, but not before a drop of thick fluid had fallen on to his breeches.

"The needle must be poisoned," Johann said, as the droplet spread over a gold button. He drew forth a handkerchief, and wiped the button clean. "The metal in which the stone is set is large enough to serve as a receptacle."

Haydn nodded, feeling gently around the bezel to see if he could discover a means of revealing the secret compartment. He inspected the wings again, tugging at the edges. "Ah! They extend outward so." A small compartment slid out of the side of the bezel as he spoke. "And that is our receptacle. Filled to the brim, as you suspected."

"Poison of some kind, I'll warrant." Johann lowered his head to examine the thick, copper-hued substance. "Herr Hipfl might be able to tell us what it is." He straightened up as Haydn pushed the wings back, allowing the small container to slide back in position.

Haydn replaced the ring in the leather purse in which they had found it. "It is a clever plan. A small poisonous pinprick delivered in the act of clasping the victim's hand in a warm greeting." A numb, cold sensation ran through his body again at the thought. It receded as another thought occurred to him.

He raised his eyes toward Johann. "But it makes even less sense, then, that István would leave his ring lying carelessly around. I can only think of one explanation, but..." He shook his head. No, that made no sense either.

———

"It is the juice of the rock poppy, gentlemen." There was a gleam of appreciation in Herr Hipfl's eyes as he looked up from his scrutiny of the reddish-brown fluid in the bezel of the ring Haydn had found.

"A medicament! Is that all it is?" Haydn could barely conceal his disappointment. There was nothing sinister in his violinist concealing a medicinal tonic in his ring. It was a discovery of no significance at all.

They were in the barber-surgeon's large, book-lined study. A faintly acrid aroma of alcohol clung to the room—arising, no doubt, from the glass jars arranged on the bookshelves. Each contained an assortment of strange blobs floating in a murky fluid.

Herr Hipfl leaned forward with the air of one about to make a revelation. "Yes, Herr Haydn, but only in strictly prescribed doses. A large amount, such as this"—he glanced down at the small, gold receptacle in his palm—"injected directly into the bloodstream could induce a sudden, but fatal cessation of the heart."

Johann turned pale. "And all the assassin would need is an opportunity to grasp the Empress's hand! A simple enough task for a virtuoso like István."

The barber-surgeon, still intent on his examination of the poison, made no reply. He had brought the gold fluid-filled receptacle up to his nose, and was sniffing curiously at it. "There is a hint of a floral fragrance—very faint, but unmistakable. The sap from Christ's crown, if I am not mistaken."

"Poisonous, too, I suppose," Haydn said flatly. What other reason could there be for its presence in the receptacle?

"It can be in sufficiently strong doses. But I doubt there is enough of it in this mixture." The barber-surgeon was still sniffing at the fluid. "It does induce drowsiness, even in small doses. Injected with this concoction, Her Majesty would be overtaken with a powerful desire to sleep. Several hours later, the juice of the rock poppy would wield its effect on her heart, and..." He spread his hands wide.

"And, given Her Majesty's advanced years and her grief-stricken state—" Johann stared at the barber-surgeon, aghast.

"The best physician in the world would have no cause for suspicion." Herr Hipfl nodded. "A fiendish plan to be sure. It is fortunate you were able to recover the ring." He turned toward Haydn, but the Kapellmeister stared straight ahead of him, his brow creased.

"If István was to act as the assassin with this ring as his weapon," he began to murmur slowly, "why..."

"—did he *leave* the ring behind?" The barber-surgeon leaned forward eagerly. "He must have been close at hand, gentlemen." He gripped the armrest of his couch. "I trust the Police Commissioner will have thought to search the neighboring farmhouses. With the houses abutting each other so closely, it would be the work of a minute to flee from one structure to the next."

"A likely enough explanation." Haydn stroked his chin pensively. "But, why leave at all? *That* is the question."

"Ach so!" the barber-surgeon responded doubtfully. The expression on his face suggesting he suspected Haydn of having abandoned his senses. He turned toward the Kapellmeister's brother as though seeking an explanation.

But Johann was gazing at his brother blankly. He opened his mouth to speak when a sharp rap on the door interrupted him.

A servant brought in a note, and handed it to the barber-surgeon.

"From the Police Commissioner," the barber-surgeon informed his visitors as he tore open the note. His features tightened as he perused its contents. Having read through the note, he set it down on his desk, and turned toward the Kapellmeister and his brother.

"Your violinist has been found, gentlemen."

CHAPTER TWENTY-SIX

"**D**ead!" Haydn stared down at the rigid form of his missing violinist lying supine within the dense undergrowth of reeds. The barber-surgeon was already on his knees, gently probing the stiff, bloated features of the dead man. The man they had known as Bartó glared sightlessly up at the Kapellmeister over Herr Hipfl's shoulder.

"Dead!" Haydn said again, recoiling slightly from the bulging eyes that held his gaze. He moved his eyes hastily down only to see a gloveless hand reaching stiffly toward the frozen waters of Lake Neusiedl. After all the trouble the man had caused, he was dead!

Haydn wrenched his gaze away from the lifeless form, and turned toward the Police Commissioner, who was standing on a dry patch of land above the tall grey-brown fronds at the edge of the lake.

"But how...?" he began to ask when the sudden realization that István's death was not so very unexpected after all made his voice falter. His eyes drifted back toward the body. To his relief, the barber-surgeon had closed the eyelids. But for his unnatural stillness, István appeared to be in a deep sleep; quite oblivious to both the barber-surgeon's examination and the Bürgermeister's avid scrutiny.

The Police Commissioner cautiously stepped forward, eyeing the reeds that surrounded him with distaste. The ruffles on his fine linen shirt and the flamboyant cut of his richly embroidered coat marked him as a city man, ill at ease in the somewhat rustic atmosphere of Eisenstadt.

"It matters not how, Herr Kapellmeister. As long as he is dead." He craned his neck forward in the direction of the barber-surgeon. "And I trust he *is* quite dead, Herr Hipfl." At the barber-surgeon's brief nod, he rubbed his hands together. "Excellent!"

How, Haydn wondered, could the man take such relish in the miserable fact? He had hoped to discover his violinist alive, and brought to justice.

"Strangled, I believe," the barber-surgeon said. He pointed to the bruising on the dead man's neck. "He did not in all likelihood see his assailant. Were it not for this cold, the body would have long since lost its stiffness."

The Bürgermeister, who had been hunched over the barber-surgeon's shoulder, straightened up.

"Well, at least the danger is over," he rumbled, a deep note of satisfaction in his voice. "To think he was lying dead here all the while we were scouring the woods in Kleinhöflein for him!" He turned toward the Police Commissioner."What made you think to look for him here, Herr Lichtenegger?"

"It was the peasant the Kapellmeister was so good as to turn over to me this morning." The Police Commissioner turned toward Haydn, his lips parted in a thin smile. "The threat of a charge of treason provided sufficient inducement to get him to talk."

"He has confessed to his involvement, then?" Johann's voice rose a third above its normal level. His eyes flickered toward his brother.

But Haydn remained quiet. What had Helmut confessed to? The momentary flare of fear he had detected that morning in the peasant's eyes had made him question whether Helmut was a willing accomplice in the dissidents' plot. Now Haydn wondered whether the poor man was involved at all. If that was the case, how could the Police Commissioner's threat have compelled him to speak?

It had not, evidently. A brief glint of anger flashed in Herr Lichtenegger's dark blue eyes in response to Johann's question. "Quite the contrary, Master Johann! He claims, in fact, to have stumbled upon that man"—he gestured toward the dead man—"on the night of the storm.

"The peasant saw him lying face down amongst the reeds, and went toward him. Discovering the man to be beyond any help, he was tempted into rifling through his pockets in search of any valuables he could find. The very items you have already recovered, Herr Haydn."

"Ach so!" Haydn nodded eagerly. Helmut's strange behavior was beginning to make sense now. "He had robbed a dead man, and failed to report the corpse. Small wonder, he was afraid! The poor man must have thought we suspected he had a hand in killing my violinist, and I must confess, the thought did cross my mind. But—"

A delicate snort interrupted the Kapellmeister. "I am glad you find his tale plausible," the Police Commissioner said. "As for myself"—he shrugged lightly—"I am more inclined to believe there was a falling out between the two men that resulted in the death of your violinist."

He shrugged again. "He would hang for it, but for the fact that it is an assassin he has made away with. As it stands, the peasant is more likely to be commended than punished."

"But the dead man was strangled from behind, was he not, Herr Hipfl?" The Bürgermeister's bushy white eyebrows came together in a puzzled frown.

"And what of that, Herr Groer?" The Police Commissioner regarded the Bürgermeister with polite disinterest.

The Bürgermeister's perpetually pink cheeks brightened to a dark shade of plum. It was the barber-surgeon who, glancing up from his examination, calmly replied, "It would suggest a premeditated crime." He traced the dark lines around the dead man's neck.

"The bruising is deep and, from the looks of it, death came swiftly to him. His assailant must have been a man as strong as he, if not stronger."

Haydn pursed his lips. "It is hardly likely to have been Helmut, then," he said, recalling the peasant's gaunt form. "A man *so* ill-fed would have been no match for my violinist. And even if they *were* well-matched," he continued, "István had the means to defend himself." He inclined his head at the leather pouch in Johann's hands.

The barber-surgeon nodded vigorously. "Poison!" he explained in response to the questioning look the Bürgermeister directed at him before turning toward the Police Commissioner.

"I examined it myself, Herr Lichtenegger," he continued as Johann brought out the ring, and illustrated its mechanism to the Police Commissioner.

The Police Commissioner peered down into the vacant receptacle. His gaze seemed to linger on the empty hollow. Then his head pivoted slowly toward the barber-surgeon, his eyes, like twin icicles, boring into the other's gray orbs, while a single eyebrow began to arch upward.

"Naturally, I took the precaution of emptying out the poison." The barber-surgeon's cheeks flushed hotly as he spoke.

"Indeed! And how, pray, was the dead man supposed to poison his attacker, if he was attacked from behind?" The Police Commissioner coldly surveyed the company around him as he asked the question.

"No." He shook his head. "I see nothing to suggest that the peasant did not kill our assassin. A mere woman, with the element of surprise on her side, could have easily overpowered your violinist, Herr Haydn." The Police Commissioner turned sharply on his heels.

"It would have to be a very tall woman, indeed!" the barber-surgeon murmured, but it was unlikely the Police Commissioner heard his words.

"I shall still expect an autopsy, Herr Hipfl," he called over his shoulder as he strode off. "And a detailed report of your findings from it."

Unwilling to venture into the Rehearsal Room while the Kapellmeister's middle brother continued to occupy it, Rosalie and Greta waited until Michael had led his troupe of singers and the musicians he had pressed into service out of the castle to the Parish Church of Kleinhöflein.

"It will take us all day to carry those heavy cases down," Greta grumbled, looking about her as she and Rosalie crossed the hallway toward the staircase. "And whatever shall we say if one of the musicians should see us?"

"Why, that His Serene Highness wants every case polished in honor of Her Majesty's visit." Rosalie hurried across the floor, her shoes lightly tapping upon the black and white tiled floor. At Greta's gasp, she stopped, and turned to face her friend.

"It is not *so* far from the truth." With a slight shrug, Rosalie spread her hands out, palms facing upward. "Herr Haydn did ask us to polish those cases. And who is to say the Prince didn't ask him to see to it?"

"Well, in that case..." Greta paused, her hand on the newel post at the foot of the staircase. Her head swiveled around, and came to rest on a young footman standing idly by one of the Chinese vases a few feet down the hallway. She regarded him speculatively for a few minutes, and then strode over, calling out in a loud voice:

"You, there! Did no one tell you? His Serene Highness wants all the violin cases brought down from the Rehearsal Room. You had better get on with it!"

214

The footman visibly blenched. "B-but..." he stammered, looking over his shoulder at the Estates Director's office.

"Well, don't just stand there!" Greta urgently prodded the young man in the ribs. "Get a move on!"

But even with the footman's help it took the better part of an hour to heft every violin case down from the Rehearsal Room to the large, well-lit room opposite the kitchen where the maids had decided to work.

The footman cast a doubtful glance at Rosalie. "Are you sure, the Prince only asked for the violin cases to be polished?"

Rosalie surveyed the stack of oblong leather and wood cases standing against the walls of the room.

"I think we had better get these polished before we bring any more down," she said at last, gently ushering the footman to the door. There was hardly any point, she thought, in bringing down every single case when all they had to do was examine Albert's.

"Mind, you don't go too far," Greta called after the departing footman. "We shall need you to carry these up again." She looked around her in dismay. They were surrounded by cases made of polished mahogany or dyed leather. "Now, which one of these is Albert's?"

"It must be one of the leather cases." Rosalie pulled out one of the wooden cases, and pointed to the golden griffin carved into the wood above the brass handle of the case. Perched on a golden crown, it carried a sword in one of its talons and three roses in the other. "All of the wooden cases have the Prince's coat of arms engraved on them."

"Well, I suppose that does narrow it down a little," Greta reluctantly conceded. She made a face as her eyes fell on the leather violin cases. Rosalie's eyes followed her friend's gaze. There were, unfortunately, far more leather cases than wooden ones.

"Let us begin with the gray ones," she suggested, pulling one of the gray cases onto the table in the center of the room. "There are not very many of those." She lifted the brass hasp, and peered inside the blue felt interior.

Greta walked around the table, peering closely at the case from all sides. "I can see no emblem of the kind Herr Haydn showed us." From her apron pocket, she pulled out the rough drawing the Kapellmeister had left with them. "A large raven, seen from the side, holding a ring in its mouth."

"And there is nothing on the lid either." Rosalie brought the lid down, and pulled the hasp over the brass loop attached to the side.

There were four more gray cases left to examine. The next two were no different from the first one. Plain on the outside with a felt lining on the inside. With a sigh, Greta went toward the remaining stack of cases and lifted up the third gray case.

"This one is Sanyi's, I think." Rosalie squinted at a small plate affixed to the side of the charcoal gray case Greta had set on the table. "His name is etched into the metal."

Greta lifted the lid, and uttered a small cry of amazement at the rich, satin-lined interior. "What a beautiful case! Wherever did your brother find the money to buy it?"

"It was given to him," Rosalie replied shortly. "By Count Nádasdy's companion—the one who was always with him when he visited the castle." Her lips puckered. To think that her brother had benefited from the patronage of a traitor like the Count!

Greta carried the last gray case to the table. "I wonder what became of him. The companion, I mean. He was always at the Count's side. But yesterday, he was nowhere to be seen." She lifted the case up to the table, and uttered another small cry.

"Look, Rosalie! This one has a large bird stitched into the leather. I suppose that could be a raven. But its wings are outspread. And it has nothing in its beak." She opened the lid.

The red satin lining of the case was even more splendid than Sándor's violin case. A name was embroidered in large, ornate letters on the side of the case below the hinge attaching the lid to the case. The maids exchanged a glance.

"*Albert!*" they cried with one voice.

Greta sniffed. "If you ask me, that emblem is close enough to be suspicious. Very suspicious, indeed! Herr Haydn asked us to look for a bird"—she jabbed at the drawing the Kapellmeister had given them—"and here is a bird!"

A glint of metal caught Rosalie's eyes. "There is something in here!" She reached into the case, and felt around the satiny interior until her fingers touched a small object.

"A ring!" Her startled gaze met Greta's. "*It looks just like Master Bartó's ring!*" Her voice was barely above a whisper.

Greta took the ring from her, and held it up to the window. A ray of light struck the ruby, illuminating the dark shape inscribed in the center.

"A raven! Just like the one in Herr Haydn's drawing." She turned toward Rosalie, holding up the drawing against the ring.

———❧———

Johann watched as the Police Commissioner stepped into his waiting carriage. "I have never met a more stubborn man," he said. "His mind seems to be quite made up on the subject. And yet all the evidence points away from the peasant."

"Not to mention that we have a more plausible suspect," Haydn murmured as Herr Lichtenegger's carriage bore him off. His mind reverted to the conversation he had overheard that morning between Herr Rahier and his nephew. His eyes rested vacantly on the dead man, idly following the barber-surgeon's movements as he conducted his examination. How could the Estates Director have known what had befallen his violinist?

"And he warned of the possibility"—the slowly dawning implication of the memory made his voice rise—"the very day before István disappeared!" His eyes drifted toward the lake. It had, in truth, been more of a threat than a warning.

He had spoken loud enough for the Bürgermeister to have caught his muttered words. "Who warned you? And of what? What are you on about, Herr Kapellmeister?" He stared at Haydn, then turned toward Johann.

But the barber-surgeon called out before either Haydn or Johann could respond. "There is a note here! In the dead man's coat pocket." He unfolded the sheet, cast his eye over it, and then looked up.

"He must have been quite genuinely in love with that poor barmaid he seduced"— he handed the note to Haydn—"If that is what called him out the night of the storm!"

"Marlene, it seems, was in danger of losing his child!" Johann peered down at the note his brother held out for him. He scanned the faces of the men around him. "But if that is what called him out—and it is a plausible enough explanation—he cannot have intended to leave his position that night."

217

CHAPTER TWENTY-SEVEN

Haydn, still frowning down at the note, made no reply. His mind, already in turmoil at the unexpected discovery of his violinist's dead body, was now reeling with the countless questions the note had raised.

It was the Bürgermeister who responded to Johann's remark. "But, his violin is still missing, is it not, Master Johann? The instrument we found in the woods belonged to the man he killed. Who else, but your violinist, could have taken the missing Stadlmann?"

The barber-surgeon was emptying out the dead man's pockets in an attempt to lighten the weight of the body. "I am surprised he even thought to take it with him, considering the state he must have been in!"

"And he was in a state!" Haydn spoke softly. "Why, even the night watchman who let him out that night remarked upon it. But..." He studied the note again.

"But he made no mention of the violin!" Johann peered down at the reeds surrounding them, as though expecting to find a violin hidden in the undergrowth. "If István brought it out with him, it should have been here."

"And it was not amongst the peasant's belongings?" The Bürgermeister peered anxiously at the Kapellmeister and his brother. His brows drew together into a deep frown when Johann shook his head. "Why would his killer steal his violin, if not to—"

"Make us believe he had left," Johann finished the sentence. His face looked white and drawn. He turned toward his brother, but Haydn was still staring at the note the barber-surgeon had found.

The Bürgermeister rubbed his chin, his brow beginning to wrinkle again. "But how could the murderer have known your violinist was off to see his mistress?" He glanced down at the corpse.

The barber-surgeon was carefully cutting open the dead man's boots. "The killer must have been stalking him," he remarked, his head still bent over his work. "Do you recall how unreasonably suspicious he was of everyone? Even to the point of accusing you of spying upon him, Herr Groer!"

The barber-surgeon's words were greeted with silence, the Bürgermeister merely nodding a response.

It was Johann who spoke a few minutes later. "That was a week before he disappeared, was it not, Herr Groer." He turned to look at Haydn. "And he made the same accusation of you a few days after, brother." His eyes turned toward the corpse, as he softly continued, "At the time, it seemed like the imaginings of an over-fevered brain. Who knows, but there may have been more to it."

The Kapellmeister nodded, but with so abstracted an air, it was clear to all he had barely been paying attention to their speculations. It was, in fact, quite another matter that had been troubling Haydn since the barber-surgeon had handed him the note.

"But if Marlene was in danger of miscarrying," he spoke at last, uttering the words so quietly, his listeners had to lean forward to hear him, "why did the Widow Heindl tell us she was not expecting István on the night of the storm?"

The wind gently rustling through the reeds on the lakeshore sounded ominously loud in the silence that followed the Kapellmeister's words. He scanned each man's face in turn. "I have a distinct memory of her saying something to that effect," he said, a little more firmly this time.

Footsteps clattered on the stone floor of the corridor outside, startling the maids. They must have stopped at the kitchen, for the next sound that came to their ears was that of the kitchen door being opened.

"Greta! Rosalie!" a voice called.

The maids looked at each other in dismay. *Albert*! What in the name of heaven was he doing down here? Rosalie jerked her chin at the ring

Greta was still holding up against the wide shaft of sunlight streaming in through the window.

"Quick! Better get rid of that thing," she hissed.

Greta dropped the ring down her blouse, and shoved the drawing of the emblem into her apron pocket just as Albert thrust his head in at the doorway. The door opened wider, revealing Albert's tall, slender form.

"Ah! There you are!" Albert entered the room, a peeved expression on his face. "I have been looking all over for you?" He gazed curiously around the room, his eyes lingering on the cases piled on the floor. "Polishing cases, are you? But where are your rags and your tin of polish?"

The maids gave a guilty start. In their eagerness to examine Albert's case, they had completely forgotten their ostensible reason for having all the violin cases brought down in the first place.

"Never you mind where the rags and polish are!" Greta tossed her head. "As though the cases didn't need to be inspected for repairs, first."

Rosalie twisted her fingers around the handle on Albert's case. He seemed too distracted to notice anything was amiss. Still, if Greta didn't stop talking, she would give the game away.

But Greta couldn't seem to help herself. She pointed to the case on the table. "Not every case is new like yours, you know! Why some of these—"

"What is it you need, Albert?" Rosalie interrupted, stemming her friend's flow of words.

"And next time, ring for one of the maids," Greta added, appearing to have regained her senses. "You've no business down here!"

Albert's chin jutted out stubbornly. "Why shouldn't I come down to the kitchen?" His eyes moved toward Rosalie. "Your brother comes down often enough. And it was he who told me you would be down here. He saw you bringing those violin cases down."

He drew nearer to the table, and peered into the satin-lined interior of the open violin case. "I wonder if it could have fallen in there?" he murmured.

"What?" croaked Greta, sending Rosalie an uneasy glance.

"My ring." Albert raised his eyes from the violin case, and gazed anxiously at them. "Have you seen it? It must have fallen off my finger. I've looked for it everywhere"—he searched his surroundings as though expecting to see his ring miraculously emerge out of thin air—"but it's nowhere to be found!"

Rosalie's eyes drifted briefly toward Greta's bosom. She forced herself to tear her eyes away, hoping Albert had not noticed the direction of her gaze. But Albert, intent on feeling around inside his violin case, appeared to have seen nothing.

"A large gold ring set with an enormous ruby. Very valuable, besides being of historic significance. The stone itself had the emblem of the great Matthias Corvinus inscribed into it!"

"The *what* of *what*!" Greta gasped out, her voice sounding quite hoarse.

"The emblem of Matthias Corvinus," Albert repeated irritably.

The maids stared expressionlessly back at him. He rolled his eyes, misinterpreting the blank look on their faces.

"Oh, how ignorant can you be? You"—he thrust his chin at Greta—"are only German, and may be excused from knowing very much of Hungarian history. But you!" He turned toward Rosalie. "What is your excuse?"

Receiving no reply, he sighed heavily. "The stone is inscribed with a raven, much like this one on my violin case." He brought down the lid, and pointed to the bird embroidered on the leather case. "But on the ring, the bird's wings are tucked in, and it holds a gold ring in its mouth."

He opened the lid, and patted down the interior again. "I had it on when I opened my violin case this morning. But..." He continued to prod at the heavily padded corners. "No, I don't suppose it is in here, after all."

He closed the case, and turned to leave. "Let me know if you should find it."

Rosalie was about to murmur a response, when Greta piped out just as Albert opened the door, "We found Master Bartó's missing travel trunk this morning. It was empty!"

Rosalie glared at her friend. What mad impulse had moved Greta to blurt out that bit of news?

Albert turned at the door, and stared coldly at Greta. "Have you two nothing better to do than to go on about an old travel trunk? It was empty!" His lips twisted into a little sneer as he repeated the words in a falsetto meant to mimic Greta's voice. His voice resumed its normal pitch as he went on. "And what wild surmises have you drawn from that, I wonder? Oh, that your Master Bartó was rushing around madly trying to retrieve an empty travel trunk!"

The Widow Heindl must have been peering out of the window, for no sooner had Haydn and Johann approached the sandstone farmhouse than the arched wooden door opened. The midwife burst out onto the street and stood with her arms folded across her ample bosom, an expression of extreme annoyance on her plump features.

"Your violinist is not here, Herr Kapellmeister. He has not been here in days. You may tell the Bürgermeister to call off his men. Standing and staring at my house all day long will not help them find your violinist!"

"No, it will not," Haydn agreed readily enough.

The widow appeared somewhat disconcerted by this remark. She looked suspiciously from the Kapellmeister to his brother. "What brings you here, then?"

Haydn brought out the note they had found in István's coat pocket. He held it out to the widow, as though intending to give it to her, but his fingers retained their firm hold upon the folded sheet of paper.

"It is no concern of ours, of course," he began, his eyes on the note, "but the last time we met, Frau Heindl, I do not recall your making mention of Marlene having nearly lost her child a day or two ago." His gaze bore into her bright blue eyes. "You sent for my violinist"—he released his hold on the note, allowing the widow to take it—"and yet you told us you were not expecting him. How could you have known he would never come?"

The widow held the note before her eyes, squinting at it. Her lips moved silently as she deciphered its contents. Having read the note, she regarded the men before her, a stern expression on her face.

"What kind of tomfoolery is this?" She thrust the note back at Haydn. "Marlene is in no danger of losing her child, delicate though she may be. Who wrote this nonsense? Where did you find it?"

"We would not be here if we knew the identity of the author of that note," Johann replied. "As to where we found it"—he glanced briefly at his brother before letting his gaze return to the widow's face—"it was on our violinist's person."

"On—" the widow seemed to be on the verge of repeating Johann's words, but stopped herself short. "Whatever can you mean, gentlemen?" A look of consternation had replaced the indignant expression on her face. Her eyes flitted from Johann to Haydn.

"Your violinist has been found? But where...?" The widow's voice seemed to crack. She stared over their shoulders as though expecting to see István appear at any moment.

"His body was discovered on the edge of the lake," Haydn said as gently as he could. The poor woman seemed to be taking the news hard. How much worse would it be for the poor barmaid in her care! "We believe he was killed on the night of the storm. He must have been on his way to see Marlene."

"But who...?" The widow's eyes fell on the note. She reached out to retrieve it from Haydn's fingers, and scrutinized it for a moment before returning it. "Then, whoever sent this note meant to lure him to his death," she murmured, seeming profoundly shocked at the thought. "But who would do that?" Her blue eyes regarded Haydn.

"I wish the widow had allowed us to put a few questions to Marlene," Haydn complained on the ride back to the castle. The midwife had, in fact, been quite adamant on the subject, strenuously insisting that Marlene be allowed to reconcile herself to the ill-tidings before being subjected to any further questions.

Haydn let out a heavy breath. "We would be further on in this matter if we could only get clarification on a few points.

"When Michael and I met her, Marlene implied István was in some kind of danger. She accused me of disregarding his pleas for help. We were unable to question her any further, then, and now..." He spread his hands wide. Obtaining the information he needed should have been a simple matter. Yet they found themselves thwarted at every turn.

Johann was gazing out the carriage window. They had left the narrow alleys of the little village of Mörbisch am See, and were now driving through open countryside dotted with vineyards and meadows. A small wine tavern, not very different from the one Gerhard owned, drifted past them.

"Did you get the impression, brother," he began, turning slowly from the window, "that Frau Heindl might have had an inkling, however faint, of the identity of the author of that note?"

The effort of recalling the midwife's response to the news of István's murder brought Haydn's brows together. Had Frau Heindl said or done anything that suggested she knew who wanted to lure his violinist to his death?

"It is quite clear that whoever sent István the note must have killed him," he said, thinking aloud. "Given the contents of the note, it must have been someone who knew of his affair with Marlene. And given the missing violin, it was someone who desperately wanted us to believe István had simply left. I can think of only one person—"

"Yes, but there is another who had the same motives. And Frau Heindl would have every reason to conceal his involvement in the matter."

Haydn's frown deepened. What was his brother seeing that he was not? "I am afraid, I do not follow, Johann."

Johann leaned forward. "Ask yourself brother, why would anyone want us to think István had left? Everyone in Eisenstadt was quite convinced he had simply gone. And what was the reason for his departure?"

Haydn had no idea where the questions were tending, but the answer was simple enough. "We assumed he sought to evade his responsibilities toward the woman he had seduced and gotten with child, but—"

"Yes, and who benefited most from that assumption?"

Haydn opened his mouth to respond only to close it a moment later. "Ach so! István had already threatened to leave. That reason would have served Herr Rahier and Albert just as well as any other reason."

A faint memory stirred in his brain. He was able to grasp it, and draw it out into the open. "When I informed Frau Heindl that István had left, she told me she had heard the news from Gerhard, but had thought it was *his envy speaking.* Those were her very words, Johann."

"She must know." Johann sat back in his seat, and nodded. "She is his mother, after all. Marlene was Gerhard's intended before she left him for István—a strong enough reason to hate the man. Besides, Gerhard has been trying to separate them ever since it came out that Marlene was with child."

"And Gerhard was not too happy to know I thought István might have come to harm," Haydn added, more convinced now that Johann was right. "He told Rosalie to inform me I was wasting my time with my suspicions!"

He took his silver timepiece out of his pocket, and gave it a quick glance. "There is time enough, I think, for us to pay Gerhard's wine tavern a visit."

CHAPTER TWENTY-EIGHT

Still muttering to himself, Albert left the room, oblivious to the stunned silence that followed his remarks. Her eyes fixed on the door, Greta leaned over toward Rosalie.

"Did you hear that?" she hissed the moment Albert had pulled the door shut behind him. "He didn't deny the travel trunk was empty!"

"No, he did not." Rosalie stared vacantly at the door. There was something about Albert's behavior that did not quite make sense.

He had practically confessed to being one of the dissidents. The ring they had found left no doubt about the fact. Yet far from being rattled at hearing about the travel trunk, the news appeared only to have elicited his contempt...

Still, they could hardly spend all day trying to make sense of Albert's strange behavior. There were more important matters at hand. With a vigorous shake of her dark curls, she turned toward Greta.

"What possessed you to mention the trunk to him?" Rosalie couldn't help being annoyed. Herr Haydn had repeatedly told them to be on their guard when he issued his instructions that morning. And here was Greta blabbing all they had learned to the very man they were trying to gather evidence against!

Greta waved a plump hand dismissively through the air. "I was only trying to gauge his reaction. I could hardly believe it when he described that ring of his. Why, he even knew what the emblem referred to. But did you see, he didn't bat an eyelid when I mentioned the trunk!"

A note of reluctant admiration sounded in her voice. "Who'd have thought he'd be so brazen?"

Rosalie mumbled out an indistinct response. Her violet eyes, fixed on the door, were shrouded in uncertainty.

"But he was right," she murmured at last. "Why *should* Master Bartó concern himself over an empty travel trunk?"

"Well, for that matter, why should Albert?" retorted Greta. "Obviously the trunk wasn't empty when Albert got his hands on it. Master Johann was right. Albert must have emptied it out before he hid it. The wily scoundrel! That way even if it were found, we'd look like fools if we showed it to His Serene Highness."

"Yes, but..." Rosalie hesitated briefly before turning to face Greta. "What if the trunk really was empty to begin with?" She ignored Greta's snort. "Those branches were so weighed down by the trunk, they would have broken had it been any heavier. And it was heavy enough, empty."

"*Oh!*" Greta stared at Rosalie, biting down on her lip while she considered the matter.

"B...but what did Albert mean by hiding the trunk, then?"

"I don't know." Rosalie absently ran her finger over the raven stitched onto Albert's violin case. "I can't see how he could have had anything to do with it, Master Bartó being a fellow dissident."

"What does that have to do with anything?" Greta demanded.

But Rosalie, still tracing the emblem on Albert's violin case, appeared not to have heard her. "There can be only one reason for anyone to go to such lengths over an empty travel trunk. And, if Albert had no cause..." She raised her eyes toward Greta. "But Gerhard did, didn't he?"

"Gerhard!" Greta sounded bewildered.

Rosalie nodded slowly. "He said the oddest thing when I told him Master Bartó had disappeared."

<hr />

A little over an hour later, the carriage conveying the Kapellmeister and his brother stopped outside Gerhard's wine tavern at the end of Weinberggasse in Kleinhöflein.

Haydn glanced around him as he stepped down from the carriage, and waited for Johann to climb down after him. The late morning sun cast a bright patch of light on the solid wooden door and the warm, grey stone of the tavern. At this early hour, the tavern-keeper was unlikely to have many customers.

Gerhard, wiping down the stone countertop at the far end of the room, looked up as the brothers pushed open the door. A desolate air hung over the empty tavern.

"What brings you here, gentlemen?" The tavern-keeper's eyes flickered briefly in the direction of the plain wooden clock standing by the doorway, before coming to rest on his visitors in an unblinking stare.

"Something you said to one of the palace maids," Haydn responded, returning the tavern-keeper's steady gaze. There was nothing for it, he had decided, but to come straight to the point.

"When my violinist first went missing, I had reason to believe he might have come to harm. Yet you wanted Rosalie, the maid, to inform me that I was wasting my time with my suspicions. What could you have meant by that remark?"

Gerhard bristled at the question. "What do you think I meant, Herr Kapellmeister? Your violinist seduced the woman I love, and then refused to believe he had fathered her child. He struck her—here in this tavern, in my presence—"

"Behavior that he subsequently repented," Johann interrupted. "You can hardly be unaware of his offer of marriage."

"Pah! An offer of marriage, indeed!" Gerhard snorted. "Well, where is he now? He has abandoned her just as I foresaw he would. It would be as well for poor Marlene to wake up to that bitter fact rather than continue to delude herself that he loves her."

"And yet it was this message that brought him out on the night of the storm," Haydn countered as he handed the note to Gerhard. He studied the tavern-keeper's features while the latter ran his eye over the note.

Gerhard was stone-faced when he looked up. "But he never arrived there, did he?" he said, an undertone of triumph lacing the contemptuous tone of his voice.

"No, he did not." Haydn's tone was soft. "He was unfortunately waylaid—"

"Waylaid!" Gerhard repeated, exhibiting the first sign of emotion at the news. He swallowed a few times, then cleared his throat before speaking again. "You have found him, then?"

Haydn nodded, but it was Johann who spoke. "On the banks of the Neusiedl. Not very far from your mother's farmhouse."

"For a man as much in love as Gerhard claims to be, he showed very little signs of concern at the news of Marlene's ill-health," Johann remarked to Haydn as the carriage drove them down the hill toward Eisenstadt.

But the Kapellmeister was not inclined to read any sinister significance into the tavern-keeper's lack of concern. It was entirely understandable, he thought.

"It *was* another man's child she was in danger of losing," he said, then realized the explanation must sound callous to someone like Johann. His younger brother had so little experience with women, he tended toward a rather idealistic notion of the intimate relations between a man and a woman.

He idly contemplated the note sent to his violinist. The hand seemed so familiar. He peered down to examine it more closely when a stray thought diverted his attention.

"Gerhard's reaction, or lack thereof, *was* rather suspicious," he conceded. "Marlene is, after all, as well as can be expected for a woman of her delicate constitution. The news of her miscarriage should have taken him completely by surprise. Yet it did not..."

He peered down at the note again. It was written in a fine hand, the letters well-formed. The hand of an educated man, Haydn reflected. Could a mere tavern-keeper like Gerhard have produced such a fine script? His mother, judging by the effort it had taken her to decipher the contents of the note, was barely literate.

"Why should he be surprised, brother? He was well-aware Marlene was in no danger. Having concocted the story himself, no doubt." Johann seemed quite convinced on the point. "I can think of no other reason for him to send a receipt for that"—he gestured toward the case of wine on the seat beside Haydn—"directly to the Prince."

Thinking that Gerhard was unlikely to willingly provide them with a sample of his penmanship, Haydn had purchased a case of wine. "To be billed to His Serene Highness," he said, offering to take the receipt to the Prince himself. But the tavern-keeper had refused the offer, turning his back on his visitors as he made a note of the order in an old, worn ledger.

Haydn gave the case a fleeting glimpse out of the corner of his eyes. "Fortunately, it is an obstacle that is easily surmounted. Gerhard made a delivery of wine the day after István disappeared. He will have left a receipt with Rosalie. That will do very well for our purposes."

His attention returned to the note. "But if it was Gerhard who killed István," he murmured more to himself than to his brother, "what role did Albert and his uncle play in this affair?" He raised his eyes toward Johann. "That they are both involved is without question."

***

Haydn had no sooner returned to the castle than he was accosted by the Estates Director. He was tempted to disregard Rahier's cold voice calling out to him as he ascended the staircase. But, recalling the Estates Director's fondness for carrying complaints to the Prince, he turned reluctantly around.

Rahier motioned toward his office down the hallway.

"A moment of your time, Herr Kapellmeister." He glared pointedly at Johann "*Alone!*"

"You are a hard man to find these days, Herr Kapellmeister," the Estates Director commented once they were in his office.

Firmly closing the door to his office, he turned toward Haydn. His icy blue eyes held the Kapellmeister's gaze.

"You have two new musicians," he continued when Haydn remained silent, gesturing toward one of the richly upholstered chairs at his desk. "And neither one of them has signed an official contract."

"Yes, but—" Haydn began, following the Estates Director to a desk stacked with papers.

Rahier, still sorting through the papers on his desk, held up a peremptory hand.

"Save your breath, Herr Kapellmeister! The order comes from the Prince himself. Your temporary contracts will not do any more." He raised his eyes briefly from his desk. "An excellent course of action, in my opinion! It will prevent just such a disaster as was recently forced upon us by your violinist's departure."

"Indeed!' Haydn pressed his lips shut. He resolutely thrust aside the memory of the Estates Director's marked lack of concern at István's disappearance. It would do no good to bring it up. But as he watched Rahier sifting through the papers on his desk, his resentment grew.

"How long will this take?" He glanced pointedly at his silver timepiece.

Rahier raised his eyes, and regarded Haydn. "It will take as long as it needs to, Herr Kapellmeister." He straightened up from his desk. "I believe the contracts are in the other chamber."

He walked toward a door behind his desk. At the doorway, he looked over his shoulder.

"I will be back shortly."

Left to himself, Haydn was about to draw out the note found on his violinist's body, when his gaze fell on a document on the Estate Director's desk. The signature at the bottom in Rahier's fine, sloping hand caught his eye. He leaned forward, trying to see if the rest of the document was in the Estates Director's hand, but most of the page was obscured by another sheet lying on top of it.

He raised his eyes, directing a surreptitious glance at the door to the inner chamber. Judging by the sounds emerging from the room, Rahier was still busy looking for his contracts. Haydn leaned forward and, careful not to make the slightest noise, slid the document out from under the paper covering it, and drew it toward himself.

Ach! It was only a receipt, and all it contained was Rahier's signature. Comparing that to the writing on the note was unlikely to yield any firm conclusions. Haydn's eyes drifted toward the top of the receipt.

The House of Stadlmann! But he had not placed an order for a new instrument. Yet, here was a bill of sale for a single violin from the Viennese luthiers...

He raised his head. His startled eyes looked straight into the Estates Director's cold blue gaze.

"What *are* you up to, Herr Kapellmeister?"

"I might ask you the same question, Herr Rahier." Haydn held the receipt up, his finger jabbing at the item listed on it. "A Stadlmann violin bought—"

"Yes, I know what it says, Herr Haydn." The Estates Director winced, seeming flustered for the first time since Haydn had known him. "I bought it for Albert, and charged it to the Prince's estate, thinking you would hire him."

Haydn glanced down at the receipt. "But this is dated September."

"Well, that is when I thought you would hire him," Rahier snapped. "But I was clearly mistaken. You hired...well, we all know *whom* you hired! I would have returned the money to His Serene Highness's exchequer, but you did eventually hire Albert—although, God knows, you took your time about it!" He shrugged. "And the violin now belongs to the Estate, in any case."

Haydn stared down at the receipt. "Then, Albert's violin is his own..." If Rahier had bought Albert his violin, then who had stolen István's instrument? *Gerhard*? But...

"Ahem..." The Estates Director coughed. "...I hope I may count on your discretion...Herr Kapellmeister...!"

"Eh...what?" Haydn looked up at the Estates Director. "Discretion? Yes, yes, of course, Herr Rahier." His eyes fell on the contract in Rahier's hands. There was no time to waste! He could examine Rahier's penmanship later.

"I have been thinking, Herr Rahier." Haydn spoke quickly. "It would be an excellent idea to have *all* our musicians sign new contracts—to avert just such a disaster as another violinist leaving so close to the imperial visit. A clause promising a bonus might do it."

The Estates Director's jaw dropped open, but Haydn left the room before he could say a word.

Released from Rahier's presence, Haydn rushed up the stairs, eager to find Johann. He thrust open the door to the Music Room. An empty room faced him. *Where* was his younger brother?

He pulled the door to a close, and looked uncertainly around him. Had Johann been called to the Rehearsal Room? But the members of the orchestra were in the concert hall below.

Haydn crossed the hallway, walking past a small chamber next to the Rehearsal Room. Out of the corner of his eye, he caught a glimpse of a figure playing the violin. His mind absently identified the strains as the solo part from one of his concertos. Sándor must be...

He stopped abruptly before the Rehearsal Room door. It was *not* Sándor, he had seen. Who then? It could not possibly be... He retraced his steps, poking his head into the doorway of the small chamber.

Albert!

"Your playing seems much-improved!" Haydn was impressed, despite himself. His eyes drifted toward the neatly stacked pile of scores on the table. "I see Sándor has finished making copies of all the music."

Albert pushed the music toward Haydn, smiling happily.

231

"He has, Herr Kapellmeister. And he has also been helping me with this piece. Under his instruction, and with diligent practice..." He lifted his shoulders in a deprecating shrug.

"Ach so!" Haydn leafed through one of the scores. Sándor had done a fine job, indeed! Both with the scores and with Albert.

He was about to say as much when his gaze fell on the wide band of pale skin on Albert's right forefinger. The imprint of a ring! And unless he was mistaken, it was the same width as the ring they had recovered earlier that morning. His eyes narrowed.

Why was Albert practicing a solo he would not be called upon to play?

He raised his eyes toward Albert's. "I trust you can play your own parts as well as you just played Sándor's," he said lightly.

"But, Sándor said I could take the solo for this concerto, Herr Kapellmeister!" Albert's voice rose in protest. "That is why I have been practicing it."

"Indeed!" Haydn's eyebrows shot up. "And why, may I ask, has my first violinist been delegating his assignments to you?"

"Because I asked him to." Albert sounded surprised, as though the matter could not be simpler to explain. Uncle said I would be taking over as first violinist, but you hired Sándor instead. Who takes any notice of a mere musician? But a solo performer... Now that is a different matter altogether!" Albert's lips stretched into a wide grin.

"Why, the Empress herself may well clasp a solo performer by the hand, may she not, Herr Kapellmeister?"

CHAPTER TWENTY-NINE

Back in the Music Room, Haydn paced the floor frantically. The danger was far from over. His Serene Highness must be warned, but what further evidence did he have against Albert? A pale band of skin where a ring was recently worn and a suspicious desire to clasp the Empress by the hand. Would these be sufficient to convince the Prince? Nothing he had said earlier had convinced His Serene Highness of Albert's involvement.

He slowed down beside the fortepiano, casting an anxious glance at the door. Where could Johann be? And where, for that matter, were Rosalie and Greta? He had rung several times for the maids, only to have someone other than those two come up.

He drummed his fingers on the lid of the fortepiano. There was the reappearance of the travel trunk, of course. Yes, that was a start! He straightened up. The sudden movement knocked his leather case off the fortepiano. Scores drifted out from the open case toward the floor.

Haydn knelt down to retrieve the case and the music. He gave the scores a casual glance as he gathered them up. They were from the set of string quartets the Count had left behind him. He rose slowly to his feet, his gaze still on the music.

His Lordship's behavior the day before had been singularly strange. His concern for the dead musician...Haydn stiffened.

Why, the Count must have known all along that István was dead!

He rushed toward the door. It opened just as he neared it, and Johann entered, almost colliding into Haydn.

"I was with the maids, brother." He held out the ring the maids had retrieved. "Albert—"

"Is that Albert's ring?" Haydn stared at the ring. It appeared to be an exact replica of István's. *God in Heaven, it was just as he had suspected!*

"Whatever you do, Johann, do not return it to him!" He tore past his younger brother, ignoring his bewildered expression. There was no time for explanations.

"Haydn!" The Prince looked up startled as the Kapellmeister burst into his chamber, unannounced. "I was about to send for you. The Police Commissioner has just made his report. The threat is fortunately over, and—"

"I am afraid it is not, Your Serene Highness. Far from it." Haydn gripped the back of a chair, breathing hard. He had so winded himself in his haste to come down, he could barely speak.

"Your former violinist is dead, Haydn." The Prince motioned toward a seat. "What further danger could there possibly be?"

Haydn sank gratefully into the chair, and took a deep breath. "Your Serene Highness, did the Police Commissioner explain how the assassination was to take place?" He brought out his former violinist's ring and, when the Prince shook his head, began to explain its operation and the poison it had contained.

"All it would need is for someone to get close enough to the Empress to grasp her by the hand—"

"Yes, but the man seeking to get close to Her Majesty is dead. The ring is safe in your hands. I fail to see where the threat lies."

"There is another very like it, Your Serene Highness," Haydn countered, wishing he had thought to bring Albert's ring down with him. "I have seen it—"

The Prince's brows came together in a displeased frown. "I trust this has nothing to do with Herr Rahier and his nephew, Haydn."

Haydn paused. It had everything to do with the Estates Director and his nephew, of course, but there would be time enough for that.

"Does Your Serene Highness recall what Count Nádasdy said when he was arrested?"

The abrupt change of subject seemed to disconcert the Prince. He responded with a slight shrug. "That he would ruin me, or something to that effect. It was only his bravado speaking," he added with an irritable wave of his hand.

"He said," Haydn spoke softly, "that Lipót György, the leader of the dissidents, would succeed in his attempt to regain the Hungarian throne."

"Yes, but his man—your violinist—is dead. Lipót György could scarcely persuade you to hire another to do the deed in his place."

Haydn made a slight gesture of assent. The thought occurred to him that Rahier as Lipót György's agent had already persuaded him to hire István's replacement, but he chose not to give voice to it. He would have to lay out a trail for His Serene Highness, allowing him to follow it and draw his own conclusions.

"Did the Count show any signs of distress or consternation, Your Serene Highness, when the Police Commissioner informed you that a violinist by the name of Bartó Daboczi had been found murdered?" he asked instead.

The Prince shook his head. "No, why should—" His voice broke off at the same time his head froze. "*Oh!*"

Haydn nodded. "If it were the real Bartó Daboczi, his game was up. The Count assumed it was the man I had hired. But *that* was István, the lynchpin of his plot, and—" He turned pale. "*There is only one way the Count could have known István was dead...*"

He stared in stupefied silence at the patterned paper on the wall opposite him. Was this the danger Marlene had feared? The reason for the mortal dread his violinist had exhibited in the days before he disappeared? What was it Maria Anna had said? István, denied the possibility of divine protection, had run from the confessional.

What crime has been committed? The words rang in his ears. Who had asked the question? The Estates Director? But why...

He was vaguely aware of the Prince speaking.

"...but who—"

Haydn turned his attention back to the Prince. "Your Serene Highness, there is only one person. We both know it. The travel trunk we mentioned to you earlier has been recovered—"

"Pah!" The Prince uttered a loud snort. "That trunk, you said, was evidence of your violinist having an accomplice within the castle. But how could a dead man send for his travel trunk?"

How, indeed! Haydn voiced the thought to himself.

"No, I don't suppose a man dead for three days could concern himself with any of his belongings," he began slowly, wondering how he could have been so blind. "But, his killer well might, if only to mislead us into believing him still alive." He raised his eyes.

"Only consider, Your Serene Highness, our entire effort has been concentrated on finding István. Were it not for the Police Commissioner arresting that poor peasant, we would still be searching for him. Meanwhile—"

The Prince held up a hand, a worried expression on his face. "I must have more concrete evidence than this Haydn." He leant back in his chair with a heavy sigh. "I need hardly remind you how delicate the situation is."

Haydn nodded, pondering the matter in silence. It was not long before he devised a strategy. He gazed into his employer's eyes, confident.

"I will need to clarify a few points, Your Serene Highness, but I believe I may have found a way."

"The pieces of this puzzle begin to fall into place at last, Johann." Haydn spoke in a satisfied tone, drumming his fingers restlessly on the side of the carriage.

Johann cast a doubtful look at his brother. "What of Gerhard? Until Rosalie finds the receipt he left with his delivery of wine, we can hardly rule him out. He knew as well as Albert that the root of your initial suspicions rested upon that travel trunk. Its disappearance from István's room made it appear he was still alive."

Haydn shook his head. "Yes, but only someone *already* within the castle would have been able to retrieve the trunk from the Musicians' Quarters, Johann." Haydn continued to tap out a rhythm on the carriage wall. "Recall that it was taken at night. *After* the drawbridge had been pulled up."

"So, it was!" Johann conceded. He stared at his brother in growing consternation. "And it was Albert who first reported its disappearance." He glanced out the window. The carriage was climbing up the steep path toward the Parish Church of Kleinhöflein. The church steeple was visible through the bare branches of the trees dotting the hillside.

"I very much doubt you will be able to persuade Pfarrer Klemens to give you any details of István's confession," he added gloomily.

"It is not the details of his confession, I am interested in," Haydn replied, following his brother's gaze. "It is the nature of the divine transaction he sought with his Maker that I am curious about."

Johann was about to speak when the carriage lurched to a stop before the church gates.

"I will only be a moment," Haydn said, climbing down from the carriage. He returned a few minutes later, a look of quiet satisfaction on his face.

"Just as I thought," he began as the carriage commenced its careful progress down the hill. "István confessed to murdering the man he impersonated, but made no mention of any plot—"

"Pfarrer Klemens told you that?" Johann's jaw had dropped open.

"Not in so many words." Haydn smiled. "But he did not deny it when I asked the question. He did say, however, that István was under the impression his confession had bought him divine protection."

"Protection from what?" Johann gaped at Haydn.

"From vengeance, from someone he referred to as the Agent of Death. That is all Pfarrer Klemens could make out. István was shaking with fear, and was barely coherent, apparently." Haydn turned toward Johann. "If I have surmised correctly, István's violin is with Marlene. He did intend to leave, but not that night."

When the carriage stopped again, it was a short distance away from the Midwife Heindl's farmhouse. As he stepped out of the carriage, Haydn caught sight of a familiar impish face staring solemnly at him.

"I believe we have a means of discovering who sent that note," he said in a low pianissimo to Johann as he beckoned the boy forward with a smile.

"Ah, Ludwig, is it not?" he asked. At the boy's nod, he continued, "You fetch and carry for Herr Heindl, I recall. Was it you he sent with a message for me on the night of the storm?" He stared into the boy's eyes, hoping his lie would trick the lad into revealing the truth. "I did not receive it."

Ludwig looked indignant. "Well, I know nothing about it. I only delivered a note for Master Bartó. And, it was not Herr Heindl who sent it, neither."

Haydn's eyes drifted toward Johann for the briefest moment. "No? Who was it, then? His mother?"

"Of course not," Ludwig replied. "She can barely write. It was Master Bartó's brother." The boy gestured back at the farmhouse. "He stayed the night here. The inn was all out of rooms, and he wasn't expected at the castle until the next day."

"Ach so!" Haydn straightened up, murmuring: "So, he came to the castle the next day, did he, after spending an *entire* night at the farmhouse? Then, Frau Heindl will remember this brother of Master Bartó's quite well, I am sure."

Marlene raised her tear-stained features toward Haydn. "If you had only listened to him," she whimpered. "Why wouldn't you listen to him?"

The Widow Heindl had been none too happy to see the Kapellmeister and his brother, but had reluctantly allowed them entry into the farmhouse.

"He said nothing to me, Marlene." Haydn's voice was gentle. "He was much too afraid to speak."

"B-but he said—" Marlene wiped her nose. "He said he had to leave— that you wouldn't believe him—"

"His fear must have prevented him from saying anything," Haydn said. He recalled his violinist's bizarre behavior. Had István been trying to get himself dismissed, after all?

Johann turned toward Marlene. "Was it you who caused his change of heart?" he asked quietly.

She nodded, a tear rolling down her cheek. "Poor István! It took him a while to see he had been duped. They said no Hungarian peasant would ever be taxed again when they took over. But until then, every kreutzer was necessary for their success. Yet not one of them bothered to reach into their own coffers!"

The barmaid's eyes blazed fiercely. "István wanted so much to believe! It was the tax-collector's demands, you see, that drove his parents from their small holding to the woods. Were it not for István's musical

238

talents, and the titles he was able to buy, who knows..." She choked on the words, pressing a handkerchief to her lips.

"He said he would ask for your help, for some money for our child, while he went into hiding..." Marlene's eyes searched Haydn's features. "They threatened to kill him. Did he say nothing of this to you?"

Haydn shook his head, his eyes drawn toward a charcoal gray violin case peeping out of a closet door. "Did István bring that here?"

⌘

"Well, have you caught him yet, husband?" Maria Anna set a tray laden with a coffee pot, cups, and a jug of cream carefully on the study table. "The killer," she repeated impatiently at Haydn's blank stare. "Have you found him?"

Haydn's face cleared. "We know who it is, and I believe we can prove it to His Serene Highness's satisfaction." He pushed aside the contracts he was working on. "It will all be over by tomorrow, Maria Anna. And nothing will mar our godson's christening, I promise."

Haydn smiled up at her, but Maria Anna stared at him unflinchingly, making no motion to leave. She wanted, no doubt, to know the identity of the killer, but Haydn had no intention of revealing any more than he already had. What little chance they had of trapping Albert would be quite lost if word were to get out that they knew it was he.

"I had better get back to these contracts," he said to preempt any further questions. "The Estates Director had every musician sign a new one."

Maria Anna harrumphed skeptically, but duly left.

Haydn poured out two cups of coffee, passed one to Johann, and drew another contract from the pile toward himself. It was Albert's. He signed it, checked to see all was in order, and put it aside. He had just signed the next one, when he noticed the musician's signature was missing.

"Whose contract is this, I wonder." He turned over the pages. Had the man remembered, at least, to add the handwritten promise to be in constant attendance during the imperial visit that Rahier had insisted upon? He located the passage.

"Ah!" he said, recognizing the writing. "It is—" The words froze in his mouth as he stared down at the exquisite penmanship.

239

"What is it, brother?" Johann raised his head in surprise at Haydn's sharp intake of breath.

But Haydn, hastily unfolding István's note, seemed not to have heard him. He held the note against the contract, peering first at the one and then at the other. He could not believe it! How was it even possible?

"It was not Albert who sent that note, Johann." Haydn's voice shook. He pushed the note and the contract across the table toward his brother.

Johann held the note against the contract, scrutinizing both. "Who then?"

Haydn's mind was working furiously. No wonder the writing on the note had seemed so familiar. It all made sense, after a fashion. But how could he have been so wrong?

"Have all the other contracts been signed, Johann? Will you please check?" He rose from his seat. "And, let me see Albert's ring. We must be sure of our facts this time."

Johann, seeming befuddled, complied without a word.

Haydn twisted and prodded at the wings attached to the bezel, until they were almost bent out of shape. But they had not been made to move. He flung the ring down.

"This is a mere replica!" he cried. "The Count must have given it to Albert to throw us off the scent."

CHAPTER THIRTY

Bright azure skies with a few drifting clouds greeted Eisenstadt on the day of the christening, but Haydn was too preoccupied to enjoy the glorious morning. With a hand prodding the small of her richly adorned back, he rushed Maria Anna into her pew within the Kleinhöflein Parish Church and, to her great annoyance, left her there with Johann, still waiting to be seated, while he hurried outside the church to await the Prince.

After a whispered consultation with His Serene Highness, he rushed back in, spoke a few words with Lorenzo, his new Konzertmeister, and his middle brother, who was to conduct the mass, before returning to his pew.

"Where are your manners, husband?" Maria Anna hissed as he sat down. "You barely greeted our godson or his parents."

"The service is to be extended," Haydn lied. He had promised her nothing would go amiss on this day, but unfortunately it would be marred in the worst way possible. "The Prince has asked for a few additional pieces to be played." He anxiously watched his musicians filing into place, hoping the additions would give the Police Commissioner sufficient time to convey Frau Heindl to the church.

Despite his best efforts, Haydn was unable to attend to either the chants that followed or the prayers Pfarrer Klemens intoned. It was in a daze that he lit the candle with Maria Anna, and watched as Pfarrer Klemens poured holy water on his godchild. His eyes kept drifting toward the church doors.

The words of dismissal had just been uttered when he saw the Police Commissioner quietly close the church doors behind him. Where was

Frau Heindl? The orchestra took up a minuet. The piece had no sooner concluded than Haydn saw the midwife's plump figure making her way down the aisle. The Police Commissioner followed her.

"Husband!" Haydn heard Maria Anna whisper urgently. "Who is that woman? Surely, you will not let her disrupt the service. Do something!"

Haydn shook Maria Anna's hand off his coat lapels. He slid forward to the edge of his seat, his gaze riveted on the midwife. She came to a halt before the musicians.

"That is he!" she cried. "You spent the night under my roof on the night of the storm." Her plump wrist stretched out from under the tassels of her shawl. But it was not Albert she was pointing to.

"Sándor!" Johann's voice rose, drowning out Maria Anna's outraged, "Husband!"

"Did you suspect as much, brother?" Johann began to ask, but Haydn was already on his feet.

Rosalie's brother looked down at the midwife as though she had lost her mind. "So, I did, my good woman. And what of it?" He looked around the congregation with a bemused air.

"You said you were his brother?" The midwife's voice, shrill with horror, filled the church. "Bartó's brother! But you were lying. You killed him!"

Sándor slowly approached the midwife, his hand outstretched as though to grasp her hand. "But I did no such thing, my good woman. Why would you say otherwise?" His right hand sought to clasp her.

His fingers were on her palm when Haydn pushed the midwife out of the way.

"Because it is the truth!" he thundered, reaching forward to grasp the violinist's wrist, and twisting it away from him. He turned toward the Police Commissioner. "Take that ring off him, man! It is poisoned."

He turned toward Sándor. "Do not try to deny it. We found the note you sent István. Your writing, the distinctive hand of a former copyist, is hard to disguise, my friend." The Kapellmeister uttered a disgusted grunt.

"What possible reason could you have to join with the dissidents? You have killed another man! What must your parents think? And what of your sister? Is she to suffer the shame of your crime?"

Sándor's cold eyes glared back at him. "There is no shame in fighting for one's country, Herr Kapellmeister."

"Assassinating your sovereign hardly qualifies as fighting for your country, young man." The Prince had come forward. "Take him away, Herr Lichtenegger!" As he turned to leave, he gave the perplexed musicians and congregation a nod of encouragement. "Carry on! Carry on! No need to disrupt the festivities.

"Haydn! When your duties here are over, I shall require your presence in my chamber!"

Rosalie set the Estates Director's mid-day meal on his desk with a thump, unable to conceal her resentment. As though there wasn't enough to do without the constant ringing of his bell! Everyone—even the Prince—was at the christening, but the Estates Director had chosen to stay on at the castle, making everyone's life miserable.

"Lunch!" she announced curtly. She glared at the back of his head, then turned around. No point waiting. She'd be waiting forever, if she expected him to look up and utter a word of thanks!

A buzz of activity caught her attention as she came out into the hallway. The musicians were trooping down the wide corridor toward the staircase, talking excitedly amongst themselves. Curious, she walked slowly past. She had almost reached the kitchen door when Albert came hurrying along.

He stopped abruptly when he saw Rosalie, seeming flustered.

"Where is Sándor?" she asked, wondering why Albert was at such pains to avoid looking at her.

"He...ehmm..." Albert tugged desperately at the ruffled cravat around his neck.

Rosalie put her hands on her hips, in no mood for his prevarications. "Where *is* he, Albert?"

Albert's eyes flitted around the hallway, apparently in desperate search of an object to alight upon before falling at last, reluctantly, upon her face. "Sándor has been arrested Rosalie! The Police Commissioner—"

"Arrested! Why?" Rosalie's voice sharpened. She looked suspiciously at Albert. How had he managed to implicate her brother in his wrongdoings? "What has he done?"

"He..." Albert swallowed. "Apparently, he...eh...killed Bartó—"

"*What!*" Rosalie stared at Albert. Could she have heard aright? Why in the name of heaven would Sándor kill Master Bartó? To be sure, he had been impatient to fill Master Bartó's position. But to go so far as to kill the man? Her brother would do no such thing.

"His ring," Albert was saying. "It was a weapon of some kind—"

"No. No, that is impossible!" Rosalie locked her fingers together, shivering as an icy draught touched her bare neck. Had Albert left the doors open again? And what nonsense was he spouting? How could Sanyi's ring be a weapon? It was merely a token of the Count's appreciation of his musical abilities.

Albert was still speaking. She stared up at him, trying to take in his words. A few isolated words penetrated the fog that clouded her mind. *Conspiracy... plot to kill the Empress...*But they made no sense. Surely, Sanyi—feckless, irresponsible Sanyi—had no interest in the dissidents and their plot? It was Albert, the man who stood before her, who had repeatedly expressed outrage on behalf of the Hungarians. It was he who openly wore the dissidents' symbol.

But even as she voiced her doubts, her mind returned to the Count's odd behavior when he encountered her in his guise as a peasant. He had known more of her than either Albert or Master Bartó could have told him. Who else could have spoken of her but Sanyi? Who else knew enough of her confidences to betray them?

As to the ring. She herself had remarked upon its similarity to Master Bartó's ring. Sanyi had come to the castle the very morning Master Bartó disappeared, certain of finding a position. How had he known Herr Haydn would have need of his services?

"Oh, Sanyi! What have you *done?*" A cold wetness stung her cheeks.

"Here, here! Don't cry!" Albert sounded alarmed. He thrust a handkerchief into her hands. She bit down on the fabric, struggling to stop the sobs that wrenched out of her as Albert frantically patted her arms and her back. Then, as she continued to weep, he drew her awkwardly into his arms.

They had been standing thus for no more than a moment when an outraged cry behind them forced them apart.

"Oh, for heaven's sake, boy!" The Estates Director's voice seemed to ring through the hallway. "If you must dally with the girl, do so in the privacy of your own quarters. And, be quick about it! The Prince requires our presence in his chamber."

Albert swiveled around, his hands still on Rosalie's shoulders. "But—"

Rahier held up his hand. "No more of your nonsense, boy!" He turned on his heels, calling over his shoulder: "And, whatever you do, be sure not to get her with child!"

———————

Haydn fought down his dismay when he saw the Estates Director and his nephew standing before the fireplace in the Prince's chamber. It was bad enough he had been subject to the recriminations that poured forth from Maria Anna's tongue the moment the Prince departed. Now he would have to contend with the Estates Director's jibes as well!

Rahier turned around just as Haydn pulled the door shut after his younger brother.

"Your proclivity for hiring the wrong person never ceases to amaze me, Herr Kapellmeister!" The Estates Director wore a smug smile. "Two violinists, both vouched for by you and your brothers"—Rahier's gaze drifted toward Johann—"and both involved in the same dastardly plot!"

"And were it not for the Kapellmeister, their involvement would never have been discovered, my dear Rahier." The Prince's quiet voice came from behind them. He lowered himself into the imposing chair beneath his grandfather's portrait, and indicated that his visitors should be seated.

"Yes, but his sister—" Rahier began, when Haydn interrupted him.

"Will stay on, Herr Rahier." Haydn looked pointedly at the Stadlmann case leaning against Albert's chair. The Estates Director had sought his discretion for that small misdemeanor. He would grant it, but not without extracting a reprieve for Rosalie. "None of this was her doing."

The Estates Director flushed. "Yes, of course, Herr Kapellmeister."

The Prince gazed curiously from his Estates Director to his Kapellmeister, but made no reference to the exchange between them when he spoke. "What was it that changed the direction of your suspicions, Haydn?"

Albert's gasp echoed through the room. "You mean you knew it was Sándor!" He sprang up from his seat, hovering over the Kapellmeister. "But you said nothing yesterday! You could have warned me, Herr Kapellmeister." He stood before Haydn, looking indignant. "To think I have spent hours—*alone*—in the company of a dangerous man!"

Haydn was mortified. How could he have warned Albert, when... He swallowed. "I knew nothing at the time. It was someone else I suspected."

"Who?" Albert wanted to know.

Haydn felt himself redden. "There were a number of other suspects," he began to mumble.

"You!" Rahier interjected before he could finish. "It was you, the Kapellmeister suspected, boy." His eyes swiveled toward Haydn. "Although I cannot imagine what put that daft idea into his head!"

"Me!" Albert gasped again, returning to his seat. "Why me? What have I done?"

Haydn sighed. He glanced at the Prince, and thought he detected the corners of His Serene Highness's mouth twitch.

"You must admit your behavior was extremely suspicious." Johann came to his brother's rescue. "The matter of the travel trunk alone pointed to you." He elaborated on Haydn's suspicions for the benefit of his listeners.

"But I did hear a noise that night—the sound of something being scraped along the floor," Albert protested. "I was only surprised Sándor slept through it all. His room, like mine, was right next to the room in which your violinist slept."

Haydn shook his head. "That was the first mistake we made." He turned to Johann. "The only reason Albert knew of my initial suspicions was because Sándor had heard of them from Rosalie."

"Yes, but Sándor was nowhere in sight when the trunk disappeared the second time." Johann looked toward Albert for an explanation.

"I was on my way back to find a gardener and to give Uncle the news when I met Sándor. He suggested I hurry back to the castle, and offered to find a gardener himself." Albert still looked peeved.

A gleam of understanding illuminated Johann's eyes. "Ach so! But what of this ring, then?" He brought Albert's ring out from his pocket. "I am afraid, the wings on the bezel are twisted. The damage is not permanent, I am sure. I will see to the repairs myself."

The Prince reached forward for the ring before Johann could return it to Albert. "Ah! The emblem of Matthias Corvinus!" he said, holding the stone up against the light.

"That was our second mistake," Haydn admitted ruefully. "The dissidents had adopted the great Hungarian king's emblem as their standard, but they would hardly be foolish enough to call attention to themselves in that manner by wearing the emblem in full view. It was the barber-surgeon's suggestion that led us astray, I am afraid."

The Estates Director held his hand out for the ring. "I still cannot understand why your first violinist left his post if he planned to assassinate the Empress herself."

"Yes, that question troubled me from the moment we found the ring and discovered the receptacle of poison it concealed." Haydn stroked his chin pensively. "It all began to make sense when I realized the Count must have had István killed. Although the letters we recovered and the conversation I overheard should have told us all we needed to know.

"You see, Marlene had effected a change of heart in István. He attempted to leave the conspiracy, but the dissidents had no intentions of letting their hired assassin go before the deed was done.

"Forced to continue with their plan, István did everything he could to get himself dismissed. And were it not the imperial visit, he would have succeeded. His desperate demand for money had its desired effect, but his dismissal would only take effect after Her Majesty's visit.

"Cornered, he threatened to leave—a threat that was all over the castle because one of the maids had overheard him. Rosalie must have passed on the gossip to her brother, unwittingly alerting the dissidents to István's decision. Of course, István had already made plans to leave. He had already removed his violin, and was surreptitiously making off with my music—thinking to sell the works, no doubt, to support Marlene and his unborn child.

"But before his plan could take effect, Sándor was dispatched to do away with him and take his place. Sándor's connection with the Count— the letters he came bearing and the ring—quite escaped our notice, I am afraid."

The Estates Director sniffed. "It was your unreasonable antipathy toward me that deceived you into suspecting my nephew, Herr Kapellmeister. Admit it!"

Haydn raised his eyes toward the Estates Director, who had risen from his seat and now stood with his back toward the fireplace. He supposed it was true, but...

"Your own behavior was not exactly calculated to dispel my suspicions, Herr Rahier." He held up a hand to stem the other's protests. "When the Police Commissioner visited the castle the day after the storm, you laid hold of me, wanting to know what crime had brought him here."

"There was talk of the imperial visit being cancelled because of the rumors of unrest, Herr Kapellmeister." Rahier's voice had risen. "Yet nothing untoward had occurred. I wondered if your violinist had not committed some unfortunate act. After all, his sentiments were all too well-known."

"As were your nephew's," Haydn retorted.

"Pah! Albert is but a young man. He spouts views he has no understanding of —Quiet, boy!" Rahier barked as Albert began to speak. "The boy is full of contradictions. You must have seen that yourself. Why one minute, he rails against the Empire, and the next he wants to grasp the Empress by the hand!"

Haydn felt an uncomfortable warmth suffuse his cheeks at the memory. Albert's desire had only deepened his suspicions against him. His eyes drifted toward the young man, who was still sputtering indignantly at his uncle's characterization of him.

"Yes, I did wonder at that. But what did you mean when you said his outspokenness would do him as much good as it had István?"

"Only that it would earn him the dislike of the townspeople—and a speedy dismissal. Albert is no virtuoso, and you would have quickly dismissed him at the first excuse, Herr Kapellmeister."

The Prince leaned forward. "You have yet to tell us what set you on the right track," he reminded Haydn.

"It was the writing on the note sent to István, Your Serene Highness. A fine, distinctive hand that was familiar to me, although I could not at first place it. Had Herr Rahier not insisted on the musicians signing new contracts, I doubt I would have recognized the writing as Sándor's.

"I knew by that time that István's killer was also the assassin the dissidents had sent to replace him. If it was Sándor who had sent the note, then it followed that Albert, despite all appearances, could not be part of the conspiracy."

Albert stared from Haydn to his uncle in dismay. "And that was all that stood between me and the executioner's axe!"

"Yes, but the midwife's testimony would have exonerated you," Johann pointed out.

"And I, young man," the Prince added, "would not have had you arrested without solid evidence." He brought his hands together, his fingertips forming a steeple. "Now, if only we could find Lipót György."

"The Count's companion?" Albert asked, his voice rising in astonishment. "Is that who you are looking for?"

"No, no." Johann shook his head. "The Count's companion was a Leopold George. This is—"

"Lipót György!" Albert repeated. "It is Hungarian for Leopold George. He—"

"I believe you might be right!" Haydn was staring at Albert. He turned toward the Prince. "The Count was never without his companion. Yet when he accompanied you to the Palace, it was without him, even though the Count came, ostensibly, to seek my opinion on the string quartets he had left behind."

"Well, as I was saying before I was so rudely interrupted," Albert continued, looking reproachfully at Haydn, "Leopold preferred the Hungarian version of his name, but no one in Vienna could pronounce it! Shameful, if you ask me! But why are you looking for him?"

Rahier clapped an exasperated hand to his forehead. "Because he is the leader of the dissidents, you nincompoop! Do you mean to say you have known all along that the man was Lipót György, and you kept it to yourself?"

Albert pouted. "Well, how was I supposed to know he was wanted! No one ever tells me anything."

"I am afraid he will have fled the country by now," Haydn said. If only he had seen the truth earlier. They had all met the man, and spoken with him, but he had eluded their grasp. "I saw the Count shaking his head in the oddest manner when he was being led away. I am quite sure now he was signaling his companion to flee. I heard carriage wheels in the distance." He shook his head regretfully. "I should have realized he was involved."

"Well, it matters not." The Prince shrugged philosophically. "He can hardly make trouble here if he has fled the country. Their wretched plot, at least, has been averted. But there is another problem that requires your attention, my dear Kapellmeister."

Haydn, about to rise to his feet, sat back down. "And what is that, Your Serene Highness?"

"The small matter of your program for the imperial visit, now that you have lost another virtuoso."

Haydn's eyes sought Johann's in dismay. It was a matter that had quite escaped his attention. With a sigh, he turned toward Albert.

"How many of his solos did Sándor teach you, young man?"

Albert's features brightened. "I am quite confident of being able to play half of them as well as the one you heard me play yesterday." He leaned forward eagerly. "Am I to be your first violinist, then, Herr Kapellmeister?"

"But what of the other half," the Prince objected before Haydn could say a word.

"I will perform them myself, Your Serene Highness." He stood up, and turned toward Albert. "We had better get to work, young man!"

The Kapellmeister and his musicians were about to leave the Prince's chamber, when the Estates Director uttered a condescending snort behind them.

"You would have been saved all this trouble, Herr Kapellmeister, had you hired my nephew in the first place!"

THE END

NOTE FROM THE AUTHOR

Although Franz Joseph Haydn (1732-1809) never donned the role of Kapell-detective—that we know of—it is not inconceivable that presented with the problems of a missing musician, instrument, and music, as he is in this novel, he would have been compelled to investigate.

As Kapellmeister or Director of Music to the powerful Esterházy family Haydn was responsible not only for providing new compositions and musical entertainment, he was also tasked with managing the musicians under him and with taking care of the musical instruments the family owned and their vast library of music. An adept and diplomatic manager of people and personalities, Haydn soon earned his musicians' trust and respect as well as the affectionate appellation of "Papa Haydn."

Loyal to both his employer and the Empress Maria Theresa, in the event that his musical problems escalated to one threatening the Habsburg Empire and his employer's fortunes, Haydn would, no doubt, have felt duty-bound to aid an enquiry in any way he could.

It is this sense of duty toward God, his employer, and his music that strikes one about Haydn's personality. Already in 1766, when the novel begins, Haydn was rapidly becoming known within and beyond Austria's borders as one of the nation's greatest composers. Yet he was singularly free of the larger-than-life, prima donna personality of men such as Mozart and Beethoven, both of whom acknowledged Haydn's influence on their music.

Indeed, Haydn is hailed as the father, if not of classical music, than of the string quartet and the symphony, having a decisive say in the shape these forms of music were to subsequently take.

Despite the considerable renown he achieved in his own lifetime, Haydn never forgot that he came from humble origins, the son of a wheelwright and his wife born in the little village of Rohrau in the present-day Austrian state of Burgenland.

As a composer, Haydn was largely self-taught, relying on his reading of Joseph Fux's *Gradus ad Parnassum*, C.P.E. Bach's *Essay on the True Art of Playing Keyboard*, and the instruction in singing, composition, and Italian he received through his work as composer Nicola Porpora's accompanist.

While his own talent and industriousness were certainly responsible for the greatness he achieved, the opportunity provided by the wealthy Esterházy family equally facilitated his accomplishments; and Haydn recognized this.

Like other Hungarian Catholic magnates, the Esterházys had been stalwartly loyal to the Austrian Habsburg family for at least four generations. Protestants and the lesser nobility of Hungary tended to be less enamored of the Habsburgs, hoping both for a re-unification with Transylvania as well as for independence.

Although Maria Theresa's reign and that of her son Joseph were largely peaceful, given the condition enforced first by the Emperor Leopold (referred to in the novel as the Empress's grandfather) and later in the Pragmatic Sanction that ensured the Habsburg line would continue through Maria Theresa and her children, it is not far beyond the realm of possibility that an attempt might have been made to eliminate the entire Habsburg line to regain Hungary's ancient right to elect her own sovereign.

When I discovered through my research that the enigmatic Comte St. Germain was in some circles—most notably by Annie Besant and other theosophists —believed to be the long-lost eldest son of an earlier Hungarian rebel leader, Ferenc II Rákóczi, making him the leader of the Hungarian faction in my novel seemed the most natural thing to do. I have used the name of Rákóczi's first-born son who died in childhood, Lipót György, for the character.

The fact that Comte St. Germain, in addition to being of possible Hungarian stock, had disappeared from France in 1760, returning a decade later, meant that it was quite possible he had spent the intervening years stirring up strife and rebellion in Royal Hungary and Transylvania.

Like the character of Lipót György in my novel, Comte St. Germain was credited with being a dazzling virtuoso violinist and having almost supernatural powers. Always suspected of creating political trouble in countries such as England and France, but never brought to justice for his supposed crimes, it was only natural to have Comte St. Germain's fictional counterpart, Lipót György, also escape Habsburg wrath for inciting treasonous behavior in Hungary.

Another nugget of information that conveniently fit my plot was that a member of the Nádasdy family, a Hungarian noble family of considerable fortune and power, had been involved in an earlier plot against the Emperor Leopold. That plot having been discovered, the Catholic families involved lost their lives and their estates. In the case of Ferenc Nádasdy, the bulk of his property was granted by royal decree to his brother-in-law, Pál Esterházy, Prince Nikolaus's grandfather.

The police system I have described in the novel, however, was not instituted until after Maria Theresa's death in 1780. Joseph II had a tendency to micro-manage, and Count Pergen's system appealed to his autocratic nature.

Readers interested in more information on Austro-Hungarian relations are referred to Bryan Cartledge's excellent history of Hungary, *The Will to Survive*. Cartledge begins with the Magyar tribe's settlement in the Carpathian Basin in 400 BC and continues on to the formation of a democratic Hungarian nation in the 1980s.

Those fascinated by the picture of Haydn's life depicted in this novel might find Vernon Gotwal's translation of two of the earliest biographies of Haydn by G.A. Griesinger and A.C. Dies interesting. Both Griesinger and Dies base their biographies on their conversations with Haydn as an old man and the anecdotes the aged composer provided them with. David Wyn Jones's *Life of Haydn* provides the latest in Haydn research, and was an invaluable resource for this novel.

Readers are also referred to my web site at WWW.NTUSTIN.COM, and my newsletter, where I share the fascinating snippets I uncover during my research.

ABOUT THE AUTHOR

A former journalist, Nupur Tustin relies upon a Ph.D. in Communication and an M.A. in English to orchestrate fictional mayhem. The Haydn mysteries are a result of her life-long passion for classical music and its history.

Childhood piano lessons and a 1903 Weber Upright share equal blame for her original compositions, available on **ntustin.musicaneo.com**.

Her writing includes work for Reuters and CNBC, short stories and freelance articles, and research published in peer-reviewed academic journals. She lives in Southern California with her husband, three rambunctious children, and a pit bull.

For details on the Haydn series and monthly blog posts on the great composer, visit the official **Haydn Mystery web site: NTUSTIN.COM**.

Printed in Great Britain
by Amazon